Patricia Angadi, who p
at the age of seventy, ha
interesting career. She aba
vative English lifestyle to marry Ayana Angadi,
an Indian writer and lecturer, Trotskyite and
intellectual. Together they founded the Asian
Music Circle in the late 1940s, organizing an
almost continuous programme of concerts and
lectures on Asian music and dance in Britain
and on the continent for many years. Through-
out this time, Patricia Angadi was establishing
herself as a talented portrait painter. At the age
of fifty she took a teacher training course and
subsequently taught at a primary school for
thirteen years. On retiring, she started to write
full time.

Her first four novels, *The Governess, The Done
Thing, The Highly-Flavoured Ladies* and *Sins
of the Mothers,* are also available from Black
Swan.

Author photograph by Shankara Angadi.

Also by Patricia Angadi

THE GOVERNESS
THE DONE THING
THE HIGHLY-FLAVOURED LADIES
SINS OF THE MOTHERS

and published by Black Swan

Playing For Real

Patricia Angadi

For Jackie - the Cornish one -
with special thanks for
all the affectionate caring -
so much appreciated.
love
Patricia.
April 1993.

BLACK SWAN

PLAYING FOR REAL
A BLACK SWAN BOOK   0 552 99464 2

Originally published in Great Britain by
Victor Gollancz Ltd

PRINTING HISTORY
Gollancz edition published 1990
Black Swan edition published 1991

This book is set in 11/12pt Melior by
County Typesetters, Margate, Kent

Black Swan Books are published by Transworld
Publishers Ltd., 61–63 Uxbridge Road, Ealing, London W5
5SA, in Australia by Transworld Publishers (Australia)
Pty. Ltd., 15–23 Helles Avenue, Moorebank, NSW 2170,
and in New Zealand by Transworld Publishers (N.Z.) Ltd.,
Cnr. Moselle and Waipareira Avenues, Henderson,
Auckland.

Made and printed in Great Britain by
Cox & Wyman Ltd., Reading, Berks.

For Fred

Author's Note

Though the name of Zennor has been used to describe the village in the story, the descriptions of the houses and farms of the district are entirely imaginary, as are the characters who live there. They have no connection with actual people, living or dead, and any similarity detected is coincidental.

1

Jenny Tremayne humped her daughter higher on her hip, and peered round the darkness of the barely lit railway station. Blackout and elimination of place names was all jolly fine, but enough was enough; English people as well as German parachutists were likely to want to know where they were on occasions. She tried, but failed, to remember the ins and outs of Penzance station from childhood memories, so made for the one, all but obliterated, hurricane lamp she could see. The ticket collector was as old as the hills; obviously all the young ones had been called up.

'I have to get to Zennor,' she said. 'Is there a taxi?'

'Taxi m'dear?' The aged man seemed to be reading every word of her ticket before tearing off the return half. 'It's late for taxis.'

'I know it's late – about an hour and a half late as it happens, but I still have to get to Zennor somehow.' She was exasperated, tired and hungry, and extremely cold. 'I can't carry you Joanne, you're too heavy. Stand there, close to me and don't move.' She let go the suitcase and bag and teddy bear so that they slid to the ground along with her protesting daughter, who clutched her skirt and tried to climb up her leg. There was a breaking point quite near, Jenny decided. 'We have to get to Zennor,' she said again.

She was shown a telephone and a directory and given the name of a taxi firm and, before too long, she had bargained with the cab driver and was sitting in the cold, clouded night on a bench outside the station, waiting for the car to turn up. The knowledge that the car was actually coming gave her strength to quell her own irascibility.

'Don't cry Jojo,' she said, giving her a hug and a kiss. 'We shall soon be there and then you can have a nice drink of hot milk and perhaps a biscuit if Gran's got any.' This urge to shift all responsibility, to get out of the present impossible situation, to run away without ever looking back – this was uppermost in her mind, and now it seemed almost within her grasp; only an hour or so more to freedom. Let someone else do the caring. There was no other feeling in her at that moment; hadn't been for some time now.

'Want to go home,' wailed Joanne.

Before, that might have brought on a blinding attack of rage and retaliation, but now, with rescue so close, she could keep her mind on the goal. The desire to punish the cause of all the misery, who didn't even appreciate the upset she created, was not any more a danger.

In the cab, Joanne slept in oblivion and Jenny stared out at the Cornish countryside in the blackness of wartime night. In truth, it did not seem so black as wartime London, because the moon, seen only occasionally through heavy rain clouds, gave glimpses of cold blue clarity to the view. Jenny tried to remember the landscape, but it was alien. Her own childhood memories were full of sea, rocks, sand and soft springboard turf under her feet; sea pinks bobbing in high wind and the smell of thyme. It had nothing in common with the menace outside the taxi window, because that was dark and threatening. Had it changed? Or had she changed? Perhaps this was no longer a place that offered safe, childhood security.

But that was hardly the point, was it? That was only the justification she handed out to herself. Wasn't it so that her four-year-old daughter might be brought up in the peace and quiet of a quiet Cornish village? Out of reach of the bombing and the shortages of East End London? Of course not; this trip was not for Joanne's benefit at all, it was for hers; it was to give her back the freedom she had lost, so that she could again do what she wanted with her life with no responsibilities and no appendages. Let's be honest.

The house came upon her unexpectedly; even her own village she had not recognized in the theatrically dimmed lighting and the unreal blue-blackness of night. No lights shining out from the windows as they used to when she came home from school in the winter, only stifling blackout, and a small sliver of escaping orange glow in one upstairs room to say that her parents had gone to bed. They would be angry with her for being so late. She switched back in time to the anxiety of coming home late after a village dance and dreading the row that would follow.

She overpaid the driver, guilty that he had had to drive so far so late, and piled the cases out into the road. Couldn't make him wait, so humped the dead weight of sleeping child, and hurried, through a sudden, drenching downpour and accompanying wind gust, to the front door. Would they answer at this time of night? She should have written to warn them, but it was such a spur of the moment journey. The driver could at least have helped her with the cases, but he drove straight off as she knocked the knocker – embarrassed at the deafening sound it made in that dark, silent night. A dog barked; not Shep, she knew Shep's bark, but he must be long dead; he was old when she had left home. A new dog then, that didn't know her.

Why didn't they come? She tried to keep the rain off Joanne's face, but there was only a small porch. The bags would be soaked out there in the road; might be stolen even – but that was ridiculous, this wasn't London. She almost laughed as she waited there in the rain, to think that she had imagined they might be pinched. She knocked again with ear-splitting force, and saw the upstairs light go out before the window was opened a crack and she heard her father's voice: 'Who is it?'

'Dad, it's Jenny; will you let me in?' What a

ridiculous thing to have to ask. Your daughter outside in the pouring rain and in the middle of the night, and you have to ask if he'll let you in.

'What in God's name—? Wait a minute then.'

She saw her mother's face appear beside her father's at the window. 'Jenny? Whatever are you doing out there? What's wrong?'

'Nothing's wrong, Mum, but I'm very wet, and so is Joanne.'

'Lord have mercy – you've got the child there? Whatever—? Your father's coming. I'll get my wrap on. I can't imagine . . .'

Bolts were being shot, a chain rattled and the dog whined and yelped and scratched at the closed door. Would it attack her, she wondered? Her arms were breaking under the strain of holding Joanne; the heaviness of the sleeping weight slipped slowly down and Jenny hoisted her knee under the load in an attempt to hold on a further moment. Wet, cold rain slid down her hair and into her eyes. Hold on just a little longer, only a second or two more.

'Come on in then. Oh bloody hell there goes the dog. Come back here Chip, come *back*!' Her father pushed past her into the rain in his slippers and dressing gown, peering into the bushes and whistling. Joanne was sliding further down towards the ground and Jenny leaned on the half closed door and stumbled into the warmth and light.

'Take her Mum, can you? I can't hold her.' She transferred the dead weight and felt the joy of relief flood through her.

'Shut the door,' said her mother. 'Quickly – the blackout. They'll be down on us as soon as you can say knife.'

'But our cases are out there, in the road.'

'In the road? Whatever have you left them there for?'

'I couldn't carry them because I had Joanne.'

This extraordinary conversation after more than a year of not seeing each other; what a farce.

'Well, you'd better go and fetch them. Where's your father?'

'He's looking for the dog.'

'Daft idiot. This child's soaking wet.' She moved over to sit by the fireplace, where the remains of the fire smouldered, wiping Joanne's hair with a cloth and unbuttoning her coat. 'How did you let her get so wet?'

'Hallo Mum.'

Her mother looked at her for the first time. There could have been the trace of a smile, but it was difficult to be sure. 'So you've come to your senses then, and not before time. You might have got her killed, putting her in all that danger.'

'I might have got killed.'

'You can choose what you do, she can't.'

Her father came back in, his hair plastered to his head with the rain, he was holding the dog by its collar. 'Blasted animal,' he said. 'Doesn't know the meaning of obedience.'

'Mind the blackout, and come over here by the fire before you get pneumonia. You should have let her go, she'd come back soon enough.'

'I'll get the cases,' Jenny said, moving towards the door.

'Mind the blackout then,' her mother was more concerned about the blackout than she was about her own daughter, Jenny thought resentfully. 'Put the kettle on, Will, can't see us getting any sleep for an hour or more.'

Jenny stepped out again into the streaming night, and was blinded by the blackness after the candlelight of the room. She stumbled off the path into a bush, before dim sight came slowly back, and she was able to grope her way to the gate. The cases were sodden and heavy, and the rain rained through her coat and ran in a rivulet down her neck. Must be like this in France. Steve was probably standing in mud with rain running down his neck, waiting for someone to kill

13

him. Her discomfort was nothing to the hell he was going through.

Her father had opened up the range when she got back, so that the fire flared and roared and the comfort and warmth made her want to cry. Joanne still slept on her grandmother's lap, oblivious of the drying out process and the removal of most of her clothing.

'Fancy turning up without a word of warning like this,' said her mother. 'Don't know what you were thinking of. Suppose we hadn't been here? Suppose we'd been away somewhere?'

But they never went away. 'Yes, I'm sorry, I should have let you know. I meant to, but I only decided to come yesterday. I just couldn't stand any more, had to get out after Steve went overseas, it was all too much.' Couldn't tell them she was going back; couldn't tell them she was only dumping Joanne; couldn't tell them that till later. Perhaps could never tell them; just do a flit one day without telling them; no point in starting up an argument and a fight that could never be won. Just flit, just go. But don't think about it now. Enjoy the warmth, the relief, the escape for a day or so, and go before it all turns sour again, as it surely would.

The kettle whistled and her father went into the back kitchen to make the tea. She remembered the silences of long ago; days of silences it seemed, looking back on it, so that she had sometimes found it necessary to rush out of the house just to hear the lark sing, or the cock crow, or to encourage Shep to bark in the exuberance of escape. Would this new dog bark for sheer exuberance? She didn't think so, it looked far too cowed and ashamed of its previous dash for freedom. It stared at her now with subdued hostility, like the Landseer dog that used to hang on her bedroom wall, eyes full of sentimental subserviency.

And Joanne slept on, her wet clothes in a steaming heap on the floor, the tartan rug off the sofa wrapped round her, her white gold hair streaming over her grandmother's arm, looking for all the world like a dead Ophelia. Able to abandon this? Jenny's breath caught momentarily in her throat, but sentiment was taboo. Joanne might be a tear-jerkingly beautiful little girl, but she could also become a material reason for her mother's suicide, or worse, for her own death by violence. So it was all for her own good; she would realize that one day. Surely she would realize that. Even if she had to endure the silences that Jenny herself had had to endure, that would merely increase her self-sufficiency. Jenny suppressed the thought of her own lack of self-confidence. Joanne was different, even at four she was already a personality which Jenny had never been; she was sure she had never been. So this was the only solution for Joanne's well-being. There was no other way.

'Still take sugar?' Will stirred the tea round in the pot before pouring it out.

'Yes, I'm afraid . . .'

'Well, I hope you've brought your ration book,' said her mother. 'We don't have any extra.'

Will held up a full spoonful, the vestige of a smile somewhere round his eyes. 'This spoonful belongs to me,' he said, 'it's got my name all over it, comes out of my particular jar, I'm lending it to you, Jenny.'

Jenny smiled back at him. There was homemade bread and honey, and as she bit into the crust he had cut for her, the whole of her childhood seemed to swim joyfully before her, all full of sun and warmth and secrets with Dad and milking time and newly hatched chickens and ducklings. But of course it wasn't like that at all; it was silences and isolation, and mud and cold and unendurable loneliness. It would be different for Joanne, she would be different and would be able to make friends with the other children in the village. It would be quite different for her.

'Oh yes,' said her mother, 'be sarcastic at my expense by all means. Pretend to be generous if you want, but just don't try taking any out of my jar to make up, that's all. Just don't try.'

15

Joanne woke early the next morning to the strange sound of wind and sea, neither of which she remembered hearing before. She remembered the swish of bombs coming out of the sky, but this swish went on and on and there was no bang at the end of it, but only this thumping and splashing somewhere in the distance, and funny screams and laughing in the air.

She pulled at Jenny's sleeping arm. 'Why is that person laughing?'

Jenny moaned and stirred and tried not to wake. She had only just fallen asleep. 'Erh? . . . Oh God . . . what?'

'Why is that person laughing? Listen, he's laughing and crying as well, listen.'

Jenny's gummed eyes opened a crack and her ears unblocked to hear the sound of sea and seagulls. Was it time for school? The wind whined through the gaps in the doors and windows, and her mind left the dream and emerged, angrily. 'Seagulls,' she said. 'It's seagulls.'

'What are seagirls?'

'Oh shut up, do. It's much too early, go back to sleep and don't wake me up again or you'll get a smack.' She hurled herself over in the bed, taking most of the bedclothes, and Joanne climbed down and went to see what was outside the window.

It gave her quite a shock. There were no houses, only grass, and trees which were small, and bent double by the wind that was moving the grass as well. They were high up and on the edge of a steep, steep hill that ended in grey-black swirling water that splashed down at the bottom and stretched away as far as the sky. But how could it? The sky was up in the air and the water was at the bottom of the hill. She looked at the sky and saw that it was dark grey with black clouds racing and birds just hanging there, being blown about like leaves in the park. Only there were no leaves here; everything was bare. It was the birds that were laughing and crying. Some were blown quite near her window and

16

she could see them opening their beaks to make the noise. She wondered if there were seaboys as well as seagirls; perhaps the boys were laughing and the girls were crying.

She felt suddenly cold and ran back to the bed, crawling in at the bottom near Jenny's feet because there was more space and more blankets down there. She put her thumb in her mouth, picked up the end of her nightdress between two fingers of her other hand, flicked it under her nose and fell asleep.

2

Will Tremayne's farm lay just outside the boundary of the Petherick estate. Petherick Manor was a big, rambling house sitting solidly atop a small hill a few miles from Zennor village. It was an isolated situation; very much the dominant residence for the whole district; always had been. Built to last, of unremitting granite, and changing only in size over the centuries with no-nonsense additions to house the growing generations of Pethericks and their increasing entourage. The house, along with its family, kept itself to itself, though there was talk that its sixteenth century owner had been a profligate squire, and many stories had come down of wild parties, even, it was said, sacrifices to the Devil and black orgies of that sort. There were plenty of tales about the ancient clan of the Pethericks; one in particular, the Polwagle Curse, was well known, and still caused occasional local banter. It was said that way back in Cornwall's early history, a certain witch, who had attached herself to the clan of the Polwagles, was insulted and derided by the daughter of a member of the Petherick clan. So incensed by her treatment was she, that she called down a curse upon the Pethericks.

Should there be no immediate male heir, then disaster would befall them, and the whole family would die within the next ten years and leave no trace – no uncles, no cousins – nothing at all.

It was commonly supposed that there must have been some good spirit in attendance at the time, in the same way that the good fairy had appeared and reduced the power of the bad fairy's curse in the case of the Sleeping Beauty, because one thing that had been peculiar to the family right up to the present generation was its propensity to produce a super-abundance of male progeny. Girls there were, over the ages, but proportionally few, so that the Petherick inheritance had somehow appeared to be an act of God: there would be Petherick gentlemen farmers in that part of Cornwall for all eternity. Generations of village gamblers had placed bets on the outcome of each new Petherick pregnancy; the odds were high, and worth a few shillings every time.

But all that changed when Humphrey Godolphin Petherick married Beatrice Pleasance Pascoe in 1913. It was then that the rot really set in. Three war babies made their appearance – Bridget in 1914, Cynthia in 1915 and Daphne in 1917. Humphrey Petherick was beside himself with rage.

'Must be something seriously wrong with your heredity, woman,' he said to Beatrice. 'Never happened before – never, in hundreds of years. In the whole history of my family there have been boys, boys, boys, with just the occasional girl, so no problem about the name being perpetuated. Can't be anything wrong with my family then; must be yours. No other explanation. Can't you see a doctor or something?'

Bea's rages were equal to those of her husband. 'What an insufferable freak you are; talking as though girls are something to be ashamed of. Not as if the name's noble or anything; Pascoe's much more histori-cally interesting. Nothing wrong with *me*, my dear, just that your bellicose little Petherick sperms have met their match at last in my aggressively obstinate Pascoe ovums – or should I say ova? Not that you would comprehend the difference.'

For Bea was an undoubted scholar. Her parents had considered her so uncompromisingly plain that they had insisted that her superior brain should be educated to the full so that at least she might be able to earn her own living when left an old maid. She was really quite grateful to Humphrey Petherick when he considered she might be the right type to carry on the Petherick tradition, even if she did consider him to be a bumptious, arrogant bore. At twenty-two, though, and because it was 1913, she had not begun to question her parents' opinion of her.

'You are the most crudely vulgar woman I have ever met,' Humphrey shouted at her. 'Your indelicate and obscene remarks never fail to disgust me.'

'Obscene? Scientific phenomena can scarcely be called vulgar, except by the uneducated.'

He was impossible. How to put up with such crass ignorance was difficult to resolve. But, when she thought about it, Bea knew that she really did prefer the comfort of being the head of a large, prosperous household, to being the ugly, intellectual misfit in a particularly good-looking, pleasure-loving bunch of five sisters – daughters of a bleakly unprosperous parson and his wife, and living in a Victorian vicarage near Penzance.

'You are a tyrant, and antediluvian into the bargain. I will talk how I like,' Bea went on, determined to have the last word.

They both rather enjoyed the bickering; Bea, because she was superior in arguing any point, and Humphrey, because he realized that Bea was unique among women, and he felt pleased that he had picked himself someone so unusual. Difficult to live with, naturally, but her intelligence never failed to intrigue him; one didn't know what to expect.

This production of girl after girl, however, was a

serious blow, and one that made him consider divorce on several occasions. Trouble was, never had been a divorce in the family and it would cause a scandal. Might set the county against him, and he didn't want that. Could see himself being labelled an Eastern Potentate or a Henry the Eighth character – produce an heir or else. Didn't want that at all.

Anyway, she was quite shrewd where the farm accounts were concerned. Would never have let her meddle if she hadn't shown such an interest. She had, on one or two occasions, picked up things he had not noticed himself – extraordinary for a woman – and the whole business had benefited greatly from her sharp observance. In fact everything was doing very nicely at the moment, thanks to her suggestions; in spite of his own father having been bamboozled on several occasions by a rascally accountant, and having been hand in glove with an untrustworthy bailiff. This had resulted in his leaving large debts to be met at his death.

So the girls went on arriving, Dorothy in 1919 and Jean in 1922, making five in all. It was then that Bea decided to call a halt to the whole thing. She found sex a messy and thoroughly unrewarding business and took it for granted that Humphrey had other outlets for his appetites apart from the occasional fling with her when nothing better was available. But she had had quite enough of babies; of that she was adamant. 'Can't stand the little blighters,' she asserted, enjoying the embarrassment her pronouncement caused among her acquaintances. 'If it hadn't been for Websie, I'd have dropped them all over the cliff years ago.' Mrs Webb had been engaged as nurse when Bridget was born and had just stayed and stayed over the years.

Imagine the shock, then, when eleven years later, after a rather drunken New Year celebration, Bea found herself pregnant again. 'It's positively indecent,' she told Humphrey. 'Said so at the time if you remember. But I never thought it would still *work*;

otherwise I would have been more careful – or insisted that you were.'

Humphrey tended to consider the whole thing a huge joke. 'Never knew I had it in me. Both pretty well past it I thought. Well, well; we've about run out of girls' names. What about Guinevere? Always rather fancied that myself.'

'Don't be flippant. Might be a boy; you never know.'

'A *boy*? Don't talk nonsense. You could never produce a boy in a hundred years.'

'*You* could never produce a boy, you mean. And just you remember what I have to go through as a result of your drunken spree; nine months misery, several hours' torture and another little horror to cope with.'

'Not much of a spree as far as I can remember.'

'I should be very surprised if you remember anything at all.'

'Rubbish, it's such an infrequent experience that I quite enjoyed it.'

'Well I didn't.'

'So you said at the time.'

Bea's smile was humourless. She felt trapped and set back in time. The child-bearing period should, by rights, be over for her now, and yet here she was, having to relive a discarded epoch of her life just when she thought she might branch out a little. It was really damnable.

The whole of the nine months was even more of a nightmare than any of the previous pregnancies; she was irritable, depressed and ill, furious with herself, with Humphrey and anyone else who happened to approach. 'Much better if I died here and now,' she told Mrs Webb. 'Everyone would be better off in the long run.'

Mrs Webb was unmoved by the outbursts. 'Don't talk so daft; 'tes a wicked sin to talk so.'

'Don't come religious with me Websie, I had too much of that in my childhood.'

'Well then, stop frettin' and worryin' everyone in arm's length of you.'

21

'It's all very well for you.'

'And it'll be all's well with you come a day or two my dear.'

And, of course, it was. The baby was a boy, and producing a son was such a totally new experience for Bea that it seemed to bear no sort of comparison to giving birth to five daughters. The event affected her in quite a different way; for the first time in her life she felt like a mother. And because the phenomenon had hit her so late in life, it manifested itself to excess. For the next few years she became neurotically maternal.

After a great deal of argument and bad feeling, they finally decided to name him Peter Enedoc Gwinnear. Gwinnear, because Humphrey had been certain that it would be a girl, and had become so keen on calling her Guinevere that he was loath to relinquish the idea completely. Enedoc, because Bea had happy childhood memories of carefree summer holidays near the Church of St Enedoc in Trebetherick. Peter had been the bone of contention; it was Bea's father's name, and one that Humphrey abominated. He only gave up the fight after several months of battle.

Peter spent the first seven years of his life in a haze of motherly devotion, fatherly pride and sisterly, barely suppressed, hate. Jean, at eleven, was the worst affected. She had enjoyed being everyone's baby sister; she had enjoyed getting the better of Dorothy because of the three years' difference in their ages. The three older girls had always vaguely radiated indulgence and benign indifference whenever she came within their ken, which wasn't often, as they went to different boarding schools and followed different pursuits in the holidays.

'He looks like a pig,' Jean said, when she first saw him, and he was consequently known as Piggy by all the sisters from that moment on.

Peter was a shock and an interloper, and both Jean and Dorothy found it hard to forgive him. Mother and Websie had transferred their affections, their time and their sympathies. Father had never liked his daughters that much, but now he seemed to enjoy rubbing in the ignominy of being a girl rather than a boy.

'He doesn't even consider that we might want to be farmers,' Jean said. 'Never lets us help or anything. It's so unfair. And now all he talks about is how he at last has a son he can pass on the family business to. Just as though we weren't there. I feel like throwing the wretched brat into the sea sometimes.'

'That's what Mother used to say about us,' said Dorothy.

'Yes, but she doesn't say it about him, does she?'

'By the time we grow up there'll probably be a law to say women are just as important as men.'

'Can't see that happening; the government's full of men. I suppose I could become a member of parliament when I grow up, and then I could make a law like that myself.'

'You couldn't ever get into Parliament. Nobody would vote for you.'

'They might, if I'm pretty and clever enough.'

'But you not in the least pretty, or clever.'

'No, but I might be, when I grow up.'

On Peter's seventh birthday, he was told that in the New Year he would be going to the prep school that his father had attended.

Amidst the love and the hate of his family, he had grown up in his own cocoon. He was serious and silent and enjoyed tucking himself into dark corners where he could not be seen. Indoors, he built long tunnels of tables, tipped chairs, cushions and any pieces of material he could find, like sheets and tablecloths and bathtowels. He would crawl down the tunnels and sit in one of the cave-like recesses at the end, where he would whisper to himself stories about a solitary rabbit who lived in a burrow and never went out at all because he wanted to keep warm and dry.

The idea of his being banished to some strange,

unknown prison was so appalling that the news froze him into total silence. In vain, the jolly governess, who had been hired to teach him and three other little boys living in the district, reading, writing and arithmetic up to prep school standard, tried to lure him out of his mute distress. 'Come now, Peter, there's nothing to be frightened of; cheer up! Be a man! All little boys have to go to school, and privileged little boys like you are able to go to special schools, getting ready to become special sort of men. Men who will become the leaders of tomorrow.' She waxed lyrical and forgot the dejected creature who sat hunched on the carpet before her. 'The judges, the generals, the politicians . . .' Her eyes sparkled at the idea that she had been the one to start this great man on his inevitable climb to the top.

And still Peter said nothing at all. How could they do this to him? Mother was always telling him she loved him, how could she send him away then? Had he done something to upset her? He remembered being cross with her sometimes when she didn't let him do something. But more likely that the sisters had told her he had to go. They didn't like him, so they would want him out of the way. But why did Mother listen to them? He had thought she was on his side. Must've been wrong. He had been anxious when she had brought Miss Bean in as governess. That meant he didn't see so much of Mother. She was often too busy since Miss Bean came; or he was cooped up having to learn to read and things. He supposed he hadn't learned fast enough so they'd decided he must be sent away to learn properly.

His father had said 'Going to follow me, old chap, are you? High time too; too much spoiling goes on here. Better to stand on your own feet you know. Expect the little blighters at St Bede's have become a bit more civilized since I was there. Hope so, for your sake, though bullying was frowned on even then. Not that it made much difference. But you need to learn to stand up for yourself. Much too dependent on women in this establishment.'

Peter did not recognize the word 'bullying' and found it difficult enough to relate to the boys who shared lessons with him at the moment to be able to contemplate the idea of living in a great houseful of boys and men. It was far too frightening. He understood that all the Petherick boys were sent away to school when they were seven, but he had thought he was different. He knew he wasn't a bit like his father had been, nor like any of the uncles he occasionally met at big family parties, so he thought they would treat him differently. They must know he wasn't clever and brave and funny like they were. He didn't tell jokes and didn't like riding or football or cricket, so there would be no sense in sending him away to learn about these things. They were bound to let him stay at home and not try to do any of the things they did. He was frightened of all the animals on the farm, so they couldn't possibly expect him to be a farmer like them. Not possibly. He made a very long, dark tunnel in his bedroom, all round the room, that ended under the bottom shelf of the cupboard in the wall under the roof, and he crawled into it and cried. They would never find him there.

But they did, and he was wrenched away from everything and everyone he knew, to be dumped in an unknown environment amid uncomprehending strangers. Some of the boys tried to be kind, but found it hard going as his answers were monosyllabic.

'*Pethe*rick?' a master shouted at roll call; he received no answer so looked up at Peter, sitting silently at the back of the class. 'Come on, boy, answer your name.'

Peter looked round him to be sure that he was the one being addressed. 'But that's not my name.'

'What?' Quick check of the list. 'What do you mean? Not your name? You're down here as Petherick P. Have you got in the wrong class or something? And say Sir when you address a master, boy.'

'My name's Peter Pe*the*rick . . . Sir.'

A sharp glance to see if insolence could be detected.

'Petherick – doesn't seem a likely pronounciation to me, boy.' A penetrating look, this time. Obviously a cheeky one, this. 'See that you answer when you're called, next time. However it's pronounced. Understand?'

'Yes.'

'Sir.'

'Sir.'

The Sunday letter-writing session was a nightmare. There was nothing to say that could be said. He could expect no support. He had been abandoned.

Dear Mother
    I am quite well I hope you and Father are quite well I miss you very much the tuck box was very nice I ate all the chocolate and I was sick in my bed it was very narsty.
    Lots of love from Peter.

3

Joanne Tremayne waited quietly in the dark, empty bed for the siren to go off. She was stiff with the fear of not having her mother within immediate clutching distance when the moment came. Mumma had vanished a day or two after they had arrived in this silent, frightening place. They had both cried a lot before she went. In fact, Joanne had screamed and clung to bits of her mother's clothing while Gran unpicked each finger in turn from Mumma's coat, and Grampa had pulled her away. Mumma was going, like she sometimes did in London, and she'd never come back. Always there was this fear: she'd never come back.

'I won't be gone long,' she'd said. Always said that

when she went out anywhere. But what was long? It was now that Joanne wanted her. But Gran and Grampa hadn't let her go, no matter how hard she cried and kicked and struggled, they hadn't let go of her, and Mumma had run away, out of the door and down the path and into a car, and the car went off down the road, into the distance and out of sight. And still they held on to her so that she couldn't go after her. Held her like she once held a cat until it scratched and bit her and she had to let it go. She sank her teeth into Gran's hand and was rewarded with a hard and painful slap.

'Little vixen!' shouted Gran. 'Bite me would you? Well you don't get away with that sort of thing with me, my girl.'

But Grampa wrapped his arms right round her, so that she was pinioned gently and could only kick his shins. 'There, there, old darling,' he said in her ear. 'Don't take on so my dear. We'll keep you safe and sound for when your Mumma can come and fetch you. Don't you fret so, little Joanie.'

The stinging slap from Gran reduced her screams to sobs which shuddered through her, and she turned towards Grampa and wept into his old, rough shirt.

But all that was days ago, and Mumma still hadn't come back. She was surely bound to be back before the siren went off? Bound to be. It had been quite a lot of nights since the siren had gone off this time. It probably hadn't gone off because Mumma wasn't there. Must be because of that because she was always there when the siren went off. But perhaps it wasn't going to go off any more because perhaps the war had stopped. Mumma said it went off because of the war. And things were different these last few days because of Mumma not being there and the siren not going off and no bangs and this funny place with no houses and Gran and Grampa and Chip the dog. She liked Chip the dog; he was soft and floppy.

Grace Tremayne looked round the door ready to

shout at any sign of wakefulness, but Joanne stayed still as a mouse so she turned and stumped downstairs like a disappointed hunter deprived of its prey. Try as she would, she was unable to get rid of the dislike she felt for this angelic-looking child she found herself in charge of. Prettiness was suspect; the pretty ones always thought too much of themselves; grew up spoilt and perky. She'd been glad that Jenny had been no oil painting. Glad she'd not put her in for all those Beautiful Baby shows they'd had when Jenny had been a little one. Kept her away from all that rubbish, and yet she still grew up like she did. And now, using her mother as nothing more than a dumping ground. Just using them, that's all. No justice in this world; none at all.

'Needs a good slap, that Joanne,' she said to Will, still smarting at the thought of Jenny's behaviour. 'Don't know the meaning of discipline she don't . . . Well, she'll learn it soon enough with me. I'm not standing for any of her spoilt ways I can tell you. Jenny's been too soft with her, that's what it is. Soft on her and hard on us. Taking off like that without so much as a by your leave. Putting on us like that. Just you find her, Will Tremayne, that's all I say; just you rouse yourself for once and get her back here. Why should we do her dirty work for her while she's gadding about somewhere?'

'You're hard on her Gracie. She were doing her best after all; and it's not fair on the little 'un to keep her up in London with all those bombs and that.'

'Oh faddle to that; your daughter's only thinking of Jenny Tremayne – or whatever her new fangled name happens to be, that's if she do happen to have changed it which I doubt – she's never thinking of her baby, nor of her parents, and that's for sure. Nothing but trouble, that one.'

It was hard to forgive one that had brought disgrace to her family; running away without a word when she was no more than seventeen, and then coming back a year or so later with a baby and no husband and expecting love and kisses – oh no! That wasn't Grace Tremayne's idea of acceptable behaviour; certainly it wasn't. And this – this new outrage now, added further insult to injury. It was unforgivable.

Will lit his pipe for the fourth time: ruddy wartime tobacco; work hard all day and then can't get a decent smoke nor an unbothered rest in the evening, even when he made the effort to come home instead of staying down the pub.

They both relapsed into the defensive silence that had been so much a part of their life together. Not much sense in airing thoughts that were so far apart: only led to more irritation and bad feeling, specially when the subject of Jenny came up.

Will remembered the disappointment that had crept up on him as Jenny had grown up and away from the life in which he had found fulfilment and contentment. But it was only to be expected; how could he ever have imagined a pretty young lass like Jenny would have been happy working on a rough old farm? She'd naturally go for a bit of excitement and fun. Only sad she had to go and get herself landed so quick, before she'd had time to think. And Grace as good as throwing her out like that – or at least making it impossible for her to stay; shouldn't never have done that. He became agitated at the memory and the disquieting knowledge of his own inability to stand up to Grace's dominance on occasions like these.

Grace and Will Tremayne were born in 1890 within ten miles and two hours of each other. Indeed the local midwife of the time was hard pressed to be in at both births, having to make the journey between the two cottages by farm cart. But Will's mother was an old hand at the game, Will was her tenth, and she rather scorned the midwife's claim to the medical title. 'Know more about it than you do Beattie Penney,' she grumbled, 'seeing as how I been through it ten times more'n you're ever likely to.' But she appreciated the company, nevertheless, and enjoyed the gossip that Susan Tucker had produced a daughter two hours earlier. 'Old George'll be towering mad he ain't got a boy, after all this long wait and all.'

'And she being past carrying now I wouldn't wonder,' Beattie Penney agreed. 'Poor old George; always wanted a boy, didn't he? But she's the non-receptive type, that Susan. Tell the truth, I was that surprised that she ever did conceive at all. Bit of a miracle you could call it.' The two women laughed together, so that Will Tremayne was born to the accompaniment of gossip and a chuckle, which may have been the reason for his later ability to relieve his otherwise bleak life with an occasional smile.

'Better have one we know rather than getting landed with one of them evacuee kids from the slums,' Will reminded his wife now. 'She's our flesh and blood, don't forget, and a lovely little kid into the bargain.' Unlike his wife, Will had been bowled over by Joanne's looks. He didn't remember ever seeing a child so stunningly beautiful. Not that he looked much at other kids, he supposed, but he didn't remember Jenny looking like it. Joanne was like the pictures of angels his mother used to pin up on the walls when he was a child himself. Took him back.

'Lovely little kid indeed; she's a brat that needs house training for one. Wets her bed you know. All that extra work; diabolical I call it.'

Strange, thought Will, to start off again with a little 'un. He quite liked the idea, remembering Jenny as a four-year-old. Never much trouble until she grew up. Poor little kid upstairs all alone. He'd have to do a lot of shielding and loving on the sly if she was to come through. He sighed, and lit his pipe again.

It had been almost a foregone conclusion, all that time ago, that he and Grace should marry; there didn't seem to have been anyone else left for one thing, and for another, his parents had thought it suitable. So much easier to go along with what was expected, and it all worked out pretty well on the whole. He never did expect too much and tended to keep himself to himself so he was able to take Grace's dour temper in his stride. Altogether, Will led a reasonable life, and together with Grace had achieved the success of owning a small holding, no mean feat at the time. His mother had always said that he would get on. 'No beating about the bush with my Will,' she said. 'Sets his mind on something and goes after it, that's my Will.' It was obvious that he was her favourite, being the last of the bunch.

Grace had had no such security to fall back on. Her father resented her from the very first; she should have been a boy, he had little interest in girls, as Beattie pointed out, so her mother never quite forgave her for disappointing him. They only had the one child, no-one knew why, but reckoned it was a just punishment for something one or other of them had done at some time.

Whatever the evil that had brought about this lack of fertility, Grace obviously carried it through into the next generation, because Jenny was the only child Grace and Will managed to produce. Unlike Grace's father, Will was delighted to have a daughter. If anyone had asked him, he would probably have admitted that he would have welcomed one or two more, but Grace wasn't keen. 'If you want me to keep the place clean, your clothes washed, the dinner cooked and the hens fed, you can't expect me to produce a crew of kids as well. Got no time for that; one's more than enough. My mother only had one, no reason why I should have more.'

There were occasions when the suspicion that this could, possibly, have been a hasty decision hovered in the back of her mind: if they had had a boy, then things would have been easier; boys looked after their mothers and worked for their fathers. A son would never have gone off like this and then expected them to support his child – no son of hers would have done that. Girls were different, and suppose she'd had another girl? That would have been disaster. She couldn't have risked having another girl.

Will listened, now, to her remarks about Joanie with a buried sense of dissent. He could not bring himself to disagree, even quietly in his own mind, but there was a lurking suspicion that Grace was wrong to look on children as a tie and a drawback.

'Commonsense,' she would say to him sharply, 'that's what you lack, Will Tremayne; much too soft you are.' And she was probably right; Grace had a lot of common sense.

It took some two to three weeks before Joanne stopped sitting by the front door, waiting for Mumma to come back; before she stopped asking anyone she happened to meet whether they had seen her Mumma who was coming to fetch her. She seemed not to hear Gran's exasperated explosions of couldn't she stop moping around asking for her mum and give a bit of credit where credit was due? Didn't she see that they were doing their best to look after her and make her happy? Not that she expected gratitude, mind, but all this crying and moping was getting her down.

Joanne looked long and hard at this grey lady with the angry face, and tried to push the fear and misery to the back of her mind. If she could think of something else for a little while, then the bad things might just go away, like they did when you fell asleep at night. Quite often you woke up the next morning and everything was all right again. It hadn't happened here yet, but it might, it just might.

Just for now, she would have to think some good thoughts and make up some nice stories that had happy endings and they might possibly come true. You never knew. But the good thoughts refused to come; there was only the suspicion, that soon became a certainty, that Gran was really a witch who had witched Mumma away. She'll put me in a cage, thought Joanne. Witches do that. She's witched Mumma away and now she'll keep me in a cage and then she'll eat me.

She put her thumb in her mouth and one finger up her nose, and started to rock backwards and forwards, crouched on her haunches in a corner of the kitchen, thinking over and over how she hadn't been clever enough to wish the right wish, so that things were now worse, and looked as though they might never get better. This nearly always happened in stories, but it usually came out right in the end with the help of some magic from somewhere else. There was often a poor farmer with three sons and the youngest one was a prince who was magic and able to rescue people. Well, Grampa was a poor farmer but he didn't have any sons. Maybe there was another poor farmer in the village whose youngest son might be able to rescue her from the wicked witch.

She met him on a Tuesday afternoon when Gran had gone into Penzance for market day.

'Not taking *her*,' Grace told Will, jerking her head in Joanne's direction. 'More trouble than it's worth and like as not she'd be sick on the bus.'

Joanne did not demur; who knew what witches might or might not do on buses? Specially when Grampa wasn't there to come to her rescue. She certainly would have been sick, she always was on buses, and anyway it was important to stay back in case Mumma took the opportunity of the witch being out, to come and snatch her back again.

Will was working round the farmyard, and told her to play near the house where he could keep an eye on her. There was a swing down by the pigsty, strung from the one tall oak that had grown in spite of the searing Atlantic wind. Joanne saw the swing ropes disappear into the soaring branches which looked to her like the roof of the church where the swifts had nested. There were some dark and frightening sheds

33

underneath, where all the log piles were, and where Grampa filled the basket that stood by the fire. She wished they weren't so near the swing, because the goblins could always dart out and get you.

And then, close by, was the barn where hay lay, left from the summer. In the barn it was warm and cosy and away from the wind if it was howling and screeching at you, and on other days you could keep dry and out of the wetness of the misty clouds of tiny rain drops that stuck on your face and your clothes and finally ran down your neck in little rivers. It was quiet and safe, and somewhere you could watch without being seen and listen for all those silent sounds that crept round you when you were alone.

Charlie was in the barn when she went in, sitting shrouded in hay so that you could only see him if you looked particularly hard, and even then you couldn't exactly make him out, because his hair looked like the hay, and he definitely had a distinct air of magic all round him. He seemed, to Joanne, the obvious saviour with magical qualities sent to solve her problems. The person she had been making impassioned wishes for every day, and for whom she had added a silent prayer on to the ones the witch made her say to Jesus every night. It was a great relief, that at least somebody had heard her, be it Jesus or the Good Fairy: didn't really matter which. She introduced herself without hesitation.

'Joanne?' he said. 'What sort of a name is that? I shall call you Jo and you can call me Charlie.'

'My gran's a witch,' she told him. 'She's gone in to Penzance today to buy a cage big enough to put me in, so that she can keep me there until I'm fat enough to eat.'

'Ar,' said Charlie.

'Have you come to rescue me and fetch my Mumma back?' she asked.

'I don't know how to fetch her back,' he said. 'I'm not magic you know.'

34

Jo was disappointed, but he probably wouldn't know that he was magic. He would suddenly realize it some time later, and then they would be able to try out all sorts of spells together.

'I expect you are really, only you haven't found out yet. We could try doing spells and things. Shall we go on the swing?' She would be safe with him because the goblins wouldn't dare to jump out on her when there was someone else there.

Jo sat on first and Charlie pushed her because she hadn't yet got the hang of working it herself. It was very good to have him there to push her because without a pusher, there was no way she could make herself move properly. He was strong too and she was soon flying exquisitely high, almost to the sky and back. The endless ropes that were attached to the sky high branch seemed to swing almost slowly from so far up, and yet she swept with breath-taking speed from the dizzy heights of the deserted rooks' nests where she could view the ground from afar, tearing downwards past the pigsties, past the hen coops, to be flung up by Charlie's jerking shove into a lying down position where she could only see clouds and seagulls hanging in the sky.

Charlie was magic all right, to be able to give her this fairy feeling of flying. This was probably the way he was going to rescue her: on one of these flights up to the sky, she would actually slide off the seat and find herself flying, along with the birds, back to London to find Mumma. In no time at all the rhythm had caught up with her, and she became her own driving force, pulling and pushing her own way to exhilaration, and possible rescue.

'Here, 'ere, 'ere . . .' She suddenly heard Will's warning shout from below and ceased the striving thrusts so that the wind in her back and then in her face became a gentle brake to slow her pace. Will grasped the rope of the swing to bring it to a halt.

'You're too small for to go so high,' he said. 'Drat it,

you'll go and break your neck you will; a little thing like you, how did you manage to get yourself up as dangerous as that? How did you manage it? A little thing like you.' He was shaken to realize the dangers of such a thing, and his heart went quite cold.

'I learned just now to work myself, Grampa. I never could before, I never could work myself at all, but now I know how to and it's wonderful, it's magic. Charlie started me off by pushing me but in the end I was doing it all myself.'

'Charlie? Who's Charlie?'

'He's a magic boy I met in the barn.' She looked round her but couldn't see him. 'He was here just now. I expect he's hiding.'

'Well I don't allow no young varmints messing around in my barn. You tell 'im that from me, and don't you go talking to no Tom Dick and Harry without they talk to me first.'

'But it wasn't Tom Dick or Harry, it was Charlie, and he's my friend.'

'Pretend friend more like. Don't know no Charlie round these parts, so don't you go talkin' to nobody, remember.' He looked round, belligerently, to search out anyone in the vicinity.

'But he's special, Grampa, because he's magic. He taught me to fly like the birds fly. I was flying like the birds. I could see all over everywhere, and I could see everyone down here just walking about, ordinary like – and I was up flying, like God.'

'Well, I didn't see no Charlie, so just you mind how you learns to fly in future. And anyway, nobody didn't have no right to push a little thing like you, Charlie or no Charlie. Nobody didn't have no right to danger you like that. You could well have broke your neck, you know that?'

'He proberly made himself invisible just so you couldn't tell him off. Could you mend me if I broke my neck or would I be dead?'

'Oh you'd be dead all right if you broke your neck.

36

Don't you be taking risks like that again, Joanie. Just you mind what I say now.'

He took her hand in his, and she felt the earth and mud caked creases as they went into tea together.

'I like your teas Grampa with splitters and cream and jam and that. We didn't have teas like that in London.'

'Your Grandma, she do make crackin' good jam.'

'Yes she do,' Jo said before remembering that Gran was a witch. She tried to think of other good points her grandmother might possess but could remember none. Witches were probably known to be good at cooking; she wondered how she cooked children; with carrots? Or beans? Onions? She hoped not, because she didn't like onions.

'Is Mumma coming here soon? Is she coming on holiday with me? When is she going to take me home?' Perhaps they could take some cream and jam with them.

'She wants you to keep out of the way of all them guns and bombs and things. She wants you to stay down here till it's all over and then she'll come and fetch you no doubt. Just now she's got to go and help win the war along with all them soldiers. To get it over quicker.'

'When will it be over then?'

'Oh, bound to be over by Christmas or Easter maybe. Sure to be over then.'

Jo hoped that Christmas or Easter would not take too long to come. 'But Christmas has just been and I got some gloves and a woollen hat.'

'Ah, so it has then; well next Christmas, bound to be over by next Christmas so they say.'

Jo froze into a distracted paralysis of horror, and all the bad old thoughts came flooding back. Next Christmas was a lifetime away.

4

Being the eldest of the Petherick tribe was no easy task. Bridget became something of a substitute mother, nurse and organizer for the rest of the family. She took over that role when Peter was born because her mother and Mrs Webb appeared to opt out of responsibility for the girls from that time on. Bridget considered it sickening and downright unfair, but she realized it wasn't such a bad thing as far as she was concerned.

She was nearly nineteen at the time of Peter's arrival, over large and masculine looking. The Petherick girls took their looks in rotation from father and mother: one, three and five having Humphrey's rather coarse features and unruly fair hair, while two and four took the straight, dark hair from their mother that went with aquiline features and grey-blue eyes. Bridget resented the serene, aristocratic looks that Cynthia and Dorothy had inherited from Bea, which she considered was at variance with their characters: Cyn was weak and Dot was smug; not in the least aristocratic. She took her position as the eldest very seriously and was considered by all as captain of the team.

She had stayed on at school far too long because she was enjoying it so much. Head girl and good at games, she was undoubtedly the Headmistress's pet. The admiration was mutual: Miss Cartwright made her feel worthwhile and appreciated. This was so much better than being looked on as the family dogsbody which was how she saw herself at home.

Mind you, she thought to herself, I did enjoy organizing things, and, because of being head girl at school, I sort of took on responsibility automatically. But at home they didn't really appreciate it; Mother and Father didn't even notice, Websie got annoyed because I was always telling her what to do, and the others thought I was bossy.

But it made me grow up pretty damn fast I can tell you, because the sisters resented the sudden neglect we all experienced in different degrees when Peter was born. Not that Mother or Father had ever paid us much heed, but we existed as a group, all together; a sort of block of inanimate matter that called itself a close-knit family. At least that was what Websie called us. ''Tes a close-knit family the Pethericks, that's to be sure,' she would say, in her good old Cornish way. 'Never ones for spreading theirselves about. Not a one of 'em.' And she was right I suppose. Though we do mix a bit now that we're older. Go to a few hunt balls and dances and sometimes tennis parties, but we tend to do things together, like picnics and riding and bathing expeditions.

She let her mind dwell on the pleasure of those family days. The feeling of clan was so strong, she thought, not a bit the same now; we all seem to be at loggerheads most of the time. It may be because Mother and Father row so much, and Mother does talk and talk and not give you much time to answer, but I suppose we've become a bit inhibited where conversation is concerned. Daphne talks a lot of nonsense, burbles on about nothing to no-one in particular and Jean is a real bore, going on all the time about socialism and equality in order to shock, but the rest of us don't talk a lot. Personally, I can't see the sense of rabbiting on unless you have something definite to say, and I like to keep my own opinions to myself anyway.

But they won't have me for much longer; now that there's a war, and Piggy has gone to school, and everyone else is old enough to look after themselves. I'm taking off to join the FANYs. Got to get away from this 'close-knit' family idea, and incidentally help to keep the bloody Germans at bay. It's not a good idea to wait until I'm called up and shoved into just anything the powers that be fancy. The FANYs are at least ladies, and it counts as war service.

Wouldn't really know there was a war on down here except for troops. As farmers we have pretty well all we want in the way of meat and eggs and vegetables; food rationing scarcely worries us. I never cared for sugar or sweets anyway, though I wouldn't give up my ration to Piggy like Mother and Websie do. That just seems silly to me, and bad for him into the bargain.

Where Bridget might be considered a rock, Cynthia Petherick was far less able to cope with life than her sister. Born eighteen months later, she never felt able to catch up. Bridget was always older and therefore cleverer. Bridget knew what to do, Cynthia never did. The idea that any of her own thoughts might be worth airing was alien to her. Bridget said all the important things before Cynthia had ever thought of them. It was easier to wait to be told things rather than think them out for herself.

'We'll ride today,' Bridget would say quite early on in the morning, so Cynthia would immediately re-adjust her mind towards a day of riding. Hadn't Bridget said so? Life was so much easier that way in any case. Opting out of decisions meant that you were never responsible for the things that went wrong. She was actually just as capable as Bridget, as long as someone told her what to do. Her marks at school were marginally better, except in English where imagination was called for, but she was never head girl, and only a prefect because she was next in seniority.

'You're such a wet, Cyn,' Bridget used to say to her quite often. 'I despair of you, really I do.'

Bea said much the same in a different sort of way. 'If Bridget goes into the FANYs, God *knows* what will happen to the rest of the family now the girls have all left school,' she said to Humphrey. 'I'm far too busy to organize everybody into worthwhile activities, and we can't have them messing around with the army types,

40

which they seem to persist in doing. Daphne and Dorothy are far too pretty for their own good and Jean will go out of her way to get herself into trouble. Why can't they get *married* for heavens sake? Can you imagine Cynthia being able to deal with any sort of situation? Can't you speak to Bridget, Humphrey? Tell her where her duties lie?'

'Depends where you think they do lie my dear.' Humphrey was sprawled in his chair, staring at the ceiling. 'With God, King and Country, or with you.'

'You're just being offensive now. And you haven't even changed out of your boots, have you.'

'No, no, can't say I have. No-one to pull them off you see.'

'Well you needn't think I'm going to.'

'I don't, my pearl, I don't.'

'What happened to the boot lever contraption I gave you for Christmas?'

'It's somewhere or other. The girls take it to remove their riding boots.'

Bea snorted with irritation; either she would have to call Cynthia – and who knew where she might be at this moment? – and tell her to remove her father's boots, or the carpets would be covered in mud for the next seven days until the daily got round to cleaning the sitting room again. It was an insoluble dilemma and one best put straight out of her thinking for the time being.

The big change in all their lives came in the summer of 1941, just after Bridget had joined the FANYs. Cynthia went into the WVS, being unable to decide which service she would dislike least if the authorities got to her age group for call-up. Daphne and Dorothy had decided to become landgirls, in order to work on the family farm, and Jean was showing alarming leanings towards the pacifists and insisting that she was applying to be exempt on moral grounds. Nobody argued with her, because they knew it only made her

41

worse. If everyone kept quiet, she might think it was not sufficiently challenging, and give up the idea.

Bridget, on a short leave, found that her organizing powers were not so much in demand at home, since everyone had been left to their own devices. As a new and inexperienced member of the First Aid Nursing Yeomanry, she missed the satisfaction of being in command. Of course, she realized that command in the services could not take all that long to achieve – promotion was quick, once they realized you were the type. Still, one last little fling with the family would round off that part of her life nicely.

'One more family picnic is a must I think,' she said aggressively, just in case any of them thought she had opted out of being head of the family. 'What about Friday? Start nine o'clock, so up early to get the horses ready. Cyn and Dottie you organize food, and I suggest we trek over to Godrevy and set up camp there. Take canvas if we think we can rely on the weather, come back following evening. Good for bathing and we can probably find a few places that aren't entirely inundated by the Military where we can let the old nags rip. Swan song, sort of thing. All nostalgia and sentimental nonsense.'

'Only if you take Piggy,' said Bea. 'It would do him so much good, and it's half term.'

Bridget groaned. 'In that case I suggest another day. Mother you *know* he hates anything like that. He loathes riding, is frightened of the horses, can't swim, gets sunburnt and would sulk from start to finish. I refuse to act as nursemaid.'

'Poor little pet,' said Daphne. 'I'll look after him. You won't even notice he's there.'

'You're mad,' Dorothy joined in. 'Wherever Piggy is, there's disaster. All those beastly tunnels everywhere – I mean to say, he just *steals* things to make them, wherever he is. He'll get us all arrested.'

'He might dig himself into a sand dune and get buried,' Jean said hopefully. 'The other day he took all

42

the blankets off all the beds: Websie nearly killed him.'

'He'll probably grow up to be famous,' Daphne insisted. 'He'll design a Maginot line that actually works, you see if he doesn't.'

'He certainly won't support any bloody war effort if *I* have anything to do with it,' said Jean. 'He's bound to be a pacifist anyway; he'd be much too frightened to fight anyone.'

'Ah – *that's* why you're a pacifist is it?'

'No it *isn't*; I just said *he* would be frightened. You know perfectly well . . .'

'For pity's sake, stop arguing, all of you,' shouted Bea, with her hands to her head. 'You'll drive me mad. I insist that you take Peter with you, and that's that.'

But as it happened, it rained all through the half term, so the expedition was put off until the following week when Peter had gone back to school. And as the five girls were racing their ponies on the downs, Humphrey Petherick dropped dead from a heart attack in the middle of one of his fields, and they returned to a household that was never quite the same again.

5

Peter Petherick sat in a corner of the Lower School Common Room, pretending to read Treasure Island. The words slotted obediently into his brain, but were immediately engulfed by the thoughts already there. It was so difficult to stop thinking.

'Once out upon the road, Black Dog, in spite of his wound, showed a wonderful clean pair of heels, and disappeared over the edge of the hill in half a minute,' he read. But even as he read it, he was thinking: They say that I've settled in at school quite well now. It took some time, but he seems happy enough now that he's older. And then they go on to say, About time he grew up a bit, he's nearly ten now, though really I'm only just nine. They're ashamed of me being so babyish. Mother is always telling her friends about me, even when I'm standing there, because I find it so difficult to answer people when they ask, How are you getting on at school then? I mean what do you say? If I said, Oh all right, it would be a lie, and I find it even more difficult to tell lies without going red. I get teased a lot about that, this going red thing; I do it whenever I'm afraid of something, and that's pretty well all the time. Always something to be afraid of, specially at school. There's always someone somewhere who's waiting to jump out at you or shout at you or trip you up and laugh. And you can't hide away at school because everyone wants to know just where you are absolutely all the time. It's beastly.

Work's all right; I like that because I can do it as long as I'm left alone. The masters are a bit horrible; wanting to din things in that you know already, and being sarcastic if you say you know. And the chaps don't like you knowing everything, so I have to keep quiet and pretend to make mistakes, because they hate people with brains. I keep wanting to make my tunnels like I did at home, so that I could get away on my own, but I can't do that here, though I do always pull the bedclothes over my head once the master's made his final round and seen that we're all lying the way they tell you to.

I think a lot when I'm on my own, so that I can forget everything that's happening and I go to this place I've made up. I call it Erehwemos, like that writer did because I thought that was such a good idea for a name, only mine is somewhere backwards, because my world is somewhere and not nowhere, if you see what I mean. I pronounce it Erry-*wee*-mos, which I think is a very good name.

I go there in a sort of bubble, made of something

that's like glass only it's light and doesn't reflect the sun so that nobody can see it and I can see out of it on all sides. I go right over the world and high, high up so that down below it's just like a map and then I go even further away and I can see the world looking like a beautiful blue ball with all the countries on it like you see on the globe in the geography room. Only it all looks so *wonderful* from up there, with clouds clinging to it, and I'm floating up here in black space. It's like a dream, only it's real – *real*.

I'm King of Erehwemos and all the people there are not like they are here on earth. For one thing, there are no girls at all – but then the boys aren't like the ones here at school, or any of the ones I know back home. At least, they're like the very quiet, kind ones; there are some like that here at St Bedes, but only a very few, and the nasty ones are always the ones that rule. So in my land everyone is forced to be kind; there are special rules, so that if you aren't nice you get put in prison straight away, or sometimes you're made a slave and have to work for the good ones.

I see that everyone obeys the rules because I am the King, and so I always know exactly what everyone ought to do. And there's nobody to say you can't do that, because nobody is cleverer or older than me. I know everything – more than anyone else, so they all come to me to be told. I am very kind and very clever, and everybody loves me. They are all my friends.

I was in Erehwemos, and feeling very happy, when one of the boys found me in the school garden and told me the Headmaster wanted to see me. 'I've been looking everywhere for you,' he panted. 'Why can't you be where other people are instead of hiding yourself away under bushes and things. I think you're potty. Anyway, Spud wants to see you, and he said immediately so I expect you're in for a whacking. I bet you are too,' and he ran away laughing like anything.

I was really worried, and tried to think all the way in to Spud's study just what I could have done wrong. I

45

mean badly wrong. I wondered if he was angry that I sat in places where people couldn't find me. 'Hiding away all the time', my form master calls it. 'Want to get out and about more, boy,' he says. 'Skiving off games like this will do you no good at all.' I don't think of it as hiding away, or skiving off games – I always play when I'm told to, even though I don't like games much. But I do like to find somewhere quiet where I can take off to Erehwemos, because whenever I'm called or found in the real world, I always have to come rushing back from Erehwemos with a bang, and that makes me jump and my heart beat so hard that it hurts.

Spud looked angry when I went in. At least he wasn't smiling, which usually meant he was angry. But he said, 'Ah, Petherick,' (and he pronounced it *Peth*erick like he always does) 'sit down, my boy.' That puzzled me, because I had never been told to sit down in his study before, so I sat on the floor like we always do when he tells us to sit down in Assembly, and he couldn't see me over the top of his desk, so he got up and peered over the top and said quite crossly, 'No no, not on the *floor*, boy, on that chair, there.'

It was quite a high chair, and my feet didn't touch the ground. I couldn't think what he was going to say, so the whole thing became a dreadful sort of wait for something bad to happen because there was quite a long silence until at last he said: 'I'm afraid I have some very bad news for you, Petherick, er . . . it's your father. I'm very sorry to have to tell you that he has died.'

Well, I didn't believe him; knew it had to be some sort of mistake, because I'd only just come back from half term and I had been round the farm with him all the time, while he was shooting crows and rabbits and talking to the farm hands. I hated seeing him shoot things, but he always wanted me to go with him so I had to. I knew he couldn't be dead because he wasn't ill. It took quite a long time for Spud to convince me, and he seemed to feel very embarrassed, and seemed to want me to cry.

I didn't actually want to cry at all, because I didn't really like Father all that much, even though he often tried to be quite kind to me. I was just very surprised by the news, and wanted to ask if someone had shot him or something, but I didn't like to in case I made Spud more embarrassed than he already was.

It was only quite a bit later, when I was sitting with Matron in her sitting room and eating her biscuits, that I suddenly felt that it was all rather awful, and found there was a sort of thing in my throat that hurt.

'But I can't tell my mother and sisters what to do like he did,' I said. 'There are six of them and only one of me.' And then I did cry a bit because I felt, somehow, kind of overpowered and helpless. Like I'd been deserted and left alone in the middle of a great big empty field.

Matron was really quite nice and put her arm round me and gave me a squeeze, which I found very embarrassing because she has such a big chest and I got my face pressed right into it so that I couldn't hardly breathe.

I had to go home alone on the train and Matron took me to the station and asked the guard to look after me but he didn't really, and a lady in the carriage put me on the right train at Exeter for St Erth. The train was very full of soldiers and sailors and airmen, and I had to sit on people's laps nearly all the way, and I kept on being sick so nobody wanted me much. In the end I just cried and cried and slept a bit and was sick every so often until I got there. I nearly didn't get out because I was asleep, but a little old lady, who had talked to me a bit and mopped up my sick, woke me up and pushed me out on to the platform, and there was Cynthia come to fetch me in the jingle with Josie, my pony, pulling it because there wasn't enough petrol for the car.

Cynthia hugged me a bit and then pushed me away and said 'Ugh! You smell of sick.' And she made me sit on the other side of the jingle. I felt better when Josie started trotting down the road, even though it was dark

47

except for the moon and I'm sometimes quite afraid of the dark. But I felt surrounded by space and quiet apart from the sound of Josie's hooves going clop clop clop, and it somehow reminded me of being in Erehwemos because there are a lot of fountains there and the water goes plip plop rather like Josie's hooves. I dropped off to sleep again before we got home and only woke up when we stopped and I heard Websie say, 'So the little lord of the manor has come 'ome to rule 'is roost then 'as 'e?' She didn't usually drop her aitches so much as that, or perhaps I wasn't used to hearing her Cornish way of speaking. I didn't understand what she said in any case.

Mother and all my sisters came out of the house and kissed me and hugged me and all of them said 'Ugh! You smell of sick,' so Websie took me upstairs and washed me and dressed me in my pyjamas and I slid right down to the end of the bed under the bedclothes and went to sleep at once.

The funeral was very grand and I quite enjoyed it. Mother cried, but the others didn't and neither did I. Everyone was dressed in black except Bridget and she had her uniform on with a black band round her arm. I had a black tie on that Websie got out of Father's wardrobe. All the village came and a lot of other people I didn't know, so that the church was full up and the village people had to stay outside unless they had worked for Father. And they had dug a grave in the churchyard and the coffin was let down gradually on long sort of rope things.

He'll be very quiet down there with all that earth on top of him. I wouldn't like to be down a hole with no way out. Before I die, I shall have them dig two tunnels into my grave, so that I can climb out if I'm not quite dead. But I *suppose* Father was quite dead. They said his heart stopped suddenly. I wouldn't like mine to stop suddenly like that. If I had a bit of warning that it was going to stop, then I could fly away to Erehwemos and go on living there for ever and ever. I should like that.

48

6

Easter came and went twice, and so did Christmas, and there was neither sight nor sound of Mumma. Jo knew nothing about the two letters that had arrived, one, eleven months after the initial handing over:

Dear Mum and Dad. Hope you are well as it leaves me at present. How is Jojo? I hope she is well. Thanks ever so much for looking after her. I'm in the army now but I can't tell you where I am because it isn't allowed. Hope to see you when I get time off but its a long way to come. Thats all I'm allowed to say. Please give Jojo a hug and kiss from me and tell her I'll see her soon. I miss her something dreadful. Ever your loving daughter, Jenny.

Grace and Will read the letter together, slowly and painfully. Tears ran down Will's cheeks, probably from the relief of knowing she was still alive. Things happened so quick these days; one minute you were there and the next minute you weren't.

Grace showed no outward sign, but relief, mixed up with rage, fumed away just below the surface. 'Selfish baggage, up there enjoying herself and leaving us to stew.'

'Can't say that, Gracie. She's doing her bit after all; she's in the war don't forget.'

'In the war, in the war! So are we in the war. And doing our bit just as much as she is – more most likely. And saddled with her responsibilities into the bargain. Selfish baggage!'

'Joanie'll be that pleased to know her Mum's still there, thinking about her.'

'You're not going to tell her nothing. What – have her set up her moaning again, just after I've managed to get her to stop it? No thank you very much. She'll have to forget her Mum if we're to do anything with her. We're not going to start all that up again. Much best that we don't remind her of it. She's just about got over it; remind her now and it would set her back a twelve month.'

Will felt a coldness in his guts to think of depriving Joanie of news that had brought on such a power of emotion in his own heart, but perhaps Grace was right; women were best suited to judge these things. They'd know what went on in a babby's mind much better than he would.

The second letter, together with a parcel, followed some two months later:

Dear Mum and Dad, Hope you are well as it leaves me at present. This is to tell you that I'm going away tomorrow but I don't know where, think it may be a long way. Would you please give this doll to Jojo because it was mine and she liked it and give her a hug and kiss from me and tell her I'll be back soon. Ever your loving daughter Jenny.

A great surge of sadness tugged at Grace as she unwrapped the limp and dirty rag doll she had all but forgotten. She found it quite impossible to speak at that moment.

Will's expression lit up as he saw the doll. 'If it ain't the old doll Ma went and made for Jenny when she were born!' he said.

Grace pulled herself together. 'No need to tell that to Joan either,' she said. 'Only set her off again. I'll say I found it.'

When Jo saw the Witch approaching with Mumma's doll, she held her breath. What was the Witch doing with Mumma's doll? She tried to control the great leap of excitement that had taken her over. *Mumma must*

50

have come to get her! But if the Witch had got the doll, what had she done with Mumma? Fear crept up her spine, but don't show it; don't let her know how much you wanted the doll. Get hold of the doll and Mumma must be there too. Don't let Gran witch her away; please, please, don't let her. Show you cared, and she might do anything; she's a witch, remember. Jo scowled, and bared her teeth, in order to frighten away anything bad.

Even when the doll was held out by an unusually smiling Gran, Jo knew it was only a trick, so she snatched it and ran out of the room into the farm yard to find Mumma; she must be there somewhere. But of course she wasn't; she'd been witched away. Jo realized that she hadn't been quick enough to beat Gran's witchery, and she fled out of the farm gate, down the lane, back over the stile into the cows' field, through the gap in the hedge and on to the wild bit near the cliff. She was choked up with crying and the despair of not managing to get the better of Gran's wickedness. She had to find Charlie.

'Ungrateful little brat,' said Grace, deeply disappointed and hating Jo for showing no sign that she was pleased. She suddenly felt she wanted to cry, because her own emotion at seeing the doll again was obviously not shared by her granddaughter. She was outraged, and furious with herself for her own reaction. But Jo should have been overjoyed, she could have shown pleasure instead of that surly, miserable face she'd had on ever since she came. Unnatural, that's what it was.

Jo searched all round the farm, but didn't find Charlie anywhere.

'Charlie,' she shouted. 'Come here, Charlie, stop hiding and come here, I know you're there somewhere, you needn't pretend you're not.'

And then she thought she saw him, sitting quite still, hiding under the hedge, all covered with branches and leaves. 'Come on out,' she said. 'I can see you, you

51

can't hide from me.' And she pounced on him, and pulled the branches away. As she did, she saw, with a jolt of shock, that it wasn't Charlie at all, but another boy she didn't know.

'Oh hallo,' she said. 'I thought you were Charlie.'

'Well I'm not,' he said, angrily. 'I'm Peter.'

Jo clutched the doll to her and stared at this strange boy who looked big and untidy, and was covered in leaves and grass and mud.

'My name's Joanne,' she said, 'and I'm looking for my friend Charlie.'

'Charlie who?'

'Charlie nothing. He doesn't have another name.'

'He must have another name, everybody does. Where does he live?'

Joanne was stumped for a moment or two. 'In the sea,' she said finally.

Peter stared at her; silly little village kid. How had she managed to find him in that favourite hiding place? No-one else had been able to spot him there, ever, no matter how near they'd been and how hard they had been searching for him.

'He can't live in the sea,' he said crossly.

Jo decided to change the subject. 'This is my Mumma's doll,' she said. 'She's just given it to me, only she couldn't do it herself because my Gran's a witch and she won't let her come and fetch me. Or she might be fighting the war and not able to get away at the minute.'

Peter wanted to get away himself from this silly little girl so that he could look for another hiding place where nobody would be able to find him, but she followed him when he started to walk towards the cliff.

'Where do you live?' she said, having to run every now and then to keep up. This was the only person near her own age she had ever spoken to in the village except Charlie. Other children were afraid of Gran and kept away.

'At Petherick Hall.'

Well, she knew that was a fib, because a Lord and a Lady lived there with a whole lot of funny women whom she also suspected of being witches.

'Go on,' she said. 'You never.'

'Yes I do, when I'm not at school.'

So he made things up, like she did. 'I live in a castle,' she said, 'with hundreds of kittens and a few soft dogs.'

'You're potty,' he said, and ran away from her as fast as he could.

She looked round to see where she was, and felt a little afraid because she was nearing the edge of the tall cliff, and she had never been so far away from the farm before.

She had been forbidden to go any distance from the house, and so only knew the village as far as the post office in Post Office Row and the fields that led to the edge of the climb down to the sea. That dangerous, frightening place that was forbidden territory without Grampa holding your hand. He had taken her once or twice, giving grumbling warnings all the time. 'Don't you ever come anywhere near here on your own, mind, or the sea'll get you. You could get blown over easy, and then down you'd go and never be heard of no more; the sea'd get you.' And Jo could well believe him. This rough, furious water that was for ever splashing its great waves up the cliffs towards her, she was scared half to death by its menace and yet fascinated. It was like a big fierce dog in a pit, leaping up towards you, snarling and showing all its teeth. Frightening, but not as bad as the siren that made you hide under the stairs or in the cold, wet shelter and shiver with fear; because wherever you hid, the war could always get you once the siren had gone.

Now she was alone, and didn't in the least know the way home. She turned her fear into anger, and made her angry snarling face. *'Charlie!'* she shouted out into the empty space round her, 'Come and save me *at once*,' and immediately he appeared up over the edge of the cliff.

'I met a stupid boy,' she said, 'and he brought me here and then ran away and left me.'

'Ar,' said Charlie, sitting down on the grass beside her. 'You don't want to have nothing to do with that scumbag.'

'How do you know who it was?'

'I seen him, didn't I.'

'What's a scumbag?'

'Nasty; wicked; no good. He'll do you mischief, that one.'

'What will he do?'

'He'll do you in. Tried to push you over the cliff just now, didn't he?'

'No he didn't, he just ran away and left me.'

'That's because he saw me coming, that's all. He's a bad one, don't want to have nothing to do with him.'

Joanne stood looking at Charlie for a moment or two, clutching the doll to her chest, and wondering if he was right about the other boy. It didn't seem at all likely. And what about Charlie himself? Why wasn't he all wet if he lived in the sea? He looked very wild, certainly, with his long brown hair blowing all over his face in the wind, and his clothes ragged and his feet bare; a sort of wild version of the silly boy who had run away from her.

'Do you live in the sea?' she asked.

'You don't know nothing,' he said.

Jo imagined him rising out of the sea like a wave and turning into a magic person as the water hissed back over the sand. He must live in a cave. 'Do you live in the cave that climbs up through the ground and comes out at the top of the cliff? Grampa told me about it; and the sea rushes in and blows all the water out of the hole at the top of the cliff.'

'Somewhere near there.'

Jo looked around her from where they were sitting under the windblown hedge beside the furrowed field. There was the faintest trace of green sifted across the brown earth. She saw a bird start from a furrow and soar, singing, into the sky until it was a speck above her head.

'Skylark,' said Charlie, 'nests on the ground that one, but you try to find her and see where it gets you.'

'I know,' said Jo, feeling pleased that she knew as much as Charlie. Grampa had told her a lot about the birds, and she had often run to the spot where the bird had taken off, never to find the sign of a nest. She stared upwards at the hovering speck in the sky. 'It must be so happy to sing like that,' she said.

'It isn't that he's happy,' said Charlie. 'It's that he don't know no better than to sing because of it being spring and that.'

It sounded a good enough reason to Jo. She had herself recently begun to feel the occasional desire to sing or dance because of some strange sort of excitement inside her that was impossible to contain. Quite a new feeling it was; probably something to do with the country and the sea, because she had never experienced such a thing in London.

'It must be singing about having a home in this nice field. Quite often I want to jump about because this is such a nice place. But I wish Mumma could be here too.'

Charlie was silent, staring out over the sea and chewing at a stalk of grass.

'I've got you, and Grampa is kind, but I'd like Gran to fly away on her broomstick for ever and then Mumma could come and we'd be happy ever after, and she wouldn't be crying or cross like she was in London.'

'Like as not she'd be crying or cross wheresoever she'd be,' Charlie said, and Joanne felt her face getting hot with anger. Charlie didn't know nothing about Mumma.

'How d'you know about Mumma?' He might be magic, but he didn't have any right to say things about Mumma if they weren't nice.

'I just do. Everyone knows something about something; you hear talk all the time about people. Come on then, I'll show you the way home.'

Later she talked to Grampa: 'Was Mumma cross when she was little?' Just to make sure; Grampa would know much more than Charlie did.

He didn't answer at first, just carried on milking as though he hadn't heard her. 'Bit of a misery she was sometimes; lot of crying and that,' he said finally, stripping down the teats for the last drop, and remembering the bad bits of Jenny's childhood: days when Jenny whined and Grace nagged till he was fair worn out with the miseries.

Joanne was impressed; how did Charlie *know* unless he was magic?

'I don't cry do I?' She felt strong and grown-up, almost as though she could look after Grampa, rather than him looking after her. 'I won't let the gander throw you down the stairs like it did in the rhyme, even if you forget to say your prayers. Why did that gander throw the old man down the stairs Grampa? Would our gander do that do you think?'

Grampa's face creased and cracked into a smile and a wheezy cackle emerged from somewhere under the cow's belly. 'Wouldn't put it past the old bugger; treats them geese shockin'. Wouldn't be at all surprised.'

He picked up the bucket of milk and moved out into the daylight, still wheezing and chuckling and shaking his head.

If only there was some way of getting rid of witchy old Gran, then Jo felt, at that moment, that she would like to live here always and for ever. If Gran wasn't here, Mumma would be sure to come back and they could all live here and be happy ever after: her and Mumma and Grampa and Charlie. Got to think of a way to get rid of Gran.

7

Peter sneaked out of the back door of Petherick Hall and fled into the bushes. So far so good; no-one had seen him. Cynthia was packing his trunk, and the others were lounging about in the morning room, reading and arguing and doing all the things they always did. Websie was dozing by the range in the kitchen. He'd even given the dogs the slip: so quiet he'd been that they hadn't even noticed his going, so there were no excited, yelping creatures, noisy with anticipation of walkies, bouncing about his feet.

There was no real plan in his head; just had to get away, that was all. Panic thoughts chased through his mind and jumbled themselves up, trying to sort themselves out. Can't go back; can't go back to school. Must think of a way; maybe tomorrow it will be better, perhaps I will be able to face it tomorrow, but not now, please not now. Maybe tomorrow I'll feel brave again, but just now I've got to think of a way of not letting them send me today.

At the back of his mind, there was the muffled realization that really, in real life, there was no escape. But it's just possible, he thought, by making the most tremendous thinking effort, I might be able to think things away. And if I send my thoughts straight into the heads of Mother and Bridget and Cynthia so that they start to think my thoughts instead of their own, then they'll forget that I have to go back to school. They might forget for ever if I think hard enough. He'd seen it done once by a conjuror; he'd made people think and do things they hadn't meant to think and do. So it is possible, he thought.

Out of breath from running all round the edge of a

field, rather than show himself up by running straight across the middle, he stopped, and leaned against the stone wall. Hypnotizing it was called, he suddenly remembered as he stood there, panting, and feeling the raw air sear down his throat. Try it again now, didn't matter how far away you were.

He shut his eyes, so that he could think better. If the Polwagle curse could work all that time ago, then like as not he could do another thought thing now. Out loud he said: 'Oh Genie of the lamp,' but he hadn't got a lamp, so decided to change the words a bit. 'Oh Genie of Saint Senara of Zennor, make all those now at Petherick Hall forget that Peter Petherick should be going back to school today. Let them forget this completely from this moment on, now and forever. Amen,' and he put his hands over his face and fairly beamed his thoughts over the field and through the garden and back into the morning room, where he had last seen his mother and his sisters. Then he switched the thoughts down to the kitchen as well, to include Websie, asleep in her chair.

Wish, wish; think, think. The effort made him giddy with the concentration of it.

When he finally took his hands away from his face and opened his eyes, he found that the little Tremayne kid was standing in front of him, staring at him in amazement. There was nothing at all he could find to say. In any case, she gave him no time to think up an explanation.

'Can you make spells then?' she asked, with obvious admiration.

'Sometimes,' he said.

'Will you show me how. I have to get rid of my grandmother who's a witch.'

'You can't learn how, you either can or you can't.'

'Charlie can.'

'Who's Charlie?'

She sighed impatiently. 'I told you about him last time I saw you.'

'Well get him to show you then.'

They stood, silently facing each other for a moment until, way in the distance, shouted voices drifted over the fields: 'Piggy! PIG – GY! Where the devil are you?'

'*Piggy!* We have to leave now.'

'For goodness sake, stop playing games – we haven't time. You'll miss the train. Come back at *once*!'

Jo looked at him sympathetically. 'It didn't work, did it?'

'I shall have to hide,' Peter said. 'Don't you dare tell them you've seen me if they come this way.' He started to run, not knowing where would be best.

'Of course I won't tell.' It was difficult to keep up. 'Why don't you hide in our barn? They'll never find you there as long as Gran don't see you.' Was he really wicked and nasty? Would he throw her down the ladder, like the gander did to the old man? She'd have to take care that he didn't catch her by the left leg, and then it would be all right.

No-one saw them, and they were soon deeply buried in the hay, surrounded by silence and safety. Joanne reached out and took hold of his hand. She didn't believe he was a scumbag: Charlie was wrong. Peter, hot with embarrassment, suffered the indignity in a grudging acknowledgement of gratitude.

'I'd best go now,' she whispered a little later, 'case they miss me because then they'd likely look up here. I expect the spell will work next time; perhaps you're not doing it quite right. I'll ask Charlie about it, but he's a bit funny and only answers the questions he wants to. He *knows*, but he don't always tell.'

'Thanks,' Peter said. 'I won't stay long; just for a bit until I think the coast's clear, and then I'll be on my way.'

She didn't ask him where he would go, but felt he would be sure to win through in the end, and she began to think up various happy endings: he could find a boat and row to Land's End or America, or he might work out a better spell, or a wizard might suddenly rescue him – anything could happen.

When the local policeman rode up on his bicycle an hour later to ask if they had seen young Peter in the district lately, she never said a word, but they caught him soon after that, climbing down the cliffs to the beach. Joanne was relieved that they didn't put him in prison, though sending him back to school could possibly have been as bad. Her inside always froze up a little as she considered this unknown thing called school that was being increasingly mentioned round the place lately. Some nasty dragon's lair that lay in wait for her in the frightening future – tomorrow? Or the next day? Anytime now it seemed.

So she put the idea to the back of her mind and thought about other things until the day that Gran took her into St Ives on one of their rare excursions. Gran took some eggs and butter to an acquaintance in the town and Joanne had some lemonade made from rather nasty tasting lemonade powder. She drank it very slowly in tiny sips so that she would taste it less. Gran and the lady were complaining about things.

'Gets worse and worse; don't know where we'd be without the butter and eggs.'

'And the odd chicken, that ekes things out a bit.'

'Certainly does, certainly does. Don't know how they manage in the city, and with all those bombs on top of it.'

'You're good to take little Joanie here out of it all. Lucky girl you are Joanie, to have such a good grandmother.'

Joanne studied the strange woman who thought her grandmother was good. Surely everyone knew she was cross and horrible? That she hardly ever smiled; that she shouted at Grampa; that she made people eat up all their tapioca. *That she was a witch.* Was this a good grandmother? Joanne switched her gaze to Gran, a small, grey old lady dressed in old black clothes with a scarf tied round her head. A witch was not at all her idea of what a grandmother should look like. She squinted her eyes and saw instead a round, smiling, pink cheeked, fairy godmother-type person with shining white curls, dressed in blue silk with white collar and cuffs and a white shawl over her shoulders. Her laugh tinkled and her eyes twinkled and Joanne smiled broadly at the metamorphosis.

Gran scowled back. 'Don't know what you think you're laughing at Miss. Laugh on the other side of your face next week.' She turned to her crony. 'Starting her at school on Tuesday,' she said.

Jo's eyes widened, and the fairy godmother changed back into a witch.

'What, at the village school?' said the witch's chum.

'No no, village school's been shut down for years.'

'But didn't I hear they opened it again just recently?'

'Ah yes, they opened it up for the evacuees. All the London children go there, but it's not for the like of her, she's native. Wouldn't let her mix with those London kids, not ever. They're a bad lot.'

'So coming in on the bus is she? My Billy did that when I lived out of town.' Witch's chum pointed to the window. 'That's where you'll be coming then.' She laughed. 'Well I never, so I expect you'll be waving to me over the wall won't you?'

Jo was stunned. Was this really true? She walked to the window and looked out on to a grey squat building on the other side of the road, and as she watched, the doors burst open and a shouting, running, indistinguishable mass of children poured out into the stone yard. She watched and listened as they shrieked and screamed and hurled themselves about the playground. She saw girls skipping and boys fighting, and the whole mass swirling and chasing about in terrifying chaos. Was she to be thrown in amongst them so soon? When was Tuesday? It could be now, in a minute. Is this what Gran had brought her into St Ives for? She was usually left behind with Grampa. Was there a possibility of running away? Peter had failed, but she might just succeed. She slid her eyes to the

61

door, but Gran and her friend were directly in the way. Perhaps if she kept very still and wished, everyone might go to sleep for a hundred years like the sleeping beauty. She might be better at spells than Peter was.

She shut her eyes and wished: make us all go to sleep for a hundred years. But the shrieks and Gran's voice and the rattle of teacups went on and on unendingly. Perhaps if only she was put to sleep – that should be easier magic for whoever was doing it: please, please make me go to sleep for a hundred years – and there was a great clanging of a bell, and the screams of the children ceased immediately. The spell was obviously working, just that sleep had hit the children instead of her; easy enough mistake to make. She opened her eyes and saw that the children were not actually asleep, just under some sort of spell that this lady with a bell had put on them, because they were all silent and still and marching sadly back through the door that was swallowing them up again into who knows what? Jo watched them from behind one of the curtains. Some sort of magic seemed to be working, but Jo felt sure it was going wrong again, the way it always did. That bell, and the sudden, shocking silence, and the crowding into lines, and the way the door just swallowed them up and was shut so firmly after them, it must be bad magic. Had she wished something bad on to these children? What would happen to them?

Jo imagined a long, dark tunnel the other side of that door leading to . . . to what? All she could think of at the end of the tunnel was a fiery furnace. The sort Gran read to her about out of the Bible. The sort Shaddack Meeshack and Tobedwego walked into when God didn't let them be hurt by the fire. She supposed God wouldn't let the children burn either. It might be quite exciting to stand in the middle of a burning fiery furnace and not be burned. But perhaps the bad ones were; perhaps it was only if you were good that you didn't get burned. The children all seemed very sad and silent when the lady rang the bell; they might well have done something very bad without even knowing it.

'Does God still save people from burning fiery furnaces?' she asked Gran that night after listening to the story of Noah and the flood, which was her favourite of the ones she had so far heard. Water was not nearly so worrying as fire; it would hold you up and help you to float. Unless of course it was angry like it sometimes was at the bottom of the cliffs. It could be angry but it wasn't wicked like fire was. Fire sometimes got out of its fireplace and it could chase you and hurt you.

'People don't get put into furnaces these days, more's the pity for some I dare say.'

'Oh but they do,' Jo said. 'They do in London. Mrs Abbot and her mother and their little girl's house had a bomb on it and it was set on fire, so it was a burning fiery furnace but God didn't save them. Do you think they'd done something very bad? Do you think they didn't say their prayers like the old man who got thrown down the stairs? Why do you think God didn't save them?'

Grace felt a little flummoxed; Jenny had never needed explanations. She suddenly found it difficult to tell this innocent to mind her manners and not to blaspheme, and anyway it would be well nigh impossible to explain the word blaspheme. Oddly enough, she found herself more put out by her own inability to answer, rather than at Jo's persistent questionings. There was the remotest glimmer that she herself might be the one at fault for forgetting how to talk to children; it was such a long time since she had done so. Quite a new sensation, this feeling at fault, and not a very comfortable one at that.

'Get on and say your prayers,' she said irritably. 'After me now: Gentle Jesus . . .'

Jo interrupted her. Here was a chance to try out some magic; she'd never get good at it if she didn't practise. The poems that Gran taught her to say on her knees every night, they were most likely spells that made it easier for Gran to keep her prisoner here. If she could say the spells while wishing her own wish, then things might turn out very different.

'I can say it by myself, Gran, I learned it – you listen.' Shutting her eyes, Jo concentrated her thoughts. Make Gran disappear now, at once, and don't let her ever come back. Now for the magic spell: 'Gentle Jesus Meekernile, Looker ponder litter chile, Pretty mice inpisserbee, Suffer meet her company. Our men.'

Grace felt a new sensation attack her; she found she wanted to laugh. 'Let's hope God understands double dutch,' she said fiercely, to quell any flippant reactions, but didn't trust her self control to criticize any further. 'They do say He moves in a mysterious way,' she said, falling back on quotation. 'His wonders to perform.'

Jo's eyes widened. So it hadn't worked this time; probably hadn't said it quite right. But *something* had certainly happened, because Gran's face was twisted into a different sort of shape; perhaps God was performing a wonder.

'What sort of way does He move?' she asked. 'Sort of hopping does He? Or turning somersaults does He? I saw some clowns do that once, only that was funny but I didn't know it was funny so I cried. Does He only move like that when He's doing wonders? What sort of way does He move Gran?'

'I should think He floats,' said Grace. There was a wheeze and a croak, and Grace Tremayne found herself laughing out loud. It was quite painful, she was so out of practice.

Jo felt excited: the spell had at least made some sort of an impression.

8

In spite of many ingeniously imaginative situations, such as being suddenly recognized as so remarkably clever that school was quite unnecessary in her case, or having a doctor diagnose a serious illness brought on by the mere thought of going, Joanne found, to her great distress, that the inevitable cannot be avoided, and school was obviously inevitable.

She discovered, however, that there was no fiery furnace behind the big doors, just two very scrubbed rooms with big windows too high to see out of, and a smell of Jeyes Fluid at the beginning of the day and a hot, dirty, stuffy smell at the end of the afternoon. The mass of children she encountered were very serious and quiet when they were inside and very noisy and exuberant when the doors opened into the play-ground. She found this difficult at first because they seemed to be two quite different sets of people: the quiet, mouse-like, Yes-Miss group and the shouting, running, laughing group. They laughed at her quite a lot, especially the boys: mainly at the way she spoke and the things she did.

She seldom went anywhere without Doll. Charlie Doll, she called it, because she could talk to it when Charlie wasn't there. And because it looked like him too, if you half shut your eyes, because it was obviously a boy doll. Charlie Doll it was – so as not to muddle it with Real Charlie. She had tied a long string round it, long enough to be tied round her own waist, under her dress so that no-one need see. He came out in the secret times when thumb-sucking became necessary. 'Please can I go to the toilet Miss?', and then a few, blissful sucking minutes on the seat, with

Charlie Doll feeling soft against her cheek. You weren't allowed to suck your thumb when anyone was there because everyone called you Suckathumb and laughed and said the Scissor Man would come and cut it off.

A fellow new girl, whose name was Charlotte, was devastated by the teasing. She wept all through play and dinner-time which was a matter of concern for Jo.

'What are you crying for?'

'These people aren't my friends so they are being nasty to me.'

'They aren't my friends too, but they aren't nasty to me. I make them laugh so they like me.'

'No they don't. They think you're silly.'

Jo looked round at a group of children playing hopscotch. They did not look as though they were thinking about her being silly; they looked as though they were thinking about the game they were playing.

'They're playing,' she said. 'They're not thinking about me being silly, and if they were, then *they* would be silly because I'm not.' She laughed at the cleverness of this idea and the silliness of people thinking her silly when she was not. Then she hopped round in a circle to see if she actually was able to do what the others did and found she could.

'Will you be my friend?' Charlotte asked her.

'Well I've *got* a friend called Charlie, but I suppose I could have two because Charlie doesn't come to school so you could be my school-friend and Charlie could be my home-friend.'

'My home's in London,' said Charlotte.

'So's mine.' Joanne said quickly.

They stared at each other, full of suspicion. How could this be?

'My mummy and I have come to stay with Nana and Grandad for the war. They live near Zennor; I come in on the bus,' said Charlotte.

Joanne was filled with silent jealousy of this person who could have her mother with her always.

'My Mumma had to stay and fight the war,' she said,

'and my Gran's a witch and can turn people into toads.'

'Does your friend Charlie live with his mummy and daddy?'

'No he doesn't. He lives by himself . . . in a tree,' she added a few moments later. Of course! It was in a tree, not in a cave; that was why he knew about birds.

'In a tree? How does he live in a tree?'

'It's easy if you are very good at climbing and can build houses in trees and he is; he is specially clever at building houses in trees.'

Charlotte was impressed and forgot about crying. 'All right, so we'll just be school-friends and go to tea with each other.'

'Yes,' said Joanne, 'we will go to tea with each other.'

'Wish you were at my school,' Jo said to Charlie a day or so later, 'because there's no-one there I like except for Charlotte, and sometimes she goes off with the others and they don't want me. They think I'm funny because I talk to Charlie Doll when you're not there and then they say I'm talking to myself so I must have a screw loose and they laugh at me.'

Tears rolled down her cheeks and drips from her nose dribbled down her lip. She caught the tears with her tongue because she liked the taste, and wiped the drip with the back of her hand, because that never tasted so good. 'School's like being in a deep dark dungeon with nobody there,' she said. 'And I got nobody to talk to except Charlie Doll.'

Charlie didn't answer, so no sympathy there.

'Can you make spells?' she asked. 'Mine never seem to work, and that Peter boy I met the other day, his don't work either. It's very important for me to learn how, so that I can get rid of Gran.'

'That would need a cracking big spell,' Charlie said, 'you'd need to mix up something good and strong to finish her off. A real good poison it'd need, her being so particular bad.'

Poison! Jo thought, rather guiltily, of the pretty blue

bottle, high up on top of the kitchen dresser that had the word written on a label. She'd asked Grampa about it, and he'd said not to touch it ever, else you might die.

'Grampa's got some poison on top of the dresser,' she said, 'but I'm not allowed to touch it in case it makes me die.'

'Nah,' said Charlie, 'you don't want to mess with that stuff; there's plenty all round you for getting rid of witches. There's deadly nightshade and there's fox-gloves and dodder . . .'

'And Lords and Ladies and toadstools – there's always toadstools.'

'Plenty of them if'n you knows where to look,' said Charlie.

Joanne told Charlotte, who was not over enthusiastic, but liked the thought of mixing up potions in a cauldron. Jo wondered what potions and cauldrons were, but didn't like to ask.

'Let's go and collect some potions,' she said. The prospect sounded even more interesting than the fun of early morning mushrooming or blackberrying at the end of summer.

'You mix potions,' Charlotte said, primly. 'You don't collect them.'

'You've got to collect them before you can mix them,' Joanne reminded her, with some heat. 'Come on, I think I know where we can find some toadstools.'

So they set off, with Joanne's beach bucket and a cardboard box, walking down the lane and into the fields near the cliff. Toadstools were not forthcoming, but they picked some buttercups and daisies, angelica and cow parsley, found a rabbit's skull, hawthorn berries, some seaweed and a whole spray of deadly nightshade. It was then that Charlotte got bored with the adventure and said she had to go home to tea.

Jo stood, deserted and alone in the field and looked round for Charlie. Probably still in his tree house. She made her way back to the clump of stunted trees in the dip behind the cliff edge, but found Peter up the tree instead, and felt disconcerted. He wouldn't know about potions and cauldrons and things.

'You're in Charlie's tree,' she said, scowling at him.

'It's my tree more than it's his because it belongs to my family; this whole field belongs to us.'

'Belong, belong,' Joanne was furious. 'Does that mean you can stop birds making their nests in it?'

Peter gave up the fight at once, and Jo remembered their last encounter. 'Did you run away again? I thought the policeman caught you. Do you want to hide in the barn again?'

'No, they've let me out for Saturday and Sunday.'

'I don't get locked in at night, they let me out every day at half-past-three.'

'Mine's a boarding school.'

'Gran calls mine a board school too.'

The enigma was left unresolved, and Jo showed him the contents of the box and the buckets. 'I've been collecting things to make a spell to get rid of my Gran because she's a witch. Do you know how to make potions?'

'You mash things up and boil them,' Peter climbed down from the tree, and squatted down beside her, picking up the rabbit skull. 'You could crush this up with a stone.'

'But how could I boil it? Gran would see me if I did it on the range, and then she'd know I was making the spell and she'd guess it was for her.'

'We could make a fire here, I've got some matches. You go and get some stones to crush things up with, and I'll get some firewood and a stick to stir it.'

The adventure was by far the most exciting Jo had ever experienced. The mashed ingredients, mixed with some water from the boggy stream that trickled through the copse, bubbled encouragingly in her bucket.

'This is sure to get rid of her,' she said.

'What are you going to do with it?' Peter asked.

'I'm going to put it into her tea.'

Peter stopped stirring. 'But it's got poison in it. She'll die if she drinks it.'

'No she *won't*, witches don't die; they disappear in a puff of smoke, or they explode or something.'

'In olden days,' Peter said, 'they threw witches in the water and if they drowned they weren't witches and if they didn't they were.'

'So—' Jo was even more confident. 'She'll only get dead if she *isn't* a witch, but she is, so she won't; she'll just disappear.'

'If she does die, the police will arrest you for murder.'

'Oh don't be so silly. She won't die because she *is* a witch. I keep telling you.'

But when Jo finally offered Gran a cup of tea that she had made herself, Gran took one look at it, said with a snort of laughter, 'Whatever do you call this when it's at home?' and threw the whole thing down the sink. So that spell didn't work either.

'That child's not improving,' Grace Tremayne told her husband. 'Tells terrible lies. Something unnatural about her I reckon; the way she looks too; real evil sometimes, the way she looks. And another thing, she's forever hanging round that scoundrel Bert.'

Roberto was the Italian prisoner of war recently assigned to them as a farm hand to whom they paid ninepence a day with no food.

'Bert's a good chap; got two kids of his own.'

'Don't know why you waste time talking to POWs. They was killing our boys out there, don't forget. Some people seem not to remember that; treat them like they weren't enemies; disgusting I call it. And I don't want my grandchild's mind perverted with Nazi talk. You tell him to leave her alone. He don't seem to understand anything I say to him.'

'Joanie understands him all right though,' Will chuckled. 'Heard him telling her stories of castles and knights on horseback.'

'Exactly. Filling her head with a lot of nonsense and

70

worse. You can't trust these Italians. No knowing what he might tell her. You've got to stop it Will.'

Will walked away from her to feed the pigs. Had the feeling of walking from muck into good wholesome pig smell. No need to carry on with that sort of talk. Joanie had enough spunk to defy rubbishy commands; more than enough to stand up to her grandmother. That Bert was a good chap; grateful to be out of the bloody war, and a willing, good-tempered worker. The sort of son Will would have liked to have had.

Grace Tremayne poured the cream into the churn with uncontained rage. Might as well talk to herself; pig-headed, the pair of them. That Joan was becoming more self-willed and disobedient with each day that passed, didn't seem to know the meaning of truth. Told Miss Bean who lived down by Pendeen way that she and Charlotte were sisters and that they lived with some boy called Charlie in a house in a tree. Said they were collecting to save the Church and Miss Bean gave them sixpence. What a disgrace! A grandchild of hers *begging* – begging money on the pretext that it was for the Church. The churning became frenzied. Had to be taught a lesson; somehow she had to be taught a lesson.

'What do you mean, my girl,' said Grace Tremayne to her granddaughter, 'by begging money off people and saying it's for the Church? Just you tell me that now, before I tan the hide off you.'

Jo's eyes widened, more with surprise than fear. 'But it *was* for the Church. Charlotte and me are knights, and knights do fight for the Church, Miss Roseveare told us so; they went out on horses to fight, and Charlotte and me wanted some armour so that we could fight too, but nobody sells armour in St Ives so I put the sixpence in the collection last Sunday. I thought the vicar might know where you could buy armour and then he could go out and fight.'

Grace was put out by the silliness of this childish idea, but more irritated by the fact that Joanne seemed to be quite unaware of her own bad behaviour. Was there no way of getting through to the child? The idea that she might seem to have redeemed herself by offering the sixpence to the Sunday collection plate only served to increase Grace's irritation. It was probably a lie anyway. But she changed her tack nonetheless: 'And what do you mean by talking to that Bert all the time? Keeping him from his work when he does little enough anyhow for all that he gets paid. Ought to be getting punished rather than paid for all the wickedness his country's doing to our soldiers in France.'

This was far too difficult for Jo to make any attempt to follow, so she brought her mind back to the present moment and the problem of getting punished for telling the truth: if Gran was going to tan the hide off her whatever she said, then there didn't seem much point in saying anything at all. What was a hide anyway? Was it something to do with hide and seek? She wondered how you tanned something. She made a quick exit from the dairy and went to find Charlie, who was sitting on the stool Roberto had made for her out of a tree stump, under the tamarisks in the churchyard.

'That spell didn't work either, Gran threw it away. In Hansel and Gretel, they put her in a pot and boiled her, but we don't have a pot big enough.'

'Ar,' said Charlie. 'Better you put her straight on the fire and burn her up like they used to; got sticks and straw and that, and burned them right up so that they was no more than a little old heap of ashes, that's probably the only way as you'd get rid of the likes of her.'

Joanne sighed. 'I think that would be a bit difficult for me to do.' She imagined herself struggling to get Gran into the kitchen range on her own, and began to giggle. Charlie joined in, so that they were soon both rocking with laughter at nothing in particular. Charlotte heard the laughter from the next field and came rushing to join in, but Charlie had bolted over the wall as she approached. 'What you running away for, Charlie?' Jo called after him, 'I want to show you to Charlotte because she's never seen you and sometimes she says she doesn't believe you're there at all.' But he'd vanished, so she and Charlotte mounted their milk-white steeds and galloped off in search of further adventure.

9

For the Pethericks, there started the beginning of a period of uncomfortable readjustment – life without Humphrey. If they had thought about it before, not one of them would have dreamed that life without Humphrey would have been so very different from life with him. But in the years of confusion immediately following his death, life slid about from day to day with only anxiety ahead. The farm and the factory seemed to be taken over by Ministry officials and bailiffs with whom Bea could never get on. She fretted, fumed and shouted, and set the world against her.

Cynthia, Daphne and Dorothy were still living at home, while Jean had moved into one of the farm cottages with an Austrian female doctor friend, recently released from internment in the Isle of Man. She was constantly fighting the authorities about her call-up.

Cynthia liked to think that her place was at home, looking after Bea. She enjoyed the way they looked alike, and were sometimes taken for sisters. It was a kind of defence against Bridget's aggression: the fact that she and her mother could somehow stand together in their dark, aristocratic hauteur, so superior to the horsey, country attitude that Bridget projected.

'She's so dishonest,' Dorothy said to Daphne. 'Trying to suck up to Mother the way she does. All she really wants is to get out of doing anything, like Jean. Only Jean at least pretends she's pacifist.'

'Cynthia's always suffered by coming so soon after

Bridget,' Daphne said. 'I mean who could assert themselves when Bridget was around? She didn't really have a chance.'

'Nobody has a chance when Bridget's around, but Cynthia doesn't even try when she does get the chance, like now, for instance. Or at least,' she added, 'she may try, but she doesn't succeed.'

'Poor Cynthia,' Daphne smiled as she said it.

'Poor nothing. You're too soft. By the way, what did you think of the dashing major Bridgie brought home?'

'He was all right I thought, but Mother didn't like him, did she?'

'Mother wouldn't like anyone, now would she? I thought he was ghastly. So pompous.'

'But she likes your John.'

'Only because he's a farmer and she thinks he might be some use to the family business. She wants us to have a double family wedding, can you imagine – Bridgie and her Harold and me and John, just like father would have insisted upon. All the village invited sort of thing.'

Daphne sighed. 'I think you should agree. It might make up for me and Hans.'

'You're never going to *marry* him, Daph? An affair, yes, if you can keep it dark, but you surely don't have to *marry* the man.'

'Yes I do. We've decided.'

'Oh my God – what's got into this family? First Jean and her Austrian woman and now you with an enemy alien.'

Daphne's eyes immediately became pink and watery, which incensed Dorothy still further. 'But Dottie, he's not an enemy alien, he's Jewish and not even interned any more.'

'What difference does that make? He's German isn't he? They've probably enlisted hundreds of Jews as spies, so that the soft-hearted English will be sorry for them and not suspect anything.'

'Dottie – *really*, that's a bit much. We are both

74

desperately in love, and he wants to farm in England after the war.'

Dorothy waved her hands in the air. 'Knows when he's on to a good thing I should say, whoever heard of a *Jew* wanting to farm?'

Daphne's eyes filled with tears. 'You're absolutely wrong. That's not it at all. He'd like to be on the management side.'

'I bet he would,' Dorothy was triumphant. 'Just like I said – knows when he's on to a good thing.'

The sisters didn't speak to each other for a week.

'I could perhaps be made the farm manager,' Cynthia said to Bea, in one of her endless anxiety conversations, which were usually one-sided dissertations on how to avoid getting called up. 'I think they would take notice of that, because it would certainly be an exempted occupation.'

Bea's expression showed total disbelief. 'But you would be worse than useless; can't see that anyone would be fooled into believing that you managing a farm would be helping the war effort. I should have thought you would be a considerable hazard to the production of food. Just like you're far too young and inexperienced to be working with all those dreadful old ladies dressed in green in the WVS. They're bound to throw you out of that pretty soon and put you in the ATS. Can't see why you're fighting it. You might develop some backbone if you spend a bit of time in the ranks.'

'Really, Mother, you are incredibly inconsiderate in your remarks. And anyway, you're not having much success in dealing with the authorities either are you?'

'Only because they're all bloody fools. No wonder we're losing the war.'

'That sort of remark could be termed as spreading alarm and despondency. You should be more careful or you'll find yourself put in prison as a Nazi sympathizer.'

Bea snorted. 'I'd like to see them try,' she said. 'Can you imagine our own PC Plod coming over here on his push bike to arrest me? Much more likely they'll be arresting that idiot Daphne for consorting with an enemy alien. Have you *seen* how she tags around with that wretched German POW? Disgusting I call it. I wish you'd speak to her.'

'He's not a prisoner of war, Mother, he was just interned for a bit, that's all. He's a Jew, remember.'

'That's worse. Whoever heard of a Jew joining the Petherick clan?'

'You are so prejudiced. I expect he's very nice.'

'So's Mussolini very nice, if you like that sort of thing. We used to know some people who met him and said he was charming. But I don't happen to want a German Jew as a son in law, so get hold of her sometime and spell it out to her. And while you're about it, you could do the same sort of thing where Jean's concerned. What's the matter with my daughters? Aren't the English good enough for them?'

Cynthia sighed noisily, feeling irritable that she should be expected to act as keeper to her sisters while her own troubles were not thought important enough to warrant any consideration. 'They wouldn't take any notice of me, now would they? Anyway, I think you're making too much of it. Jean's a lost cause, though she may grow out of it, and Daphne's not stupid – well, I suppose she is – but she wouldn't be so silly as to get herself hitched to a German, be he Jewish or Gentile, in the present wartime situation.' She paused, thinking that that was just the sort of idiot thing Daphne might do. She switched her thoughts quickly and in panic: it didn't bear consideration. 'Of course,' she said quickly, to take Bea's mind off the subject, 'to revert to me for an instant, I could go and teach in the village school. Teachers are exempt. But I would have thought I was far more valuable dealing with the evacuees and the British Restaurant in Penzance.'

The thought of Cynthia being valuable made Bea laugh more than the contemplation of her own arrest for careless talk, and provisionally took her mind off

76

the horror of German Jewish sons-in-law, though she did have the tact to refrain from commenting further.

It was the business of preparing for the double wedding of Bridget to a Major Harold Markham of the Pay Corps, previously an accountant with a large firm in Truro, and Dorothy to John Giles, a Devonshire farmer, that made the difference to the lives of the Pethericks. Whether the re-introduction of males into the family was the underlying reason or not, it was with all the grand celebrations that the Petherick family started to pull itself together. The double wedding was the grandest affair that wartime conditions could run to.

'I intend to show the district that the Pethericks are not in any danger of collapse just because the male heir is dead,' Bea said at the first planning session. 'The whole village is waiting for us all to die because women are running the place. Put paid to that damn curse once and for all. We'll give a village party. If they come and drink our drink and eat our food, perhaps that will stop them gossiping.'

'The male heir isn't actually dead, darling. The king is dead, long live Piggy, remember,' Bridget reminded her. 'And I don't really relish being used as propaganda. Even if the local peasants are superstitious enough to believe we are all doomed for daring to run the place in spite of the witch of Polwagle – we are actually doing it, aren't we? And none of us have dropped dead yet . . .'

'Touch wood touch wood!' screamed Dorothy, touching every table and chair within reach.

'Wood or no wood. I don't mind betting that we shall long continue to do so. Where we *might* be laying ourselves open to death and destruction would be if we ever did let Piggy get his useless little hands on anything to do with the business. We all know that.'

Daphne reproved her. 'Don't be so unkind. Poor little Piggy may grow up to be the world's best organizer; you just never can tell with these silent children, he's probably absolutely brilliant underneath it all.'

Bea joined in the rather raucous laughter. 'No need to go over the top to prove your point, dear.'

'A big wedding would be a terrible waste of money,' Cynthia said. 'Think how many bombs could be made for the same cost.'

'Don't be such a drag, Cyn,' Dorothy said. 'Any excuse for a knees-up in the midst of wartime restrictions and gloom can only be good for the soul.'

'Well, I shall wear uniform,' Bridget said, but uproar followed that statement.

'Oh Bridgie, you *can't*,' from Daphne.

'You'd spoil the symmetry,' Dorothy complained. 'I've managed to get a whole parachute, and Miss Wriggle in St Ives has already started on my dress. You can't be so boring as to want to wear uniform, it would ruin everything. We can share bridesmaids. John's got three sisters all lined up.'

'Oh God, how frightful,' Bridget said. 'I suppose Piggy will have to be page.'

'But you can't dress him in parachute silk.'

'Can't see why not, for a shirt at least.'

'He'd never do it. Probably run away and hide all day.'

'Peter will do as he's told,' Bea said sharply. 'He's much improved since he's been to school. We could get him up in one of the old family costumes with buckled shoes.'

The arrangement went without a hitch. Black market champagne flowed at the reception for several hundred guests at the Hall, and beer and cider appeared from nowhere at the accompanying party at the village hall for locals and other ranks stationed there.

Joanne watched and listened to the proceedings in a state of wonder. The sisters coming out of the church in their white dresses, tulle veils, flower wreaths and bouquets, the church bells ringing out, a military band playing on the green, people dancing on the grass, a special tea outside at long trestle tables for the children – it was really beyond anything she had experienced before. Better than the village fête, better than the school Christmas party. She was angry with Charlie for refusing to come.

Peter, dressed in one of the 18th century Petherick boy's midshipman's costumes, borrowed back from a museum for the occasion, suffered agonies of embarrassment and distress but, as Bea said he would, behaved with all the controlled conduct that had been instilled into him at school. And Daphne attended with her husband, Hans Herrmann, whom she had married the week before when no-one had had the time to pay any attention.

Once the Petherick family as a whole had readjusted to the new challenge of running the farm and the business after Humphrey's death, and once Harold Markham, John Giles and Hans Herrmann had been, grudgingly, accepted as part of the Petherick team, Bea found herself adrift and disconcerted with no-one to fight with. With all of them, except Cynthia, now living away from home, the very thought of her family irritated her more than usual: they were so ineffectual and disorganized. And Peter was not coming up to expectations either. He was never going to be capable of organizing his family or the family business. As a team, she and the girls would probably be able to make it. Bridget had leadership qualities, and the others, including the husbands, would tag along. That bloody curse; why should anyone believe in such things these days? The whole thing was absurd; but she couldn't bring herself to suggest taking any chances. Perhaps a serious talk with Peter before he went back for the Autumn term might make some sort of impression.

Humphrey had always dodged the issue; preferred to infer rather than bring the whole thing out into the open. Would mutter the family motto whenever she faced him with arguments: 'Man in the image of God' he would say, as though he was wielding a shield against the hammer blows of commonsense.

'You do realize, darling boy,' she said to Peter, having managed to corner him, alone, before he slid away from the breakfast table to the safety of some remote launching point for Erehwemos, 'how pleased we should all be if you began to take a teeny bit of interest in farms and farming and country life? You are getting quite big now, soon be going on to Winchester, and then, we hope, to some Agricultural College if you want to. But darling, you could be starting to learn now, you know. So many interesting things you could be finding out just by walking round the farms a bit, talking to people. Asking Daphne and Dorothy what sort of things they have to do as Land Girls, having a go at something yourself perhaps.'

Peter clung to the sides of the dining room chair he was sitting on. He had stopped chewing the piece of toast in his mouth when Bea began to talk, and it was now soggy and unmanageable but still rather large for swallowing. It also made speech difficult, so he leaned forward and spat it on to his plate.

Bea recoiled quite visibly. '*Really*, Peter, do you have to be so basic? One doesn't have to be physically sick when confronted with the idea of a healthy outdoor life, surely.' And she left the room in fury.

Peter wondered, for a moment or two, whether he should follow her out and try to explain that it wasn't actually sick, but just a chewed bit of toast he didn't want to swallow, but decided against it. She was not in a listening mood, and it would only make things worse. There followed a great desire to get away from the fear and the disturbance in his mind that his mother had caused, so he slipped off his chair and ran out of the room, through the French windows in the garden, down the driveway, across the field with the cows, over the slate wall into the fallow field and down into the hollow where the brambles fought with the gorse and hawthorns.

Nettles stung his legs and thorns scratched him, punishment, he felt sure, for not doing what he was told; for not wanting to do what he was expected to; for wanting to run right away from the dislike he had, at that moment, of his home and family. The desire to escape from them was wrong, that he knew, but how to deal with it?

Emerging, breathless, and near to tears on to the cliff path, he stared down at the sea below. The beach was a forbidden place on one's own, but he was already guilty of so much, a further sin could scarcely worsen the situation, and he had need of darkness and quiet and knew just where he could find it.

The cave had always been a favourite place of his, but he was never able to be there on his own. Older sisters were forever urging him out of it when they took him to the beach. 'Come *out* of there, Piggy, it smells.' 'For God's sake, Piggy, come out. Everyone pees in caves – and worse. Go and fetch him, Jean. I can't go in, it gives me claustrophobia.' And Jean would come in and haul him out before he'd been able to enjoy it all. But it had been wonderful, he remembered that; the walls had seemed to be lit with green fire and the darkness lured him on.

It took no time at all to slither down the path and over the rocks, and there it was – black, inviting and forbidden. A safe and unfindable hiding place, waiting to be found.

It was quite a long time later that fear caught up with him. The cave was deep, but he felt sure that sooner or later he would come to a way out to the cliffs at the other end. He had heard of such caves; smugglers used them, and spies, landing unseen on the beaches at night. There was bound to be another way out. He remembered his father's funeral and thought of the two tunnels he was going to insist on for himself. It was then that he became suddenly afraid and wished that he had brought a torch. Just walk back the way he'd come; nothing easier; just follow the way back by feeling the walls. But the walls didn't seem to end. The green fire shone out from them, but the further he walked the less he could see. Had it been as far as this? Surely not.

He squatted down on the wet floor and realized that he had an urgent desire to widdle. Websie called it widdling; you said pee at school, or even piss if you were older. He heard it trickling away, but couldn't see it. So it was true, everyone did pee in caves. His heart was beating so loudly he almost could hear the sound bouncing off the walls. Nobody would find him here because it was unfindable. He had even lost himself and the fear he felt made it suddenly impossible to get to Erehwemos. He put his hands over his face and let out a great wail of despair before burying his head in his arms and sobbing silently and despairingly.

It was very soon afterwards that he heard a small, high-pitched scream and a childish voice say 'What was *that* Charlie?' He strained to hear more but there was only the sound of waves and sea, a long way off, and then the tiny voice wafted back again: 'I've got to go home. They'll think I'm lost.' Clear as a bell it was, and Peter at once got up and followed in the direction from which it came. 'I've got to go home,' he thought. 'They'll think I'm lost.'

A long time elapsed before he began to see daylight: a heart-pounding, panicky time of groping along streaming walls, sometimes bent double, often uncertain which of two tunnels to follow. But he now had no real doubt that he was going to succeed. He felt he was following the voice rather than trying to find his way – the voice must have got out, because it didn't call out again. He only had to follow the voice. It was getting lighter all the time and, finally, as he rounded a bend, there was the bright, tiny spot of light that was the entrance. He hadn't been lost at all, only mislaid for a moment or two. He had just had an adventure, that was all.

10

On the same day that Bea was lecturing Peter about his responsibilities, Charlie suggested he might take Jo down the cliffs on to the beach. Joanne told Charlotte: 'He says there's a cave down there that's all lit up with magic green moss on the walls. He says you sometimes hear the Zennor mermaid singing down there.'

'Who's the Zennor mermaid?'

'She's a mermaid who heard a beautiful young man singing in the church here and she came every Sunday to listen to him singing, and then one day she got him to follow her down to the beach and he went in the water after her and he was never heard of again because he went and lived with her under the sea.'

'Human beings can't live under the sea.'

'Well he did and you can sometimes hear him and her singing under the sea.'

'But he'd be dead by now if it was a long time ago.'

'Oh don't be so *silly*, people can do anything in fairy stories.'

'But fairy stories aren't true and anyway, we aren't allowed to go down to the beach; not down the cliff path. It's dangerous, you get cut off by the tide. We're not allowed.'

'But Charlie's with us, that makes it all right because he knows everything about tides and things. We're allowed if we're with someone.'

Charlotte hesitated, rubbing one foot against her leg. 'But Charlie isn't here, I can't see him anyway.'

'Yes he is here but likes hiding when there's anyone around.'

'I think that's silly and I'm not coming.' Charlotte ran back over the grass and on into the village.

Joanne watched her getting smaller and smaller with a mixture of exasperation and scorn.

'Cowardy cowardy custard,' she shouted. She turned to Charlie: 'Who wants her anyway?' she said. 'We'll be better on our own because she can't climb, and anyway, she's much too afraid.'

'Nothing to be afraid of,' said Charlie. 'Come on then, let's get started.'

The climb down the cliff path was long and quite alarming. Not many tackled it these days, unless there was a wreck, when the whole village turned out to salvage what they could. Joanne remembered an enormous quantity of tinned peaches which suddenly filled Gran's larder once and set off her dislike of what was once her favourite pudding. She remembered Grampa repeating, 'Lovely wreck that were,' over and over again, but she had not been allowed near the cliff path even then.

The beach looked small below them and her feet kept slipping on the stones and rough sand of the overgrown path. She slid on her bottom some of the way and winced at the scratches on her legs and hands. But there was no going back; Charlie was way ahead, leaping, swerving and bouncing along with ease. If he could do it, there was no reason why she couldn't. It was just a question of following Charlie.

The pleasure and satisfaction of finally feeling the sand soft beneath her feet was all bound up with pride of achievement. She looked sideways at Charlie to see if he appreciated her success, but he seemed to take it for granted. He knew she was brave and clever, didn't he? He knew she could do anything that he could do.

The smooth, slippery rocks at the bottom were easier on the feet, and the sand seemed like silk after the roughness of the cliff path.

'It's nice down here,' she said, sitting down in the sand and wanting to show she appreciated his bringing her here. 'I'm glad you brought me.'

The cave was a little way along the beach. It was dark and deep and the walls glowed with phosphorescence. Charlie led her by the hand to show her. 'It goes deep,' he said. 'Can't tell how deep it goes until you try.'

Joanne was paralysed with fear. 'Do we have to go in?' she asked Charlie who was pulling her into the blackness beyond.

'Not if you're frightened we don't.'

'I'm not frightened exactly, not if you're here with me, but . . .' she tried to find some other excuse, but there really was none. And anyway, Charlie would know how she was feeling; there was no hiding anything from him.

He suddenly produced a lantern. 'Keep this here for where it gets real dark,' he said, lighting the wick. But the light made the darkness even more frightening, because it made shadows that leaped and danced, Joanne's terror encased her like a block of ice, but her legs continued to move and, bent double, she followed the stealthily creeping Charlie and his lantern further and further into the darkness.

Their emergence into an immense chamber took her completely by surprise, so that she lost her balance, and fell among the rocks surrounding a still, black pool, to which she could see no end. 'It's the quiet you see,' Charlie said, seeming not to notice that she had fallen over. 'It's so quiet in here that it makes it easier to hear the singing.' He squatted down where he was and remained perfectly still. 'You just listen real deep like. Make trumpets for your ears so they catch the sound. It's far away, remember, and deep under the sea where they sing; takes a deal of listening to hear.'

Joanne squatted beside him and trumpeted both her ears with her hands. The sides of the cavern that they could see in the dim light glistened, and cold drops dripped on them and into the pool in the silence. Plip . . . Plip . . . Plop . . . and then after what seemed like hours, she heard it . . . far, far away and out of nowhere, a tiny, high pitched moan that slid minutely into her ear. She stopped breathing and stretched her listening beyond the ultimate to catch the faint wailing whisper. 'I hear it,' she mouthed silently at Charlie, whose eyes winked back at her. They smiled their mutual pleasure.

'We could go and find her,' Charlie whispered. 'Shouldn't be difficult; just follow the sound. They do say she's like a queen and can grant you wishes and that.'

'Grant wishes? Could she get rid of Gran?'

'Easy enough I reckon.'

'But how? How could we find her? Where is she?'

Charlie pointed into the pool. 'Down there, they do say. If'n we dived in and just swam and swam, we'd find her. That's what they say.'

'But I don't swim very well, and I don't like going underneath.'

'They say the mermaid makes that all right; she makes it so as you can swim and breathe under the water.' He took hold of Joanne's hand and began to pull her towards the still, black pool.

There was a sudden freezing of the insubstantial into cramped limbs and aching cupped hands and stark terror. A sensation that all was not well, and exactly at that same moment, a long, high-pitched wail came out of nowhere and echoed and echoed through the cave. Jo leaped to her feet and let out a scream of fright that seemed to have been pent up inside her for a long, unspecified time.

'What was *that*, Charlie?' she said in a high, shrill voice.

'No need to be afrighted,' Charlie said softly. ' 'Tes only the poor lost soul calling out to be rescued.'

But Jo scarcely heard him in her haste to get away from her fear. 'I've got to go home,' she shouted out, so that it echoed round the cavern. 'They'll think I'm lost.'

The drips and the damp and the darkness dogged her as she slipped and scrambled her way out of the cavern and back through the tunnels into the real world again. The tide had come in and there was very little beach left, so she ran, plunging clumsily in the sand, and then scrambled up the rocks to where the path started.

Climbing up the cliff was slower and very much harder. Fear again clamped Joanne into a paroxysm of terror. 'Charlie,' she shouted, 'Charlie, where are you?' but he didn't seem to hear and she slipped back the three steps which had taken so long to achieve. The sea had rushed in and swirled just below her feet. It splashed and sucked and roared at her as she clung to tussocks of grass and points of rock. The sea will get you if you don't watch out, Grampa had said. Don't you ever go down there, Grampa had said.

This was surely where God should come in; He saved those three in the burning fiery furnace didn't He? Trouble was, she couldn't put her hands together nor kneel down, but perhaps it wouldn't matter. Please dear God help me to get up the cliff and tell Charlie to come and rescue me. Her bare feet scrabbled on the shingly slope. She seemed to have dropped her shoes in the rush to the path and consequently progress was very painful, but God had obviously heard, because suddenly there were more secure footholds, large tufts to grasp with her hands. It must be possible specially if God was lending a hand. Things were no longer so frightening, though still exhausting, and half way up she started to cry very loudly and quite angrily. 'Charlie!' she shouted in between sobs and wherever she could get her breath together. 'Charlie . . . Grampa . . . help me.'

She sat down on a small stony ledge, overhung with a tussock of coarse grass. It was comfortable and sheltered her a little from the tearing wind. She could perhaps wait here until someone came; the sea wouldn't reach here. Someone was bound to come soon. Grampa would come looking for her. She shut her eyes and thought of sitting on Mumma's lap; it was fairly easy to imagine, the sea made almost as much noise as the bombs when they weren't too near, and the grass over her head tickled like the scarf Mumma sometimes wore when it was very cold.

Jo started to sing like Mumma used to when they sat in the shelter together, and she rocked to and fro in time to the tune, 'Early one morning just as the sun was rising . . .' Her rocking movements dislodged the gravel ledge that had been Mumma's lap and all the security was once more swept away. Jo found herself sprawled on her face, and sliding backwards down the cliff face. Stinging grazes burned her knees and hands and she screamed out against the wind and the surf sound, 'Mumma – Mumma don't go – don't leave me here Mumma – don't let the sea get me Mumma.' Surely God didn't really walk away from people like this? He was surely supposed to help you, not just make it easier for a bit and then snatch away the helping hand and watch you thrash about and hurt yourself.

She clutched at a clump of dry grass and stopped her slide down towards the sea. Perhaps if she kept very still and clung tight to the grass and tried not to think about the hurts to her hands and her legs; if she tried to think about nice things, like soft hay and being on the swing, and lying in her bed when the sun came through the curtains in the early morning, then that might make it better and help to pass the time till Grampa or Charlie came to find her. God would probably get word to both of them and make them understand where she was. God had quite enough magic powers for that at least.

But it was not Charlie, nor Grampa that found her first, but that Peter Petherick boy.

When he had followed the sound of the voice and found his way out of the cave, he had scrambled towards the cliff path with some difficulty. The incoming tide was splashing viciously against the rocks and swirled round his legs, pulling him backwards as it ebbed, but once above the water level, the footholds were less slippery and fairly easy to manoeuvre.

Half way up the cliff, as he stopped to catch his breath and rest his aching legs for a moment, he caught sight of her, sprawled flat against the side of the cliff under overhanging tussocks. At first, he thought she was a dead body, and his heart gave a great lurch of shock. But she was alive all right, and wailing, and he then saw it was the Tremayne girl.

'What's the matter with you?' he shouted.

'I can't climb any more.'

'Don't be daft. You've done the worst part, the rest's easy.'

'I can't, I'm tired, and Charlie just went and left me to die.'

'Oh rot, there's no reason to die just because you're half way up a cliff. Come on.'

He hauled her to her feet and pulled and pushed her, protesting loudly, the rest of the way to the top.

As they approached the end of the climb, with Peter a few feet behind, to catch her if she should slip, there was the sound of voices and a shout, 'It's all right! She's here – she's all right. I bring her up.'

Peter dodged quickly behind a jutting rock: couldn't be found here and get himself into more trouble at home. He saw Roberto, the Eyetye POW, pick her up, and he looked beyond and saw the cliff top full of people, talking, running up and down, searching. Could they be looking for him? He didn't wait to see. Quick – get back home and pretend you'd been there all the time; so he hid for a while, and then ran, ran like a hare with the dogs after it, and found Websie in the kitchen just dishing up the dinner.

'Dear life and what's put you in this fine lather I'd like to know? Just you get yourself together and tidied up and down to the dinner table quick, sharp smart and no dawdlin'.'

But Peter had no breath to answer. He was feeling, for about the first time in his life, that his home, in spite of all the terrors of female dominance and expectations, was perhaps a haven, and a safe place to run to. The realization gave him quite a shock as well as a small glow of comfort.

For Joanne, the end of the adventure was more dramatic. After being pushed and hauled by Peter up the last bit of the cliff, it was only when Roberto found her, dishevelled and tear sodden, that she felt really safe.

'Little one, little one, how did this come about? Don't cry now carissima. You are safe, safe with Berto.' And he lifted her up and over his shoulder and climbed to the top of the cliff path.

Grampa came, almost running, to meet them and she saw Charlotte and some other people from the village, but no Charlie. He would know how angry she would be with him. Obviously he was hiding, the horrid pig. Roberto carried her home, with Grampa walking beside and looking and sounding like he was crying: 'How could you do that Joanie? I've told you so many times. You could have been killed easy. I been near dead with worry Joanie.'

Gran, on the other hand, was not crying; more like spitting she was, spitting like some wild she-cat. Gran took Joanne and shook her until she thought her head might drop off. 'And what d'you think you were doing, you wicked, disobedient minx? Running off like that without a word and causing all this trouble? Whole village out looking for you, you bad, no-good brat. If it hadn't been for that Charlotte telling us where you'd gone, you'd likely as not be dead as a doornail by now which would have been God's justice on you for all your wickedness.'

But God had been on *her* side hadn't He? So Gran didn't have any right to scold her like this. Charlie was the real one to blame. If it hadn't been for Charlie, she would never have . . . just you wait, Charlie . . . just you wait till I get my hands on you.

Charlie finally turned up in the hayloft where she had gone one Sunday afternoon to escape the burdensome care that was still being handed out.

'Can I go and help Grampa milk the cows?' Because now she had to report where she was going.

But Gran was loath to allow her any sort of treat; she had to pay for her naughtiness. 'Your grandad don't need help and he don't need you getting under his feet either, though I don't see why he should get out of his share of keeping an eye on you. I don't get any let up these days, forever watching out for you in case you should slink off. See what extra burden you put on us by your wicked, thoughtless ways.' Gran stared angrily at Jo for a moment. 'Get on then, but don't make a nuisance of yourself else he'll give you what for.'

Jo watched Grampa milking for a while, enjoying the thin, silvery ping sound of the milk hitting the white froth in the bucket, and giggling when he directed a jet towards the waiting cat; they were both so clever, Grampa and the cat, the jet seldom missed its mark. But then boredom caught up with her, she wanted to run in the fields again, or play on the swing, or look for Charlie, even though she was so angry with his shocking behaviour.

'Can I go and play in the hayloft?'

Grampa considered; Grace had said don't let her out of your sight, but it was a bit too much, that. Couldn't for ever keep after her like a bloody shadow. She'd learned her lesson; wouldn't be so silly again. Couldn't come to much harm in the hayloft after all.

'Reckon so, if you don't go nowhere else.'

Jo climbed the ladder with relief, just to get away from all the eyes, forever watching. Mice shot away with tiny rustles as she approached, and the soft warm smell of the hay embraced her and made her smile with the pleasure of it.

She saw Charlie at once, even though he was half hidden in the hay.

'It's no good you trying to hide from me,' she said. 'Why did you leave me to die like that?'

'You didn't die.'

'I nearly did.'

'You never. You were just being weak and feeble and pretending you couldn't do something when you could've. And anyway, that Petherick boy came to the rescue.'

Of course the Petherick boy had actually helped her: she had to admit that, but he hadn't been much better than Charlie, because he'd made her do it herself, instead of rescuing her like a real rescuer would have done.

'He didn't rescue me, he just found me. You both could at least have rescued me properly.'

'No we couldn't've; you've got to do things for yourself and not be afraid of doing what you really want to do or you'll never get on. You're a scaredy cat, always trying to run away or give up, and you won't ever get anywhere if you do that.'

'But you were trying to make me drown.'

'Don't talk so silly, I was taking you on a great adventure so as you could bring about your heart's desire.'

'But it would have made me dead.'

'No it wouldn't've.'

'Yes it would've.'

'No it wouldn't've.'

She'd made her point; no sense in carrying on. 'Let's make a house,' she suggested, so they did.

11

The end of the war approached and at the same time, buried anxieties for both Joanne and her grandparents began to surface. At seven years old, Jo had not succeeded in making friends at school. She was usually too wrapped in her own imaginings so that school life tended to pass her by. Charlotte, who lived at the other end of the village, was the only one she kept up with, out of school.

Grace grumbled on: grumblings that by now floated past Jo's hearing altogether, without beginning to penetrate her consciousness.

'Reckon we're expected to keep 'er here for good.' Grace refused to consider that there might be other reasons for Jenny's silence. *She* wouldn't get herself killed, that one. Much too smart.

'Good mind to take it up with them as should know,' she said to Will, 'since you won't stir yourself. Get 'er traced somehow.'

Will had much less certainty. 'Best leave things alone. She'll come back if she's able. We'd have been told if anything bad had happened, rest assured. She'll be back, you see if she isn't. Any day, she'll phone up and tell us she's coming down right away.' That meant any day now, little Joanie might be whisked away from them; didn't bear thinking on.

Charlotte's mother, who had been made a war widow in the early part of the war, was now engaged to an American GI.

'We have to go and live in a place in America called Detroit,' Charlotte told Jo, her eyes pink with unhappiness.

'It will probably be very nice,' Jo told her. 'You'll be

93

able to eat lots of sweets and chewing gum and bananas.' She was devastated at the thought of losing one of her two friends. However irritating Charlotte might be at times, they had had some good fun together. They had moved, in the course of their play, from galloping their pretend horse through the fields to exchanging gossip in the hayloft which they found far more comfortable and a great deal warmer. Their interests had evolved into a passion for horses and dogs, for which they were considering setting up a hospital and training centre.

'I hate chewing gum,' Charlotte said, the tears now running down her cheeks.

'So do I, but you'll probably learn to like it.'

Charlotte vaguely and uncomfortably guessed that Jo's parents were not able to collect her when the war was over. 'What will you do when the war's over?' she asked. 'Will you be able to go back to London?'

Jo did not hesitate. She suddenly wanted to be shot of this place and go back and pick up where she'd left off, all those years ago. Explanations flashed into her mind as she spoke. 'I'm going back to live with my Mumma,' she said.

Charlotte's eyes widened. Since the day they met, Jo hadn't ever talked about her Mummy. 'But I thought . . . I thought . . .' She had always imagined that perhaps she didn't have one any more.

'My real Daddy got killed in the war,' Jo said, 'and then my Mummy married another soldier who is very rich, so I shall go and live with them when they get back.'

Something like that *must* happen, surely. This father business was more puzzling. She just remembered someone called Steve; but you don't call your father Steve, you call him Daddy or Dad, and she had never called anyone that. She'd asked once, but Gran had only snapped, 'That Steve wasn't your Dad my girl; your Dad was a Cornishman, so you're Cornish through and through and don't you ever forget it,' and then had refused to say anything more. After that, a great empty space often seemed to engulf and imprison her.

'When my new Daddy gets back,' she said to Charlotte, rather slowly, so that the ideas could form themselves before they made themselves into words, 'he's going to buy a very big house in the country where he's going to keep a lot of horses and a lot of dogs and my Mumma and I are going to live there with him.'

'Is he a farmer then?'

'No, he's a vet, but we shall have a farm too and my Mumma and me will run that and we shall have sheep as well as cows and we shall have kennels for stray dogs that get lost. And cats too,' she added as an after-thought. 'And birds that break their wings or get caught by the cats, we shall have a hospital for them too.'

'When will they come for you do you think?'

'Oh I don't know, because Mumma is in the war too and she has had to be in a foreign country all this time, so that she couldn't come and see me at all, so I don't know when she will be able to come back to England, and my Dad is a prisoner in Japan so it's sure to take him a very long time to get back.'

She could see the house they would soon occupy. Very big indeed with long drives up to the front door and it would look like a castle. In fact it *was* really a castle which had once belonged to a knight and his lady, and there was a moat round it and a drawbridge and it would be completely surrounded by forest, and there would be fields full of buttercups and hills for the sheep and a lake with boats on it and an island in the middle where she would have a special cottage of her very own.

She could not bring herself to question either of her grandparents about the future; she was afraid to break the comfortable silence that gave her the chance to make her own arrangements in her head.

'Charlotte's going to live in America,' she finally said at tea one day. 'When the war's over.' There, it was out. She had shown that she knew life was going to end;

given them the chance to tell her the worst, or the best. But the silence seemed to grow for many minutes until Grampa took his pipe out of his mouth. 'Don't reckon things is going to change much down here.'

Now what did that mean?

'Got no sense, some of these young women,' said Gran. 'Think they're going to get it better over there, but they won't. You mark my words, they won't get it better at all.'

Nothing about Mumma coming back to fetch her. And what about her Cornish father? Perhaps he had been killed and they didn't like to tell her. That was it, he was killed while rescuing one of his friends from deadly danger. Probably from the sea, because he was sure to have been a sailor. He must have dived into terrible seas, just like the ones they had round here when the boats were wrecked on the cliffs. Dived in to rescue his best friend who had been blown overboard. Jo saw his fair, beautiful head engulfed in mountainous waves, she saw him finally go under and come up three times – because you always came up three times before you finally drowned – and then he would have raised both his arms above his head because that's what drowning people did too. She saw quite distinctly, the waves break over his head and the last she saw of him was the tips of his ten fingers as he sank beneath the restless waves, the sort that God doth calm. Only He didn't this time. Tears welled up in her eyes and throat at the thought.

But the war ended and, as Grampa had said, nothing much changed at all. Most of the troops had moved out anyway just before D-Day; that remarkable period when the population of St Ives and district had seemed to halve and become ninety per cent female within the space of one week. Even the children had remarked on it. 'Where have the soldiers gone Miss? Did the Germans kill them all Miss?' 'Why aren't there any big lorries any more Miss?' 'Won't we get any more chewing gum Miss?' And the answers: 'It's the invasion dear, the troops have

96

gone to help the French soldiers chase the Germans out.' 'Let's make a map, children and then we can put pins into the places where our troops win battles.'

The actual cessation of hostilities seemed to make no immediate difference at all to begin with. Only for Jo the panic built up with each successive day and was held fiercely in check in case terrors should become reality. The stately home to which they might soon be moving, stayed sublimely in her mind's eye, welcoming and waiting for her – and yet, did she really want to go?

The flags came out on VE-Day and the school had a party and the town had a party. Charlotte went away to Detroit and Jo grieved, Bert fell in love with a Cornish girl and became involved with his own problems. Jo thought how lucky that Charlie remained, so that the loss of the other two was not so bad as it might have been. She didn't see Peter again, after the episode on the cliff, and had somehow so confused him in her mind with Charlie, she was no longer sure that she had actually ever met him. She made no new friends at school. The other children jeered at anything she told them about Charlie, or how she was going to live in a castle. The whisper went round:

'Jo Tremayne's a liar!'

'Jo Tremayne smells of pigs!'

'Jo Tremayne's soft in the head!' And even,

'Jo Tremayne's a bastard! She ain't got no Dad.'

Jo heard the words but, likely as not, would be imagining herself riding round a paddock on the snow-white pony her new father would have bought for her. The vision made a mockery of their words: of course she had a father – she had had two, in fact, and was therefore luckier than most.

She tried to discuss the situation with Charlie, but he seemed to become more and more critical of her as time went on: 'Well you ask for it don't you? You're not as clever as they are, are you? Not grown up are you? No wonder they laugh at you, can't expect them to do nothing else.' She cried a lot when he said this, because of course it was true.

'Don't suppose I shall ever have a friend again, Charlie.'

'You got me.'

'Yes but you're not nice to me any more.'

'I just say what you expect to hear, that's all. Anyways, you won't need me much longer.'

'What do you *mean* not need you? I haven't got anybody else, of course I need you.'

Charlie didn't argue with this. 'You'll throw me over before too long,' was all he said.

Jo demurred, 'As long as I'm here and you're here, I shan't. But I may have to go away to live in my castle with Mumma. Or my real father might take me on his ship to India and we'll live on a beach with palm trees and have elephants to pull our carriages.'

'You won't leave here till you're growed.'

'How do you know that? You don't know any more than I do. Mumma will come any day now, as soon as she gets back to England, or my Dad will come in his boat to St Ives or Penzance, you see if he doesn't.'

The only thing to be done in the meantime, was to live life as it was, which Joanne proceeded to do. She caught the eight-thirty bus into school in St Ives every morning and the four-fifteen back again every evening. She cried when Bert was repatriated, and treasured the withy basket he had made for her out of willow switches, and rescued his little carved crucifix that Gran threw away saying it was wicked idolatry. She lit the oil lamps for Gran every evening and helped her to pick in the washing when she came back from school. She was once or twice allowed to go to the Socials in the village hall with Gran and Grampa, where at Christmas the ladies wore long dresses and there was a real band called Jimmie Rickard's Entertainment Company, and they all took part in the Zennor Feast in May for St Senara.

She was glad that Grampa didn't have to grow broccoli once the war stopped because she hated broccoli anyway. He kept on the potatoes, though, and bought some more cows, and Gran went on making butter and collecting and selling eggs, and they rolled out the milk churn every day for the Ministry to collect and take in to Penzance. And Grampa went on milking the cows and feeding the pigs, and sending calves, tied up in a sack with their heads sticking out, into Penzance market on the bus in charge of the driver.

It was a reasonably satisfactory life, where gradually, gradually, the fear and panic subsided, and with them, the original ideas of castle and ponies and riches, Gran turned, quite slowly, from a wicked witch into a bad-tempered old lady with the Devil in her, whose bark was worse than her bite. She could be dealt with quite well if you followed Grampa's lead, and kept reminding yourself to be sorry for her, rather than angry with her.

There was a new golden dream that one of her fathers would provide large sums of money for Jo to set up an animal hospital of her own, in the immediate district, to care for all the lost, ailing and abandoned birds, animals and even insects she was constantly finding in her ramblings round the farm and cliff. There were only the twinges of regret that Mumma didn't come.

'But if she did come,' she said to Charlie, 'I don't think I would really want to go away from here. It would be so dreadful to leave everyone, wouldn't it?'

'She won't come,' said Charlie. 'You mark my words, she won't never come here no more.'

12

The transition from prep to public school was, for Peter, just another inevitable fact of life that swept over him and carried him along, regardless. There was no running away, no hiding in the barn, no losing himself in the cave; no satisfactory Erehwemos anywhere any more.

The despair was sometimes overwhelming, particularly the week before term started, but usually his distress took the form of fatalistic resignation. He crept through his life, clinging to the belief that there was not much that could make it worse than it already was. He was almost completely mute, having no-one with whom he chose to share his thoughts.

'For God's sake Pigs,' Jean screamed at him once, 'stop this ghastly sulking. If you want to rebel, then rebel. I can't stand this martyred attitude of yours.'

'I – I'm not sulking,' Peter stammered. 'Really I'm not, I'm – I'm just thinking.'

'Well try thinking of something funny for a change, then you might *look* a bit more acceptable at least. Remember when the Lord Lieutenant and his lady came to visit and Cynthia slid on the parquet and ended up in a heap at his feet? That was hilarious,' and she started to gurgle with laughter.

'You always did have a warped sense of humour, Jean,' Cynthia said. 'You know my back has never been the same since.' And the quick flash of amusement that Peter had felt when he remembered the incident was immediately swallowed up in feeling sorry for Cynthia.

Jean was aggressive that morning. 'Do you hate us all so much?' she asked.

'No, of course I don't hate you.' Peter felt the blush creeping up his neck.

'So smile, little brother, smile sometimes – or even laugh. It would do us all a power of good.'

Peter did his best, but the smile soon made his face muscles ache. The flair he had had for pretending himself into his own imagination did not run to pretending into reality.

In that sense, school was not such a strain, once the trauma of going back had been endured. He was at least less noticeable in the huge crowd; people were not bothered as to whether or not he smiled or looked as though he was sulking. He was thus more able to concentrate on the business of existing in a hostile environment.

Just one voice was out of step with the multitude. 'Are you ailing, boy?' Ian Dalrymple-Smythe had taught classics for many years, and was Peter's housemaster. 'Mooning about the way you do – not healthy you know.'

The cover of anonymity was breached and Peter's heart sank.

'Sir?' he said, hoping the encounter might end quickly.

'Sir nothing,' Dalrymple-Smythe glowered down at him. 'Questions should be answered. Present yourself in my study at teatime.'

The summons had to be obeyed, and Peter sat unhappily on the hard high chair placed opposite the collapsed and crumpled figure in the sagging leather armchair. It struck him how old and worn out both chair and man appeared: they matched so well, a study of faded black and dusty brown.

'Well *Peth*erick?'

'Peth*e*rick, sir.'

There was a blast of cracked laughter. 'Ever the pedantic and fussbudget I note. Look beyond, boy, look beyond. Life goes on out there you know; might just as well join in, what?'

'Yes sir.'

'God's truth, what a boring little runt you are. Good mind to give you a whacking to wake you up a bit. Would brighten my day, I can tell you.'

Peter felt an unfamiliar flicker of amusement in spite of himself; he was suddenly unafraid of the old creature sprawled out in front of him who reminded him of his father. If Humphrey had lived, they might have been able to share this sort of relationship together. An absurd wave of relief swept through him as he considered the idea of having a father and being a son.

Dalrymple-Smythe pushed a tome of a book towards him. 'Y'Greek's about the only thing you're any good at,' he said.

'And biology, sir.'

'Bugger biology, boy; messing about with the bloody innards of rats never did anybody any good, but wrap yourself around Plato's ramblings in the original language and you'll come out educated, no matter what sort of little wimp you may be. I shall expect a paper on it by the end of term, and that's on top of your regular school work. Understand?'

'Yes sir.'

'Right, now scoot, but you can come and see me to talk about it any time; in fact I shall expect to see you every Friday at this time; and you can bring some buns for us to eat. You've probably got far more money than I have, so you can provide the buns.'

Peter walked away from the interview exhilarated and not at all overawed. He felt that he had discovered an ally, and that life might from now on be lived rather than endured, centred as it could be on Greek philosophy and biology – for which he continued to have an enduring fascination – and long-distance running, the one sport in which he excelled. He had, after all, been running away all his life, and to have the running now not only permitted, but actually encouraged, was a tremendous bonus. Even if he only ran, inevitably, in a circle, and always ended up where he started, the relative scale of the route was big enough to allow him to consider the path out as an escape away from absolute being, while the finishing line became the anticipated haven of rest where he could sink into the exhausted analgesia of sleep and occasionally be accorded the plaudits of the community: something achieved by his own effort.

And the progression held for a time. Though authority always insisted he should attend classes that could achieve exam results likely to take him to University, he merely sat in on subjects in which he had no interest, and achieved precisely nothing. 'Rather naughty, dearest boy,' Dalrymple-Smythe – known by now, out of his actual hearing, as Dimple – told him. 'Should at least try, you know. Could perfectly well get English, anyone can get English unless they are dead, and there's no way one can combine Greats with *Biology*. Ugh – what a revolting idea! Told you time and time again. Such a pity; once you've got to Oxford, you'll never have to move again; from undergraduate to graduate to tutor to professor. Live your life within hallowed precincts. Would suit a hermit like you down to the ground.'

Peter didn't bother to argue. In spite of his continued bias towards an isolated withdrawal from life in general, the thought of incarceration within some ancient seat of learning was claustrophobic in the extreme. He needed air and sea and rocks and birds; and at once gooseflesh crept up his arms and his l gs as he was transported to cliff top and smell of thyme and sound of sea and call of birds. His whole being ached for the nostalgia of familiar memory; it was overpowering.

The weekly sessions with Dimple continued as oases in the desert, and an obsession with philosophy improved his Greek, but he did little to appease the other members of the school staff apart from those in the biology department. For the first time in his life, he began to experience the sensation of affection towards another human being.

'I'm very grateful, sir, for all you've done for me.'

How painfully embarrassing that sounded; how did one express anything that meant anything? 'I was – er – I was finding life increasingly – ah, I mean – didn't see the point of going on somehow. But with these sessions with you, well – well, I really do enjoy them and look forward to them. I mean, well, it's good to have something to look forward to.'

He ended the speech in an agony of confusion and embarrassment, twisting his hands together behind his back.

Dimple seemed to melt quite visibly. 'Well, well; that absurd little speech must have cost any amount of guts to get off your chest. I congratulate you; next week we'll practise delivery and voice production. You have to proclaim, boy; strike gestures, present yourself. Am I to understand by this peroration that you have at least decided, far too late, mind you, to prepare yourself for University?'

'Well, no, I don't really want to do that. I just want to – want to – just sit and think a bit.'

'Stupid boy!' roared Dimple. 'Don't know what's good for you; never did, and probably never will. Go off and waste your life, then, if you must, but don't say I didn't warn you.'

He sat, glowering, his face full of acute disappointment, and Peter curled up with guilt.

'I'm sorry, sir.'

'And that's a bloody stupid thing to say; you're not sorry at all, you're glad, or you should be at least. Chosen what you don't want to do and told me to bugger off and mind my own business. Should be damn pleased with yourself. Stood on your own feet for once; about time too, if you ask me.'

Peter saw a tear trickle down his cheek from under his spectacles, but couldn't be sure it wasn't just the result of a rheumy eye. They stayed, staring at each other for what seemed like an age, and then Dimple held out his hand. 'Come here, boy, and sit beside me.' He took hold of Peter's hand as he approached, and pulled him down to sit on the arm of his chair.

'You won't really be needing to come to these little tea parties of ours any more. Gone beyond me now, perfectly capable of dealing with the subject yourself.' He held Peter's hand against his cheek. 'Truth is, I'd be desolate if you stopped coming.'

Peter's mind switched painfully back to his first year at the school: the older boys, mostly those only a year or two above him, had seemed to know that he was an incorrigible innocent and had set upon him like vultures. In time he had learned how to deal with situations, but the memory of it was safer pushed into the void and lost.

'Second truth is, Peter, I love angelic little boys, but when they get bigger, the whole thing becomes more serious, and I start losing my heart. These sessions have meant so much to me; thought they might have meant something to you too. Bloody silly, I know. Could you find it within your heart to indulge me just a little? Nothing nasty, darling boy, just a little love, that's all.'

Peter snatched his hand away with exaggerated violence and fled from the room; down to the changing rooms, into running gear and out, far out across the playing fields, over the wall and into the country beyond. Just away, away, into the unforeseeable, the unpredictable, to Erehwemos – or was it now Erehwon?

It was summer and it was hot, and the precipitous flight soon turned into a stumbling, gasping stagger. Had to bring himself under control if he was to avoid collapse: slow down, breathe deeply, get a rhythm, and gradually he found himself padding more easily, eating up the ground with regular loping strides. Into a second wind now, with the breeze blowing gently against the sweat on his face and torso. Time for thought, time for contemplation, time to consider.

Why be so *afraid*, for God's sake? A pathetic old man, who had given him so much, and for whom he felt great affection and gratitude, wanted a little love in return.

As he loped along the well-known track that would eventually bring him back to the playing fields, it dawned upon him what a position of strength and responsibility he was now in; poor old Dimple had compromised himself totally, which left Peter in complete control and able to call the tune. So how easy it was to respond. All part of a debt – you looked after your own when they got old. Make life good for Dimple, and at the same time repay something of what he owed to him. Distaste was a small price to pay; to do something for somebody was an entirely new conception for Peter, and he padded back across the fields and into the school, filled with a certain excitement at having discovered another small reason for living.

'Why were you not at prep this evening?' Billowing black robes met him as he made for the changing rooms.

'Needed an extra practice for the inter-school sports, sir.'

'Should have asked permission. Can't just take off when you think fit.'

'No sir. Sorry sir.' And he heard in his head Dimple shouting: 'Bloody silly thing to say – you're not sorry at all.'

13

There was only a modified sense of let-down in the fact that nobody had yet come to Zennor to collect Joanne and whisk her away to her castle in the air, because, as she reminded herself, it was only a dream in a small girl's head. Had she ever really expected it to happen?

'Told you many a time,' Grace said to her husband. 'Can't think why you ever kept the notion that that Jenny might turn up one day. Trusting old ninny, that's what you are; ought to know better by now, you've lived long enough to learn some sense.' There was something akin to affection in Grace's voice. Will noticed the different inflexion, but couldn't recognize it for what it was.

'See how right I was when I said don't tell her about them letters? Would only've got her worked up for nothing. Don't trust that daughter of yours with her "Give my love to Joanie" line. Let her show herself ready to do something herself. Why don't she get in touch now the war's over? No, no, she's a sly one – won't let us know where she is just so as she can go on making use of us. Disgraceful, that's what it is.'

The emphasis on the wickedness of others gave Grace proof of her own good nature. She knew that her short temper meant that some might dismiss her as hard, but it was just that she couldn't abide sentimentality: gave her the creeps, that did. No good pretending mother-love for a no-good daughter. Best come out with it and blow the disappointment in what might have been.

Later that day Joanne came striding across the yard in her school uniform. At twelve years old, she was a big, fresh-faced girl, with fair, tousled hair escaping from her beret, and her round pink face shining with minute mist droplets. Will's heart missed a beat or two. How could he hope to keep this beauty to himself, caged up like some wild thing? It surely wouldn't be long before she flew.

'Hallo Grampa. They let us out early. Shall I do the pigs?'

'No, you'd best go in and help your Gran.'

Jo wrinkled her nose and then giggled. 'But that'll mean I have to do something awful like fishing the washing out of the copper and putting it through the mangle, you know how I hate that. Go on Grampa, let me do the pigs.'

'Well don't you spoil them clothes, you know what a rumpus there'll be if you get messed.' Satisfactorily secret misbehaviour; made him feel young.

Jo had resigned herself to life without Charlotte and

without parents. Zennor was home for the present at any rate.

'Can't ask you back home,' she would say to the few school friends who attempted any sort of companionship. 'My Gran's a bit difficult; she don't like me bringing no-one home, says it makes too much work.'

It was likely that's what she would have said anyway. On occasions, Jo would assume a limp as she approached the school playground. 'Didn't get out of the way quick enough,' she would explain, with a rueful smile. 'My Gran's a dab hand with the broom handle if you don't get to muck out the cowshed quick enough.'

Her very fair skin bruised and scratched easily and often in the course of her everyday, energetic bouncing and scrambling over walls and rocks and through heather and brambles and other small obstacles: she seldom went round, but rather through or over anything that obstructed her path.

'You mean she *hits* you?'

'Misses more likely. I'm a fast mover.'

'But you're always covered in bruises and things.'

Jo blushed. Couldn't really blame that on Gran; not actually say it because that would be a downright flat-out lie. 'I'm just a clumsy great clot, that's all, can't blame anyone but me for that.'

Respect increased; didn't even blame her torturer. 'Do you *have* to live with your gran?'

'Yes, well you see my dad was drowned while he was rescuing a friend after they was torpedoed, and my mum, she was caught in a bombing raid on a hospital in Tripoli where she was nursing. But she never felt nothing, they say, just disappeared – pouf – like that.'

After she had said it, Jo felt uncomfortable because she remembered once thinking that that was the way witches disintegrated: in a puff of smoke. The way she thought Gran was going to go at one time. The memory made her want to giggle, but that would have ruined the effect of the drama. She had decided, soon after she had joined the big school, to forestall any jibes from school mates, and she let fall stimulating stories about her home life almost as throw-away remarks to classmates. Let them enlarge on them if they wished.

The ploy worked. She was now poor Jo, an oddball maybe, and not one you'd want to make a friend of, but not many had had the misfortune to lose both parents, and be bashed up by her gran into the bargain; she was held in a kind of muted respect. It was understood that she had to work desperately hard as soon as she got home from school, in constant fear of this aged grandmother; cleaning the house, cooking, washing, ironing, as well as feeding the poultry and the pigs and dealing with the accounts and paperwork from the Ministry. No wonder she was a bit odd.

'Don't know how you do it Jo.' Some of the girls felt they ought to make a gesture.

Even the teachers were impressed. 'I wondered, Miss Delaney,' the word had got round to one of the younger teachers, who felt it her duty to inform the head-mistress, 'whether we should visit Joanne Tremayne's grandparents. They do seem to expect her to undertake too much work in the home.'

Miss Delaney had been in the area as head teacher for a good many years, and glanced at Joanne's reports before answering. 'Mr Tremayne is a good, kind man, Miss Thomas, with a great deal of understanding, I don't believe he would approve of slave-driving. Mrs Tremayne has a sharp tongue and very little humour, I know, but actual inhumanity? I wouldn't have thought . . .'

Miss Thomas persisted. 'She seems to suffer a great many accidents in the home – er – often unable to take part in PT or games because of a painful arm or leg . . .'

'Are you saying they ill-treat the child?'

'It would appear a possibility.'

'I can't believe such a thing would go unnoticed in such a small community. Mrs Tremayne is certainly a big of a dragon but – well – I wouldn't have thought . . . Send Joanne to me, Miss Thomas. I'll see if I can get to the bottom of the matter.'

'Ah Joanne, Miss Thomas tells me you've been in the wars lately; how do you manage to get yourself injured so frequently?'

Were they on to her then? Did they suspect her of pretending?

'Oh I do fall about a bit – er – like down the ladder in the hayloft, and then the cows get a bit wild sometimes when you milk them.' Grampa never let her milk the cows but old Delooney wasn't to know that.

'You are a little young to be milking the cows, does your grandfather allow . . .'

'No he doesn't really, but my gran likes me to help him out now and then. He doesn't want me to do anything, but my gran thinks I should do my share of helping out.' And make sure it was all the boring jobs too, didn't she just.

'I see, and what sort of things does your grand-mother expect you to do?'

'Well there's the chickens and the pigs and getting the hay down for the cows and hanging the washing out and doing the mangling and the washing up and cleaning up the house and that.'

Miss Delaney searched for probability in the herculean catalogue, but felt her doubts waver in the wide-open unworldliness that gazed back at her.

'Is this why you're behind with your homework?'

Jo smiled expansively. 'I don't get that much time,' she said. And it was true; there were always so many other much more interesting things to do.

'But the accidents? How do you manage to have quite so many bumps and bruises?'

'Well – I'm a bit slow you see, and a bit clumsy.' That was sort of true, and old Delooney could take it to mean anything she liked.

They sent the inspector round fairly soon, which was very embarrassing.

'I didn't say *nothing* Gran,' Jo insisted to a furious

Grace after the visit. 'Really I didn't. They just were on at me about homework, that's all.' And that was nearly true, after all; she hadn't told them how evil Gran really was.

She fled into the barn in a storm of weeping and called for Charlie because she knew he was hiding in there somewhere. 'It's not fair,' she sobbed. 'Even Grampa's cross with me, just as if I'd done something wrong when it's her what's done the wrong things and her what makes miseries of both of us, me and Grampa both. She ought to be done away with, that's what.'

'You make up it's worse than what it is,' Charlie said, chewing away at the straw in his mouth. 'You used to pretend things was better than what they were, and that's a much easier way to live.'

'I don't pretend anything,' Jo shouted at him. 'It's all true and real and happening, and it isn't fair I get blamed for telling the truth.'

'You don't never tell the truth just how it is,' Charlie said, and he laughed at her and made her angrier than ever.

14

The time came, rather later to Jo than to other girls, when boys ceased to be shouting, teasing little pests and became provocative, if spotty objects to be impressed by prettiness, pertness and lipstick if you could get hold of it. Jo found herself listening to some of the school chatter, being reluctantly drawn into the general obsession with boys, rock and roll and clothes. The music dinned rather pleasantly into her ears: something utterly new and oddly satisfactory. She saw other girls looking pretty, and began to resent her own patched and jumbled sweaters, shirts and ill-fitting skirts. She began to like the look of some of the boys, especially the big, clean, tall ones.

'That George Brown,' she told Charlie, 'he's gone on Sylvia Penhallet. Can't think why, she's so *ugly*.'

'Why should you mind if he's gone on her?'

'I don't mind, silly, I just think it's strange, because he's quite good looking himself and he could have anyone.'

'You, for instance?'

'Aw don't be stupid. I wouldn't touch him with a bargepole.'

'But you might kiss him down by Zennor beach.'

'I wouldn't kiss him. Not ever. Not if he was the last boy on earth I wouldn't.'

'Bet you would,' said Charlie.

Charlie had been better tempered with her lately. They sometimes had small arguments like this on the subject of boys and Jo's reaction to them, but they usually ended up walking hand in hand along the cliff top, loving the sea below them and the sky above and thinking where else was there such a perfect place as this to pass the time of day. There was no-one in the world who understood her better than Charlie did; there was no-one she would rather talk to or be with. She even started to talk about him: 'He's wonderful,' she told the girls at school. 'Ever so tall and good looking with a smashing smile, and he's always around and asks me out all the time.'

'Really? Does he really? Where d'you go? Does he take you to the flicks? Do you go dancing?'

Jo laughed at them. 'Oh no, he's not like that at all. Doesn't like the cinema or dancing. He's clever and we go for long walks and he's just *in*teresting.'

'I wouldn't find long walks interesting, not unless you got a kiss and a cuddle on the way.'

Jo blushed. 'Well of *course* we do that too,' she said.

When George Brown did finally ask her out, Joanne was delighted. It was not that she was particularly impressed by George Brown himself, in spite of what she had said to Charlie. But maybe she was missing out on something; it didn't do to be thought lacking; didn't want people to think she couldn't attract the boys; as good as those silly girls any day.

'I'm pretty broke,' he told her. 'Not enough for the movies. We could have an ice cream if you pay for yourself.'

'Yes, of course, I'd like that.'

'Saturday then?'

'All right.'

'At the caff, three o'clock.'

Two whole days to wait.

'Got to go into St Ives to do some shopping for the school play,' she told Gran. 'I'll be late back.'

'Shopping? School play? Is this the sort of teaching they hand out today? Don't bother with sums and reading and that; expect you to go out shopping do they?' She stormed round the kitchen, muttering: 'Shopping indeed; school play . . . don't teach'm these days, don't teach'm nothing at all. What a waste of time. I was working for me living by the time I was your age; won't even let you leave school now; keep you on to play act and do shopping. I'll write to that Delaney woman; not that it'll do much good; proper smarmy school-marm type that one. Looks down her nose at us country folk . . . shopping indeed.'

Joanne held her breath until the tirade began to die down. Would Gran write to Mrs Delaney? Hardly likely, no real chance, so the lie would not be found out – unless anything went wrong. Someone might see her of course, the colour rushed into her face, they could report back. But she could always invent something; so many possibilities of what she was doing in the caff with a boy: learning her lines for the school play? Checking her homework? Waiting for one of the teachers? Lots of possible excuses, 'I'll go on my bike,' she said.

'And who's going to feed the chickens then? As if I didn't know.'

'But Gran, it's only this once.'

'This once, yes, then this twice and this three times and your grandfather and me getting older and not able to keep up with the work, but do we get help? Oh no, you go gadding off to do shopping don't you.'

'I'll do extra on Sunday, really I will. You get something special for me to do on Sunday.'

'Farm animals can't wait till Sunday, so what good's that?'

Jo went outside to walk on the cliffs. Was it worth her while? All this fuss because she wanted to have an ice cream, with George Brown in a caff. Was it really worth it?

She saw Charlie approaching and greeted him miserably. 'You'd think I was about to do a murder,' she said, 'the way Gran's creating.'

'Well so you are, as good as.'

'What do you *mean*, as good as? I'm having an ice-cream with George Brown in a caff, is that the same as murdering someone?'

'You're murdering time,' Charlie said. 'Wasting your time with that turnip-head. You mind him, that's all I'll say to you, you just mind him.'

'All right, so I'll mind him. You're just jealous. Why don't you take me out somewhere then if you don't want me to go with him?'

'Jealous? Me jealous? That's a good one – and we do go out don't we? All the time we go out and see the things that's worth seeing, like the sunset over the sea, and the buzzards wheeling and smell the smells and feel the wind and the rain and see the sun making things golden and the shadows long. What more do you want than these?'

Jo tilted her nose in the air. 'Country life isn't everything you know. I want to live a bit, not just moulder away here on the farm.'

'Come into the barn.' Charlie said as they approached the farm. 'I'll show you what life is all about.'

Jo followed him with a sense of curiosity. What was

114

there to find out about in the barn that she didn't know already? She was unprepared for the fact that he put his arms round her when they had climbed the ladder into the hayloft, and she was totally unprepared for the glow and the tingling excitement that took over when he kissed her. It was breath-taking, and chased all other sensations from her.

Thinking back on it afterwards, she found she could remember very little of what happened; a sort of dream memory of warmth, light, racing heartbeat, softness and feverish excitement came to her mind whenever she thought of it. But how long did it last? What was it exactly? What did they do to create this exhilaration? That, she could never recall. And then why did she suddenly find herself, flushed and pulsing with an unknown exuberance, in the kitchen of the farm, lighting the lamps for Gran? How had she got there? How did she leave Charlie and the barn without remembering?

Whatever had happened, there, suddenly, was Grampa sitting in his chair with Gran cooking the supper. Jo was confused and a little frightened. Had she actually experienced what life was all about? Was she any the wiser? Inexplicably, she felt that she was – much wiser, much more experienced and possessed of some great new secret. But that, of course, was only this active imagination that her teachers were for ever telling her she had to control, it was just that that had taken her over for those few lost moments. It wasn't anything unusual really, she just imagined that it was.

So she went out with George Brown two days later, and they sat, eating strawberry ice creams in the Quayside Café. Jo found the experience disappointingly boring. There was no-one she knew there to show off to, she could think of nothing at all to say to her companion, and the strawberry ice made her feel a little sick.

'You're all right you know,' George Brown said, after quite a long silence. 'We might go to one of the Saturday night hops, what do you say?'

115

'I haven't done much dancing.'

'I could teach you if you like.'

'Well all right, I wouldn't mind.'

There was another long silence and Jo thought of Charlie. There were never boring silences with Charlie, but she couldn't think of anything that would interest George. She knew nothing about football.

'I could take you part the way home if you like,' George said at length, 'and we could say good night by that bus shelter. There's a bench there and there's no buses at this time.'

'If you like.' She was quite keen to get going before it got too dark. Gran had said to be sure to get home before dark. She had never done the journey by bike in the dark, not that there was really a problem, she knew the road well enough.

She got up. 'Come on then.'

She handed over the money for her ice cream, and he paid the bill.

I won't do this again, Jo thought, it's really not much fun. Wonder what I'm doing wrong. Bet he won't ask me again, and the other girls will think I'm pretending if I say it was boring. I shall have to say it was wonderful and smashing, but that I decided, he was no good for me. As they rode silently through the streets of St Ives, she thought out what she would say to her classmates on Monday. 'Oh it was smashing really. We had a superduper time; sausages and chips and then a Knickerbocker Glory, and he told me all about his family and where he lives and what he likes doing. And he squeezed my hand in the caff, and he was really swish the way he ordered the food and paid the bill and that. And his kisses – oh my eye, they're a bit of all right, I can tell you.'

'Let's stop here then,' said George Brown, rather out of breath from pedalling up the hill.

'Here? Oh all right.' Jo got off her bicycle, and looked to see what George would do.

He opened a gate into a field, and held it open for

116

her. Did he know of a short cut across here? She followed, and watched him prop his bike against the stone wall.

'This is better than the old bus shelter,' he said. 'Let's sit down here.'

The kiss was awkward and uncomfortable. Jo found it impossible to sit upright and kiss at the same time, and she overbalanced and ended with her head in his lap. She felt undignified and embarrassed but didn't like to say anything because he seemed quite at ease. She kept remembering Charlie's kiss and the amazing effect it had seemed to have on her – it *was* the kiss that had given rise to the sensation, she supposed. With her mouth clamped to George's, she speculated why this particular manoeuvre should seem so uninteresting, and she let her eyes wander round to make sure there was no-one in the vicinity. Have to watch the time; she considered looking at her watch, but realized this would be impossible. She watched starlings gathering on the telegraph wires above. What a racket they made. Funny if one of them did a mess on them; she felt an urge to laugh but controlled it. What was he doing with his hand up her skirt? Was this what they meant when they giggled and asked each other How far did he go then? Was this really what they meant?

She struggled to sit up rather quickly, but lost her balance again and landed on her hands and knees in the grass. This was no fun at all – nothing like it had been with Charlie. That had been magic, this had no connection with magic.

'Well goodbye,' she said, getting to her feet rather inelegantly and brushing the grass off her skirt. 'I've got to get home and it'll take me quite a time from here. Thank you for . . .' but she had paid for her ice cream so there was nothing to thank him for. She disentangled her bicycle from his and wheeled it out of the field. 'Goodbye,' she said again, and pedalled off towards home.

It was a wonderful evening, and the heather looked

golden as she approached the village. Charlie would have loved that vista; pity he wasn't here with her to enjoy it.

15

The Jenny Tremayne who was the daughter of Grace and Will and mother of Joanne, was now Mrs Jennifer Bowen, living in Woking, Surrey, wife of an ex-captain Martin Bowen, late of the Parachute Regiment, at present Managing Director of a successful sports shop in the town.

Jenny had only very recently begun to feel at home in her startlingly unaccustomed surroundings, and there were still moments when she stopped short in the middle of any particular chore in which she was engaged to stare blankly around her and wonder what on earth she was doing there. The metamorphosis had been gradual, but after convincing herself that it would never take place, it was difficult to believe anything could possibly last. Something was sure to impinge and wreck the whole thing, so she hadn't taken anything for granted for the whole five years since her world had, miraculously, turned upside down.

The bad memories were still so vivid, that was the trouble; getting less now, perhaps, but they still came flooding back every now and then to throw her off balance yet again. The memory, for instance, of the delight of that escape to the freedom of working in a shop in St Ives when she was sixteen. Done their best to stop her of course; couldn't understand why she didn't want to work on the farm. *Work on the farm! Ugh!* Instead, there was the fun and excitement of parties and dancing and encounters with boys that led to giggling, breathless couplings with whoever took your fancy, whenever the opportunity presented itself. It was heady stuff.

But how could she have been so grossly innocent? Hard to imagine it now, but she hadn't the first idea of the facts of life at the time; they'd even kept her away from the mating of the farm animals as something not right for her to witness. Anyway, you couldn't relate what animals might do to what people did; animals didn't make love, they mated; people only had babies when they fell in love and when they experienced The Feeling, and she'd never had any sort of feeling in that respect that was worthy of note.

She remembered, even now, the astonishment she had felt to discover that one painful session in a field of a summer evening could end up with her being pregnant: it didn't seem possible. Didn't even realize it until it was too late to do anything about it, so flight was the only alternative: escape to London and the Salvation Army, her friend Susan told her. The Salvation Army had homes for people like her, she said, and it was true.

They tried to get her to have Joanne adopted, but then she met Steve, and life for two years was almost like heaven; that was real, true love, and no mistake, but of course it didn't last. The war came, and Steve was into uniform before he could catch his breath. She'd tried taking Joanne home to Zennor soon after she'd met Steve, but her mother's resentment was too much to take, so back to London to try to make a go of being a working mother.

It was the blitz that finally broke her, and parking Jo with the parents had seemed the only answer then, because it got rid of so many of the frustrations and anxieties at one and the same time. Could even pretend it was the best thing for Jo. But the guilt had never quite gone away; it had been the unadmitted query that had hung about in the offing the whole time. Seemed to tinge everything she did after that. Blotted out for a time when she heard about Steve: posted missing, presumed dead just five weeks after he'd gone overseas. She'd had to search out the news too, because no-one would have told her, she was just a casual girl friend, after all.

By that time she had joined the ATS, as friend Susan had advised. 'Just what you need,' Susan had said. 'Take you out of yourself and make you forget all the disasters. You'll be too busy fighting the war to think about anything else.'

But it didn't let her forget. She cried her way through her duties whenever there was no-one there to see, though she was glad that her days were mapped out for her. That made things easier, not having to think. Everything was ordered and automatic. You were told what to do and when to do it: no need to think at all. Very comforting it was. You had to get up out of bed because the bugle blew; you had to eat because you were told to. If it hadn't been for orders, she would never have bothered to get up out of bed ever again. What was the point?

Even when she met Martin Bowen, a second lieutenant in the Paras two years later, in one of the canteens near where she was stationed, she still moved, zombie-like through the motions of being picked up, dancing, necking in odd places wherever and whenever the opportunity arose, and going to bed together whenever there was a time or place. All part of her war duties which, she kept reminding herself, were keeping her alive – though for what, she could not decide. Anytime now, a German bomb would find her and dispose of her; the same would happen to Martin, and when he was dispatched on a special mission to Arnhem, she knew that that was the end of him and that would be that. No real regrets because there were no regrets for anything these days. One day you were here, and the next day you weren't. Her turn next, so what the Hell?

Martin Bowen had been a very ordinary man before the war. Quite an ordinary, everyday schoolboy, brought up with an ordinary sense of duty, so that he joined up before he was called up because he knew that these bloody Nazis had to be stopped. It was everybody's duty to join up and stop them. He joined the Paras because this sounded an exciting way to fight the war. He gained courage from the fact that others thought him brave and tough, and he wouldn't dare to prove them wrong.

When he met Jenny, he had completed the harsh training, and realized how unsuited he was to the appalling rigours he had to endure. But there was no backing out; just had to stick it the best he could. Bound to be killed before too long; you were a hanging, rather than a sitting target, floating about in the sky like that.

He saw this dream of a girl in the NAAFI canteen one evening, a real cut above the usual ATS girl; she looked a million dollars, with no hint of the breezy bawdiness that so many of these girls seemed to have. He'd always preferred the WAAFs to either of the other women's services, but Jenny had stood out a mile, and he was instantly attracted. He liked the way she remained aloof and a little distant, even when he got to know her; made him consider her as somehow a bit superior, and he enjoyed the challenge of trying to get her interested.

He concentrated all his energies and his thoughts on her while they were stationed near each other. Helped him to forget the worst of the horrors he was having to endure, and the sex was an excellent diversion and restorative. He disliked promiscuity and the idea of having someone to himself made life liveable in all the squalor and degradation. It was a feeling he had never experienced before: it was obviously true love.

Even when the posting overseas came through and parting was imminent, he was no longer so certain that he was going to die; there was something and someone to come back to, and he was bloody well going to make it back. As it turned out, he was perfectly right. He survived to become a hero, promoted on the field of battle, and to escape, miraculously, back to England from the carnage of Arnhem. He was decorated and fêted, and Jenny, at this same time, found that she was pregnant with Martin's baby.

For her, it could still have ended there, because who would suppose a successful war hero would remember the girl he left behind him? Jenny certainly didn't expect him to; she was just waiting for the bomb with her name on it, as she mechanically got up every morning to fulfil her duties. But quite suddenly, he appeared again, out of all the chaos, writing to her, phoning her, taking her out, loving her and giving her something to live for.

She was so grateful to him that she didn't at first think it would be fair to tell him about the baby. None of this would last, after all; she was very likely to be killed, and so was he, so why upset everything for nothing? And there was the possibility that he might take flight if she told him – and who could blame him for that? She blamed herself, and so, probably would he. He wouldn't want to be tied down to someone like her for the rest of his life when he'd made something of himself and was a hero and an officer, but when they managed a leave together, he took her to London with him for a weekend. For Jenny it was like being introduced to heaven. In fact she wasn't absolutely sure that she wasn't dead and that the whole thing was a heavenly illusion. It was the beginning of the slow awakening from total despondency that even now, four years later, was not positively completed.

They had danced and dined at a night club, a thing that Jenny had never done before, and which she found unbelievably glamorous. She hadn't known he was rich; she had never tangled with anyone rich before, she wasn't at all sure how to behave.

'You know, Jenny, it was you that got me out of that hell-hole,' he said, making an effort to control the extraordinary effect she had on him.

She thought he was joking. 'Me? How? How could I

possibly have got you out of that?'

'Because I thought of you and that made me go on, otherwise I might have given up, I was so bloody scared.' The whole thing came back to him with horrifying intensity, as it had done, periodically, ever since it happened. How long did it take for the horrors to fade?

'But you're a hero, you can't have been frightened.'

'Well I was, so I kept thinking of you and how pretty you were, and how wonderful you were in bed, and that made me determined to get back so as to demand more of the same medicine.'

Couldn't very well tell him now, Jenny decided; not the right time at all; spoil the whole thing. He probably didn't mean what he said, and knowing that she was pregnant would scare him away for good – immediately. So she smiled and said nothing. Couldn't think of anything appropriate.

'You know what is so splendid about you?' he said. 'It's your amazing calm and confidence. You give the impression that you are quite aloof to the ghastly things that go on around you. You just exude a kind of serenity that positively enfolds one.' He had never met anyone like her, and found her still silences had the effect of a tranquilizing drug in the midst of all the chaos and confusion.

She turned her head to look fully at him to see if he were making fun of her. She was still considering the effect that telling him about the pregnancy might have. 'I do?' she said, and thought, how mad can you get? Me, *calm?* Me *confident?* Why can't he see I'm just a dithering mass of uncertainty and doubt, not knowing what to say or do next. How can anyone be so wrong? But she couldn't bring herself to disillusion him; not yet anyway. Bound to find out for himself before too long.

'You must be from the country,' he said next, because her quietude reminded him, absurdly, of the peace of the Scottish Highlands.

Jenny blushed. He had obviously realized that she was just a poor farmer's daughter; she'd have to watch her talk. Thought she'd quite lost the old accent; but then cockney was just as bad. She'd have to watch her talk.

'Parents came from Cornwall,' she said. Might as well admit to that. 'But I haven't been back for an age; they're dead, so no reason to go back.'

No reason? No reason? Only a daughter of seven and two old peasant crones, that's all. Couldn't tell him that! That would just about put the tin lid on everything. Just let things take their course and they'd fizzle out before too long, so no need to go into details.

'Ah, Cornwall! That's pre-war holidays to me. Wonderful sailing holidays at Fowey. Do you know Fowey?'

'Course I do. We had a boat there once.' She'd never been, of course; never sailed a boat in her life, but best to string along with him for the time being. It was only a passing phase; get the most out of it that you can before it flickers out. And in the meantime see about an abortion; it shouldn't be too difficult. Perhaps borrow some money from him and get it done quick before anyone noticed. She'd known other girls who'd had it done. After that, back to fetch Jojo and start a new life somewhere or other. Her heart sank as the thoughts formed themselves. What sort of life could she go back to? How would it be possible to start up again with a daughter she hardly knew, with no money and no hope of a decent job? The thought of all the difficulties was stifling.

And what about Jojo? There had only been stiff, unfeeling acknowledgements from her mother to the letters she'd sent; nothing about Jojo at all; nothing to say what she thought about getting the old doll that Jenny had found such difficulty to part with; nothing at all, only a tirade of vicious abuse about her behaviour. They must have impressed on Jo how wicked she was. What hope was there, then, of weaning her away from them now? She'd never written off her own bat or, presumably, been allowed to take any interest in who

124

her mother really was, or where she was and what she was doing. Obviously she was so attached to her grandparents by now that she wouldn't want to know about anything else. Much better to leave her there now; much better not to uproot her. Jenny decided she just had to deal with her own miseries and not push them on to a little girl who was settled and happy without her useless mother.

But arranging an abortion wasn't as easy as she had hoped; expensive, dangerous, painful. She kept putting it off and putting it off, and all the time Martin wrote and telephoned and made love to her until she became thoroughly bemused and bewildered and more and more reliant on him to keep her going at all. Finally she started being sick, and there was no hiding it then, everyone at the base knew, and Jenny was swept back again into the depression and devastation of hopelessness. Martin noticed it fairly soon, and told her so.

'You don't look well, darling Jenny. What's the matter? You seem sad and upset. Tell me what's the matter so that I can do something about it.'

It was all too much, and the self-control broke. She burst into tears on the decorated and pipped regimental shoulder as he drove her back to her base and told him all – or nearly all. Anyway the immediate, most relevant news. He would obviously now disappear without trace, she knew that, but there was no way she could keep it to herself any longer, and he might just help her to have the abortion before he took off.

It never ceased to amaze her how wrong she could have been. From that moment on, she was churned along in a great flurry of turmoil, excitement and urgency that ended in a rushed registry office wedding and subsequent release from the armed forces on account of her pregnancy. Martin organized it all, she scarcely took part, but was delightedly swept through the whole business on a tide of disbelief.

'We'll get a little flat in Surrey somewhere, where you'll be safe and I can come when I'm on leave, my

125

darling. My parents will look after you when I'm not there; we'll find somewhere near so that you won't be alone and you'll be safe. I'm so happy – you can't imagine! You should have told me at once – fancy thinking I wouldn't be pleased. I'm over the moon.'

So was there any wonder that Jenny still found the whole thing too good to be true? Even now, with four-year old Lucy, and another due in three months' time. Everything, it seemed, had turned out for the best, and from the dejected, despairing, down and out, the magic wand had been waved, and she was the princess at the ball.

There was only that black dread still hanging about whenever she allowed herself to think. All this good fortune could so easily collapse. The least little thing might prick the balloon and she could be right back where she started. The important thing was not to let yourself think. Just hang on to what you've got, Jenny Bowen, push everything else under the carpet until you're strong enough to deal with it.

16

Jo had grown up knowing about the Petherick family story as well as she knew the stories from the Bible. Few, except for one or two of the Pethericks them-selves knew how far back the family went. 'They reckon they'd be able to trace theirselves back to King Arthur,' Will would occasionally suggest, in one of his more expansive moods, and then would add, ''Bout as much truth in that as in King Arthur belonging to Tintagel anyways.' And he would wheeze and cackle at the joke.

Jo was fascinated by the stories she had managed to pick up concerning this family. Will had told her of the curse that was supposed to surround the family with mystery. 'The ol' Polwagle witch, she saw to it that there weren't goin' to be no Petherick female in charge,' he told her. 'Put paid to the women good and proper; put them right in their place and no mistake.' He was seized with another burst of laughter. 'Seems to have slipped up in this generation, though. With all that crowd of women up there, the men don't have no chance,' he mopped at his eyes, 'no chance at all,' and he relapsed again into a state of mirth, coughing and nose-blowing. There seemed always to be a snigger in anybody's description. 'That mother, Bea, she be the queen bee I reckon where them girls is concerned.'

The five girls were sometimes known as the Amazons, and it did seem that way, the sheer numbers of them. Jo had learned their names – Bridget, Daphne and Jean, the untidy, boyish-looking ones, who usually wore breeches and riding boots, and walked with long strides and a kind of lofty swagger, and Cynthia and Dorothy, dark and smooth-looking, for ever looking down their noses at the likes of her. Peter was the only one of the family she knew, but she hadn't seen him for a long time and he didn't look like anything much at all: none of the swagger, none of the haughty self-confidence of his sisters or his parents. A nothing sort of boy to look at she had always thought, but nice enough in spite of that.

There had been a real fuss in the village when the father had died. Jo remembered the funeral when the whole village was full of strange people all wearing black. She remembered the flowers and the digging of the grave, which she had watched from the hidden corner of the churchyard under the tamarisks. The whole thing was an Event, like the Summer Fair and the church jumble sale and the time when a troupe of dancers had come to give a show in the village hall.

The girls, who were no longer girls by at least ten years, were to be seen quite often in the district, particularly in Penzance on market days. Jo knew the ones that were married, because Bridget's and Dorothy's weddings had been Events, too; much more fun than the funeral. Daphne's marriage had been a secret one — everybody talked about it at the time because it had taken them by surprise. It was a hushed-up affair that had made people angry, so that women of the village had gathered in small groups, full of secret, under-the-breath talk. But it died down in time, and rather than breaking away from the hierarchy, all the husbands seemed to have been swept up into the Petherick aura. Names may have changed officially but the Miss Pethericks were still the Miss Pethericks to all who had known them before. They divided, ran and expanded their late father's farm with a dedication that ensured their unassailable domination of the district. Bea, who was still active in the affairs of the family corporation, appeared as an autocratic empress, unquestionably in control of all she surveyed.

Jo found their importance impressive and enviable. Even if the family could not actually trace its roots quite as far back as it claimed, nobody was able to prove them wrong. After she had relinquished the idea that they were all witches, Jo had not been able to believe that they could possibly be ordinary, down to earth human beings. 'Why are they so important?' she asked Will. 'They're like the Barons and we're serfs just the way we was all that time ago.'

'What's this "serfs"? What's these things they teach you? They're farmers, same as we're farmers. They got money, that's all.'

'I suppose they've just hung on to what they've always had by sticking together the way they do. If they'd all split up and done something else, then likely they'd be as poor as us. It must be upsetting to have to do what your family's done since forever, no matter what you want to do yourself.'

'Can't see much wrong with it, doing what your father did.'

'If you want to do it, yes, but supposing you don't.'

'Best to keep to what you're fitted for; what you been brung up to do. Much best.'

'But all those Miss Pethericks – surely they can't all have been best fitted to be farmers, even if they was brought up to believe they was. And what about Peter? You never hear nothing about Peter. Is he going to be a farmer too?' She tried to remember the odd boy she'd helped to save from his rampaging, witchy sisters, but could only remember him looking like Charlie.

'They do say the boy wants out they say. Weak-kneed ninny, they say, who don't want nothing to do with farming. But then he don't have much chance with all them women around.'

'Don't see why not, he's a *person*, same as they are, why don't he have much chance?'

'Not with all them women around.'

Jo relapsed into silence, a state she had learned from Will to be the most comfortable when up against argument. Since leaving school she found she had also left the company of her peers and felt that she was being forced into leaving life itself.

She talked to Charlie sometimes, but not so often as before, and she began to feel that he was trying to avoid her. She hardly ever saw him these days, but was forever hearing his voice, and it was quite often criticizing her or making fun of her. Shouted at her, sometimes he did, but was never there, so that she couldn't go back at him, because what was the point of shouting out into thin air? She didn't even know if he ever bothered to listen. And anyway, people would think she was daft if they heard her shouting at someone who wasn't there.

But there was no-one else she could share her thoughts with – no-one at all. Mumma had abandoned her, hadn't she? And now Charlie didn't want her any more. But then, had he ever wanted her? She was the one who'd done all the wanting wasn't she? An opaque, despairing blackness shrouded her.

'Don't know what's the matter with the girl,' Grace

129

complained. 'Sitting there like some dumb animal. Unnatural, that's what it is. What's she got to be so miserable about? Got all she wants; a good home, good food, ready-made job. And us with no-one to leave the farm to but her. Sitting pretty she is, and all she can do is mope. Doesn't seem to have friends now that girl Charlotte's gone away.'

Grace felt uncomfortable and angry with this ungrateful lump of a girl who had changed so radically, and in a relatively short time, from the tiresome, lively brat into this silent sulker. Not that you could find fault with her in practical ways. Did everything that was expected of her, but just lately, she was somehow like a dead thing; never talking, never laughing, just going about her business. So unusual it was, that Grace found herself occasionally feeling sorry for the girl – a feeling she really despised in herself because there was no good reason to pity someone who was being so contrary when she was lucky enough to have a good home and caring grandparents. Others might not have been so generous to a bastard grandchild foisted on them. No reason at all to be sorry for her.

There were long walks for Jo; along the top of the cliffs, away to Gurnard's Point, watching the buzzards hover and wheel. How wonderful to do just that, wheel and soar on the rising air currents. Must be easy. Take off gently from the overhanging ledge and sail blissfully away, twitching an occasional feather finger now and then to change direction. So easy, so gentle. She held her arms out and felt the breeze lift and fill her jacket. Probably wouldn't even have to step off the top, just lean a little and the thermals would do the rest.

It was then that she heard Charlie's voice, stronger than ever, taunting, shouting at her: vengeful, contemptuous, terrifying. 'Well, go on then. What you waiting for? Get on with it – jump – go on! I dare you. There's nothing here for you; no-one cares, do they? Lean a bit, go on *lean*: you'll see how easy it is to fly.

Fly off, why don't you? Fly off with them buzzards. No-one would care if you never came back, would they?' She crouched down, ready to spring. Charlie wanted rid of her just like everyone else. He wasn't no different; no more a friend than any of the others. So why not? So easy, so easy. Float out over the sea. Leave the earth for ever, leave everything behind and just float away.

The force that jerked her downwards and flung her on her face on the grass was rough and painful. What did Charlie think he was playing at? Goading her on and then jumping on her with such murderous violence? She screamed out in pain as her face hit the ground: 'What are you *doing*? Why tell me to go and then stop me? You hurt me!' Her eyes streamed with the painful bang on her nose, and she started to scream hysterically and kick out wildly, but she was pinioned by the body on her back and unable to move further.

Her frustration and rage increased a hundredfold. 'What are you *doing*, Charlie?' she screamed.

But in spite of her fury, or perhaps because of it, she found the unyielding body that was restricting her own writhing, struggling movements, strangely exciting. There was a certain exhilaration in the effort needed to throw off this surprise assailant. It was vital to fight free of the tight hold he had on her. A fight to the death!

She wrestled, kicked, and bit at interfering hands, oblivious to everything except the joy of battle. Finally, by dint of bringing her knees up suddenly, and arching her back, she managed to roll over so that their positions were reversed, and she was stretched out on top of her antagonist.

'That'll teach you to try and run my life, Charlie boy,' she panted in triumph, and discovered, with an ice-cold deluge of shock, that it was not Charlie at all, but Peter Petherick on whom she now sat jubilantly astride.

'Oh God,' she said, in agonizing confusion and

embarrassment, scrambling off him with lightning speed, to sit a few feet away, out of breath, dishevelled, and with a trickle of blood running from her nose.

There was an extremely long silence, while both cast about in their minds as to how they could possibly extricate themselves from the appalling situation in which they found themselves.

'Terribly sorry,' she gasped at last, trying, without much success, to control her breathing and the pounding of her heart; it was painful.

Peter's breathing was equally uncontrolled. 'No – really. My fault entirely – I shouldn't have – I mean – I must have hurt you. I'm so sorry, here, take my handkerchief.' He fumbled in his pocket without success. 'I don't seem to have one.'

A flicker of laughter emerged between Joanne's gasps for breath. She dabbed at the flow of blood with the end of her shirt. 'Shouldn't wonder if you hadn't got a few battle scars yourself,' she said. 'Seems a bit daft, sitting here apologizing to each other, doesn't it, when I might have been dead by now if we hadn't had that little shindy.'

'I've sometimes thought about jumping,' he said. 'Well, not jumping exactly, rather floating off the top with the birds.'

What was he saying? It struck him painfully, that he had not communicated even one of his own thoughts to anyone else – let alone two at one time – since the tea-time sessions with Dimple. Darling old Dimple. They had said goodbye when Peter left school; Peter's decision, of course, like all the other decisions that had been made during their intimate encounters. Gentle, loving decisions that Dimple had agreed to almost before they had been voiced. 'Of course, darling boy. Total agreement, dear heart.' So important not to hurt his feelings more than was absolutely necessary, because they both knew so well that Peter held all the cards.

But all that was in the past tense, so that one of the

reasons for living had slipped away. And the secret despair Peter sometimes felt, plus the private fantasy he had long had of flying out over these cliffs, had today spilled out in front of a total stranger. Was it something to do with the fact that he had just stopped her from killing herself? The realization that he had managed, on his own, and without any help from others, to prevent a tragedy taking place, pumped through his being with heartbeats that had not yet slowed to their normal rate.

He glanced surreptitiously at the girl who was still alive when she might have been dead, and thought she looked rather like a collapsed scarecrow. Mud-spattered, ochre-coloured breeches and something woollen on top, olive green and purple and holed at the elbows and overlaid by strands of straw-like hair. A scarecrow, perfectly camouflaged among the gorse and the heather, perfectly co-ordinated with the countryside. She wasn't really a person, just a scarecrow or some wild animal in a wild landscape.

It took time before Joanne was able to overcome the effects of having experienced so many crises in such a short time. 'I suppose,' she said, mopping at her face with the sleeves of her jacket, 'that I have lived through all the worst moments in my life in the last hour or so.' She paused and looked out over the sea with a feeling of despair. 'And I suppose I should thank you for doing what you did.' She couldn't bring herself to say, 'thank you for rescuing me,' because it was no rescue, it was just that he had changed the course of her life. No romance, just fact.

'By some extraordinary coincidence,' he said, 'if I hadn't seen you and known straightaway you were preparing to jump, I might well have gone over myself. Felt it very strongly today; I often do. I didn't want to face up to any more bad moments. Life didn't seem worth enduring any longer.'

Out of character, out of character! Where had discretion flown to? How was it possible to voice such

privacies? She might resemble a camouflaged scarecrow, but that was no reason for such an outburst from
him.

'That's just what I felt,' said the scarecrow.

'Don't you feel it now?'

'Yes – no – I mean I don't feel like I did twenty
minutes ago; then, I wanted to float with them birds
and leave the earth altogether. Leave life and just float
with them birds. I thought that would be real nice.'

'But you don't think that now?'

'Well – no, because I wouldn't float, would I? I'd fall
– splat, and that would be horrible.'

'Dying is never nice, but once dying is over, death is
final and peaceful.'

'You don't know that; there might really be a hell
with no peace at all.'

'It couldn't be worse than hell on earth.'

'Yes it could, of course it could.' Joanne turned to
look at him, and remembered, with a deep sense of
shock, that this was Peter Petherick saying these
things. Could this actually be the boy with whom she
had so intimately stirred the witches' brew in the
immense cauldron of her sand bucket? The one she
had saved from a fate worse than death? The one who
had found (but not rescued) her on the cliff path? How
embarrassing to remember the closeness they had
shared. He was a stranger now: the rich boy who had
everything and who had prevented her from flying off
the cliff top into oblivion. How extraordinary.

'You're Peter Petherick aren't you?'

'Yes.'

'With all those sisters.'

'Yes.'

There was a long silence. Did he remember? Of
course he didn't. He would never recognize her as the
scruffy six-year-old, or the tear sodden cliff climber;
she'd scarcely recognized him, so keep quiet.

Peter knew exactly who she was. From the moment
she'd said, 'You're Peter Petherick,' he knew, and

it made him smile to himself. Could this earthy, dishevelled girl really be the little kid who'd held his hand in the barn? It seemed she didn't remember the incident; no point in reminding her – too embarrassing.

'I seen your sisters round the village, but I never seen you . . .' Since that day on the cliff she was going to say, but pulled herself up sharply. 'Don't you work on the farms?'

'I hate everything to do with farming.'

Joanne considered this statement. You surely couldn't hate everything to do with farming. Could you hate the smell of hay? And the horses? Could you hate the horses? And the milk in the pail? And the very early morning sun coming up? And the mist? And the calves? And the cock crowing? And the mice? You couldn't hate everything.

Then she thought of the mud and the rain and the freezing cold, and the exhaustion, and the silly hens and the cows' dirty backsides, and the rats and, above all, the deadly boredom of the day after day's hard slog.

'Can't see why you should be unhappy with all that family round you and all that money and that big house and you not wanting for anything. What you got to moan about?'

'The family round me – that's what I'm moaning about. I feel a prisoner; all that responsibility, it's suffocating.'

Jo sat silent on the grass with her feet sticking out in front of her. She stared out over the sea to the horizon, a vista that always made her think of herself as an isolated, unattached speck in a hurrying, heedless world: a teacher's words came back to her, as they invariably did at such moments, 'Our world in the universe is no bigger than a tiny speck of dust in Paddington Station'. She did not know Paddington Station, but she had seen the million dust specks floating in a single sunbeam piercing early morning

135

curtains, and could imagine. How small she was, and how alone. Could a family be suffocating? She couldn't imagine that. It would at least add bulk to the solitary speck; make it less alone.

'You think I'm an ungracious, spoilt brat I suppose?' he said.

Jo was shocked; it would never have occurred to her to think of Peter Petherick in such a way. She had thought him lucky to have so many advantages, but there were obviously some disadvantages to being surrounded by a rich and doting family. She had never suspected it, that was all.

'Of course I don't think that. It's just that I don't have no mother nor father nor brothers nor sisters, so I can't sort of imagine it being suffocating to have them.'

'I'm sorry, I didn't mean . . .'

'You needn't be sorry. I'm all right because I never had it.'

But she had had it, hadn't she? Something soft against her cheek, arms tight round her when the bombs came, a far off, almost unremembered smell, and she wanted it back.

'Families can be suffocating,' he said. 'Specially when they expect things of you. Having people expect things of you makes you want to run away and shirk the responsibility of it all. I can't stand up to them you see. I'm a weak-kneed ninny.'

'That's what Grampa said.'

'Everyone says it.'

She wanted to comfort him. 'They say I'm a miserable, ungrateful lump of a girl, at least Gran does. She doesn't really want me at all and Grampa wouldn't mind all that much if I wasn't there. It's better to be wanted and have people expect things of you than for people not to care whether you're there or not.'

'Not really, because not doing what people expect of you makes you feel guilty all the time, and that's soul-destroying.'

'But *I* feel guilty too; I'm supposed to be grateful to

my grandparents for bringing me up, and I'm not.'
Guilt made her face colour up, 'At least I am, and I love
Grampa, but they looked after me because they *had* to,
not because they wanted me.'

They smiled together at their shared guilt.

Peter was in a state of suspended disbelief. From the
depths, he found himself elevated into something
touching on hysterical excitement. He was actually
communicating! Not just answering yes or no, but
communicating. Effortless communication, too; no
anxiety, no embarrassment, no fear. It was a moment
to be savoured and enjoyed. The last time it had
happened, he had been eating buns in Dimple's study.
He wanted to hug this adorable scarecrow and tell her
all about it, but she couldn't possibly be expected to
realize how he felt, so hang on.

'You've cheered me up,' he said instead. 'Made me
feel much better than I did. Can't think why.'

Jo laughed and rubbed her nose. 'I suppose you
done the same for me, so we're quits.'

'No need to be grateful.'

She got to her feet and wondered what sort of a mess
she was in after rolling about on the ground. 'Is my
face dirty?'

'Filthy. I thought you were a . . .' He was going to say
scarecrow but stopped in time. 'I thought you were a
frightened animal when I first saw you today, I came to
rescue you.'

She smiled at him and held out her hand. 'Rescue's
not the right word, but thank you all the same.'

'Mutual thanks,' he said, taking her hand in both of
his.

'Best be getting back,' Jo said, awkwardly, pushing
her hair out of her eyes and brushing grass off her
breeches. She wondered how best to take her leave:
turn and run? Shake hands again and say goodbye?
Wave and turn abruptly?

'I'll walk back with you,' he said. 'That is, if you
don't mind.'

137

But the euphoria had melted; they both became seized up in their own closed worlds, and the walk back was silent and uncomfortable.

17

Bridget Petherick called it the family pow wow. She phoned her sister, Cynthia, who lived at home with mother.

'Hullo? Cyn? Bridgie here. About time we called a pow wow don't you think? It seems an age since we all got together.'

'Yes, I suppose it is, Mother's been fussing, but I really don't know if I can manage it on my own. Such a palaver. Catering for fifteen or sixteen's no fun you know and Websie gets into quite a state about it. One of these days she'll actually leave when she gives notice, and then where would we be?'

God. Here she goes, moan moan moan. 'Oh come on, darling, you know she loves having us there, makes her remember the old days when we were kids. And Mike and Jamie are on holiday so they can wash up, and we'll get Piggy to play with them after, while we talk to Bea. She can never concentrate with my kids milling around, positively manic in case they touch any of her precious belongings, and shouting at them if they do.'

'Pigs *play* with them? Bridgie, darling, he *is* eighteen remember, and when has Pigs ever played with anyone?'

'He may be eighteen, but he isn't any more grown-up than he ever was, is he? We'll tell him he'll have to play cricket with them, or tennis or something. Say either that, or he'll have to come to the family meeting.'

Cynthia laughed at the idea. 'We probably shan't be

able to lure him out of his room. You know Websie won't clean in there any more because he shouts at her if any of his precious books are so much as an inch out of place.'

'God, what a bore the boy is. We ought to have him seen to. Does he actually *read* them do you think? Or does he just build them up like bricks to hide behind?'

'Can't tell, but it does look as though he chooses them for size rather than content. *No*body could actually read let alone understand them; they're all about philosophy and Eastern religions and things like that. I think he gets them to show off.'

'Well, at least we don't have to clear up after him like we used to; at least he doesn't build up his hidey-holes with the family furniture and linen any more.'

Cynthia sniffed her irritation. 'What a disaster he is.'

'So don't let's dwell on him. What about Sunday week? I'll alert the others. With any luck I can get hold of a side of beef, everybody can chip in. Isn't there a little village kid who'd like to act as kitchen maid for the day? We could offer a pricely sum.'

'There is that Tremayne child who might give a hand.'

'Splendid idea; she'd jump at a respite from those grim old grandparents I should think.'

So it was set up, this inevitable reunion that all felt obliged, however unwillingly, to attend. It was something to do with the tenuous strands of family feeling, the imbued acceptance of background and continuity, the sense of duty and an overpowering need for a recharging of batteries.

Grace Tremayne was approached by Cynthia. 'We just *wondered*, Mrs Tremayne, if you could possibly spare your granddaughter to help us out. I've got the whole family descending on us, and Mrs Webb finds it pretty difficult to manage such a large number. If Joanne could possibly lend a hand we'd be tremendously grateful. We thought of her because Mrs Webb's very fond of her.'

Grace looked at Cynthia incredulously; Edith Webb *fond* of anyone? That was a laugh for a start. And why should that stuck-up Petherick lot think they could call on any granddaughter of hers to act as their skivvy? Her lips tautened into a thin line: 'I don't think . . .' At which moment Jo came into the dairy with the milk and was amazed to see Cynthia Petherick there. There flashed through her mind a vision of Peter Petherick pressing a note into his sister's hand and whispering, 'Deliver this to that beautiful girl at Tremayne's Farm.'

'Ah, Joanne, I was asking your grandmother if you would care to help our Mrs Webb to prepare for a family party we're having next Sunday. Even though my nephews are coming, we could do with an extra pair of hands, and I thought you might like to earn a bit of extra pocket money.'

Grace directed a furious stare at Jo: how did the Petherick woman dare? But Jo was filled with pleasure at the idea of being able to see inside the big house at last and discover how this extraordinary family lived. See Peter being a young brother rather than an exciting new friend. And earn some money into the bargain – what a chance!

'Oh I should love to, Miss Petherick. What time shall I come?'

Grace's subsequent tirade had very little effect on Jo. She found that these days she was able to erect a guard fence of other thoughts against these onslaughts, and remain impervious to and aloof from them; she enjoyed using this talent.

'How can you stand there . . .' Fun to find out if her fantasies about all these strange sisters were correct. '. . . expecting my granddaughter . . .' And what about the mother? She had only seen her once or twice, at the weddings and at the funeral and at the St Senara Fair; behaved like a queen, with all those funny old women buzzing round her. How could they be young enough to be Peter's sisters? They looked ancient. '. . . got no pride you haven't . . .' Cynthia was the one Jo found

hardest to fathom: she should have been beautiful –
tall, willowy, almost eastern-looking – but somehow
the personality etched its way through to give extra
length to the nose, and peevish, dissatisfied furrows
beside the mouth. With all the good fortune she and
the family enjoyed, what had she got to be dissatisfied
about? And Peter, that odd, awkward boy, how would
Peter behave? '. . . ashamed of you. I've a good mind
to . . .' It would be good fun. Like the Prince and the
Beggar Maid. She saw herself dressed in brown rags
amidst all the rich trappings of a castle, like the picture
in the book: very romantic.

In fact, they gave her a dress to wear, with a little
frilly apron. 'Might get your nice clothes dirty,'
Cynthia said, narrowing her eyes to take in the
corduroy trousers and sweater top. 'Rather fun to dress
up as a proper waitress don't you think?' Jo was
delighted; it was like being given a part in the school
play.

She met Peter on the cliff two days before the
reunion was to take place. 'It's so funny,' she said.
'Shall I act like the French maid in that radio play they
did last year? Or more like the funny one in the play
the Penzance Players did? You know, it was called
George and Margaret, they took some of us from
school.'

But Peter seemed to be on Gran's side. 'I think it's
absolutely monstrous,' he said. 'I'm really so ashamed
of my wretched family that they should get you to do
this. They're patronizing you, don't you see? You're as
good as they are any day.'

'I know that, so you could just as well say I'm
patronizing them; but I want to get in and view them
close up sort of thing. I can't see that it's any worse
being a maid for a day than cleaning out the pigs for
Grampa.'

'It would be all right if you look on it as a piece of
research I suppose. You could write it up for the local
paper.'

'*Write* about it?' Jo gave an explosion of laughter. 'What would I be doing *writing* about it? That'd be a daft thing to do. If ever I was to write anything, it'd be a story. I might write about how a poor little kitchen maid was treated bad by the wicked squire and his lady; like the Little Princess.' She looked at him and decided not to add the idea of the Prince and the Beggar Maid because it might embarrass him.

She hid the dress and apron from Gran, who continued to scold, and she smiled at Grampa when he warned her, 'Don't you be gettin' ideas of service being an easy way. Tain't a good way to live that. First you'd be 'umbled and that ain't good, and second you'd be slaving away, morning till night and no let up and without so much as a breath of fresh air all day. That ain't no good at all.'

'I won't Grampa, I promise. I couldn't do without my fresh air either. I just want to see, that's all. I never met anyone like them before.'

'You talk as if they was different creatures from us child. Where do you get them ideas? Talk as if they had four legs and three eyes you do. Too much imagining is what you got girl. Far too much imagining you got.'

He was probably right. It most likely wouldn't be as much fun as she'd hoped; wouldn't be near so exciting as the plays on radio, and certainly wouldn't approach the thrill of the occasional movie she had been allowed to go to. Real things never seemed to live up to expectations.

The inside of the big house was large, dark and gloomy, with the exception of the kitchen which was the first room she saw.

'You come to the back door mind,' Mrs Webb had told her. 'I'm not coming traipsing up them stairs to answer the bell for you. You come straight round the back at half-past-eight in the morning and not a minute later because there'll be more than enough to do, don't you worry about that; and no slacking mind, because you got to earn your keep, though I can't think why they should think I'm not able to do the work myself with a bit of a hand from Miss Cynthia, even though she do do little enough and leaves all the dirty jobs to me. Suppose *she* thinks she's getting past it all though why she should beats me I must say, half my age; always was a bit of a weakling though when she was a child that one, nearly as bad as that Peter, now he never did have no staying power; I blame it on his mother; never should have had him at her age but they was so keen to get an heir, would of gone on for ever I don't doubt.'

Jo stared round the kitchen while the monologue was in progress. Mrs Webb was really quite kind underneath all the talk, and one didn't really have to listen to what she said. The room could scarcely have changed since it was built – how long, she wondered, possibly two hundred years ago? Stone flags on the floor, high windows close to the ceiling, huge range with modern Aga stove looking lost and out of place; some large implements, long unused, hung high, way out of reach, scrubbed white wood kitchen table, uneven and undulating through years of chopping, kneading and pounding.

'Going to stand there all day then? Whatever you got in your hand there, put it in the outhouse, and I want a scrubbed table and then you can start chopping the carrots after you washed 'em.'

'It's my dress and apron, shall I put them on now?'

Mrs Webb's large, barrel-like stomach bounced with laughter. 'Bless the Lord no, don't want to go messing up the finery do you? You can keep that fancy dress for when you go upstairs. Put this flour sack round you to keep you dry while you scrub.'

If only she had clogs, it would be very like a Dutch kitchen picture she'd seen in one of her school books. There was even a cat, and they always had a cat somewhere in the painting, often fighting with a dog, and usually a few children stealing food and crawling

143

under the table. This experience at least was no let-down, it was a real situation from the past and she prepared to take part.

Cynthia came down later with Bridget. 'Ah Joanne, Mrs Webb has set you to work I see, splendid. Bridgie, you remember Joanne – Grace Tremayne's grand-daughter.'

Bridget was the one who would have worn plum-red velvet in the olden days, and would always have had the dogs at her side – Great Danes and Afghans, and she would ride side saddle to the hunt.

'Of course, of course, jolly good you could come along. How are your grandparents keeping these days? Splendid. Everything all right Websie? I'll send the kids down to help with the washing up. Not a bad piece of beef eh?'

Mrs Webb smiled along with them; they were good girls on the whole. Having watched them grow up made you indulgent, in spite of some of them taking off and marrying no-good husbands. She couldn't abide Bridgie's Harold, and Daphne's Hans was of course a disgrace, a *German* of all things. Bridgie had always been her favourite, being the eldest.

'Your kids'll be more trouble than they're worth I shouldn't wonder,' she said. 'Only get under my feet if you send them down here.'

Everyone laughed and smiled and behaved as though they were all the best of friends. Jo wondered if the Petherick ladies would ever dare to talk to Gran like they did to Mrs Webb, just as though she was a friend, and she went on to wonder how Gran would respond if they did.

Peter came in when she was peeling potatoes – hundreds of them it seemed. Her hands were frozen from the cold water.

'Oh I say, you can't do that; here, let me.' He took a knife from the drawer and started to peel a potato as you would peel an apple.

Mrs Webb looked up from decorating the trifle.

144

'What do you think . . . ? Well I'm blessed . . . since when have you turned chef eh?' She started to laugh as she watched his efforts. 'So this is what happens when we have a pretty girl in the kitchen is it? But you come on now, master Peter, we don't have no time for playing around what with all the lunch to prepare. Can't have you cluttering up my kitchen at this time. You can come down later perhaps with them kids to clear up the mess. Now be off with you upstairs and let me get on in peace. Go on now.'

'But she shouldn't – I mean, if she can I can. I could be helpful Websie, I could carry heavy dishes and things.'

'I've no doubt you could, but so can Joanne here and she's more able than you'll ever be, being used to mucking out and loading hay and swilling out the pigs and that. Far more able.'

It *was* a bit like preparing the cattle and pig fodder, Jo supposed, certainly not more difficult, and on the whole pleasanter. She felt sorry for Peter who seemed prepared to accept that he was not as clever as she was. A long curl of potato peeling dangled in a spiral twist from his hand.

'You've peeled half the potato away,' she said.

Peter frowned down at his potato. 'I'm not very good at it. But I'd get better with practice and I could help you.'

'Don't need any practising helpers around today,' said Mrs Webb. 'Far too much to do, so off you go upstairs and leave us downstairs folks to get on with our work.'

She was treating him like a child. Jo was shocked, and felt embarrassed that she could dare to talk to him like this, but Peter just smiled at Jo, put the knife and half-peeled potato on the draining board, and backed towards the door. 'All right,' he said. 'I'll see you later then.'

He should have told Mrs Webb off; surely he should have shown her who was boss. Because Peter was the

145

brave young squire, the gallant son who would replace his father who had been slain in battle; the one who would don the armour, wield the sword and shield and avenge that death. The tune of the hymn they had sung in primary school came floating back: 'When a knight won his spurs in the stories of old, he was gentle and brave, he was gallant and bold . . .'

'Don't dawdle girl, get them potatoes finished and then there's the sprouts. Get a move on.'

Collapse of another dream. Couldn't even pretend that one any more, Bridget in red velvet with a tall pointed hat and Afghans! It was ludicrous! Cynthia playing the lute! Peter dolled up in armour! She gave a great explosion of laughter. What a daft idiot she was. Must remember to tell Charlie all about it.

18

Bea presided over her brood at the lunch table with supreme satisfaction. No matter that they weren't all roaring successes, no matter that some of them were not even particularly good-looking, she, at least had done her duty by producing them in the first place. To the extent that she had even finally achieved the boy that Henry had insisted she was incapable of doing.

Sitting at the head of the table every few months, with the six results of her long-suffering labours, gave her immense pleasure as she grew older. Humphrey, the invincible, had been proved not only wrong, but also her inferior. Having produced the son he had thought was beyond her, she had also outlived the infuriatingly self-important old bugger whom she, oddly enough, had happened to love. Outlived him, so far, for twelve years, and run everything far better than he ever had. The only annoying thing about it was that he was not here to see how well she had managed, damn him.

'Business pretty good, mother,' said Bridget, because this was really one of the reasons for the pow wow: keeping mother informed on business matters. No need to tell much, no need to be absolutely truthful, just keep her happy and give her the impression that she was still in charge.

'Booming, my dear,' Harold, had a way of affirming the things his wife said, specially where Bea was concerned. He liked keeping on the right side of people, to be the big, affable one that had his head screwed on the right way. Being an accountant, he felt fairly secure in the closed shop he had married into, but you never knew with Bea, she could take against you for no reason, and that would have made life uncomfortable. He beamed at her to make sure she had registered.

'You sold those heifers far too cheap,' said Bea, with a cold stare in his direction. Smarmy toad; lazy as sin. He needn't think she couldn't see through his ingratiating ways. Not even certain he didn't embezzle some of the profits; always made the accounts unintelligible so that you couldn't tell what was going on. 'We're surely not doing so well that we can afford to give our herd away.'

'That was a bad week Mother,' Daphne came bumbling in to the rescue, always anxious to save faces and support the outsiders in case the family could be called cliquish. She disliked the way Bea saw no wrong in this attitude that condemned anyone other than immediate family to a status of lesser breed without the law. It was shameful and something she herself had suffered ever since she and Hans fell in love. Even when she persisted and married him, Mother did not attempt to hide her distaste. Shameful; no other word for it. Specially when he was the most gifted and the most intellectual of the lot of them. The one who was instrumental in managing the whole

147

farm in such a tactful way that no-one realized he was doing it. She seethed inside that nobody recognized this fact – or if they did, they didn't admit to it. Couldn't admit to a German managing this so English farm better than any Englishman, and certainly better than five Cornish women. 'Those heifers had to be sold then, there was no choice. It just so happened that prices were low that day. We've done extremely well over the year.'

'That's as may be.' What a stupid girl Daphne was; always had been, come to that. No mind of her own, that was her trouble, just swayed this way and that by whoever took her fancy, to the extent of letting the whole family down by marrying a p.o.w., and a Jew into the bargain. Incredible. And a more self-opinionated, big-headed, Hun that *he* was, she had yet to meet. Anyone would think *he'd* won the war.

Jo had been holding the dish of carrots, unnoticed, at Bea's elbow for some minutes and her arm was beginning to ache.

'Carrots?' she said, giving Bea a nudge.

'What? Oh – who on earth are you?'

'I'm Joanne Tremayne. I'm the maid.' She remembered the girl who had played the part in that play last year. She was really very funny, though she hadn't said anything at all, everyone had rocked with laughter. Must be wonderful to be able to make people laugh at will. Peter was smiling at her. Bridget looked very angry. Would she set the dogs on her? Jo wondered, and she looked over at Peter and smiled back at him.

'Joanne Tremayne, Mother. You know, Will and Grace Tremayne's granddaughter. Just come in for the day to help Websie with the chores.'

Bea turned round in her chair and stared hard at Jo over the carrots. 'Tremayne? Tremayne? Is that the couple whose daughter went to the bad and had illegitimate babies all over the place?'

The dish of carrots suddenly became impossibly heavy, and Jo rested her hand on the table, balancing the sprouts in her other hand on her shoulder. Gone to the bad? Illegitimate? What did that mean?

'She only had the one,' she said, 'and I'm it. Could you possibly help yourself to the carrots because otherwise I'm going to drop something.'

Bea looked down at the carrots. 'Oh – yes – I see. But I can't stand carrots, never could. You know I can't stand carrots, Bridget, surely you know that by now.'

'Of course I know, Mother, but we all love them. Cynthia ordered sprouts for you.'

Bridget made a concerted attempt to dissipate her embarrassment by clutching at the commonplace. 'Brussels have been jolly good this year, thank God we can give up the broccoli growing – can't stand the stuff myself, never could.'

The rest of the company were not so adept at making the switch from the acute discomfort of the previous moments. Daphne silently entreated Hans to sail in and save the situation; he could quite well talk them through it, she was certain.

'The weather certainly has been kind to sprouts this year,' said Hans.

Bridget looked at him coldly, and no-one else spoke for several minutes. Bea was still staring at Jo with an expression of perplexed anger. 'Well come on then girl, hand me the sprouts.'

Jo swung her body round, and changed arms, the carrots being lodged on the left shoulder and the sprouts coming to rest by Bea's plate. The whole situation was suddenly for real and she found she had to quell a desire to laugh. Here was the Baron's lady expressing contempt for the servant girl, but if they had actually all been living in those long ago times, the Baron himself might likely have made up to the beautiful goose girl, who doubled as a serving wench, and they might have rode off together on a white horse. Or the young squire, training to be a knight, might have run off with her.

Jo switched her gaze and her thoughts to Peter, and

was shocked by his expression. She had never seen anyone look so angry: Gran always looked angry, but not this sort of angry. Gran was continually morose or bad-tempered, but Peter seemed about to explode with fury. She found it difficult to understand why he should be so cross. Couldn't he see how funny the situation was?

While Bea was delving for the sprouts, Jo looked round at the rest of the family. Bridget had obviously dismissed the incident and her flash of embarrassment and was smiling confidently to the assembled company. Funny, Jo thought, how it embarrassed these folk when someone spoke their mind. Almost as though speaking one's mind was a bad thing. That Miss Daphne still looked as though she might cry and Miss Dorothy just stared down at her plate, and Miss Jean, who looked like a man and, like Miss Cynthia, didn't have a husband, was shaking with suppressed laughter. Miss Cynthia was just looking at her, Jo, with a worried frown, so she smiled back at her to reassure her. Likely these folk would have thought that Mumma had gone to the bad, same as Gran thought. The old lady just spoke her mind, that was all.

Bea had a spoonful of sprouts poised between dish and plate when Peter flung his chair to the ground and stood by the door.

'You are all consummate bastards!' he shouted. 'You could as well be living in the middle ages for all the consideration and good breeding you seem to have acquired. I'm ashamed to be a member of such a family.' And he stormed from the room, banging the door behind him.

Just fancy, Jo thought, he had the same sort of dreams that I had, thinking about his family as though they lived in the middle ages, and she blushed with pleasure to know that they thought alike.

'Whatever's the matter with Peter?' asked Bea. 'Such bad manners in the middle of lunch.'

'Shall I go after him?' Daphne began to move her

chair back. 'But perhaps it would be better for Hans to go, as man to man.'

Jean exploded into hysterical laughter, and Dorothy, who seldom spoke at all at family gatherings, picked up the gravy boat and held it out to Jo. 'Leave the vegetables dear,' she said. 'We can help ourselves and you can take this down to Mrs Webb so that she can heat up the gravy for us. It's got cold.'

There was a still silence as Jo left the room, then Dorothy rounded on her family. 'If you have to discuss the bad manners of the family, for goodness sake do it in private. Certainly not in front of the child. It will probably be all over the village the minute she gets home.'

She considered remonstrating with Bea, but thought it wiser to keep silent as the subsequent unavoidable argument would be sure to be noisy and take longer than a trip to the kitchen to heat up the gravy. The three husbands, Bridget's Harold, Daphne's Hans and Dorothy's John, joined in Jean's amusement in a muted and apologetic fashion.

'It's all jolly well for you to laugh,' Bridget fumed, 'but, like Dottie, I don't particularly like the family to become the laughing stock of all and sundry which, thanks to Mother and Pigs, seems fairly likely.'

Harold pulled himself together. 'A molehill is fast becoming a mountain,' he said. 'A small family explosion doesn't necessarily become an international incident.'

Bea looked up from her plate on which she had been concentrating to the exclusion of the events of the past few moments. 'What?' she said. 'What are you all talking about? You make a point of mumbling whenever you don't want me to hear. What was the matter with Peter? It was monstrous the way he behaved just now. You girls have spoiled him, that's the trouble. Thinks he can get away with anything. I blame all of you, whenever I tried to discipline him, you used to rally round him like a flock of crows.'

'Rooks,' said Jean. 'A crow in a crowd is a rook.' She continued to laugh, but silently.

'What?' Bea felt herself alienated within the family group and became more incensed than before. 'This ganging up against me has got to stop. I don't know why you do it. It's most hurtful. Always muttering things you think I can't hear and not telling me anything. Really most hurtful. Peter used to be the only one that loved me and stuck up for me after your father died and now it seems even he has turned against me. Most hurtful.'

'Don't be so ridiculous mother,' Bridget took up her role of spokesman. 'You know perfectly well we always include you in everything. We certainly don't keep anything from you.'

'That would be impossible anyway,' Jean said, admittedly very much under her breath.

'And we fall over backwards in order to pool all our ideas and resources where the farm's concerned.'

'We certainly don't pander to Piggy and his absurd ideas,' said Dorothy. 'John and I are for ever telling him off and trying to get him to do something with his life.'

'He should never have spoken like that,' said Daphne, 'but of course he is still fairly young. He just doesn't seem to grow up.'

'Expects to be waited on hand and foot,' said Cynthia. 'You know I still have to do his washing for him. He seems to think we have the same staff as we had before the war.'

'Pity he was too unhealthy to serve in the forces during the war,' John said. 'That's what he needs to buck him up. Couple of years as a conscript would do him a power of good.'

Jo arrived back with the heated gravy, and all conversation stopped dead for several uneasy moments.

'This beef is really excellent,' Harold said at length.

'And Websie's made a great big summer pudding, of

course,' Cynthia escaped gratefully from the insoluble arguments about Peter and the embarrassment about Bea's tactless remarks into her own domestic bliss of successful organization.

'With a great deal of smooth, delicious custard I sincerely hope,' said John. There was some measure of relieved laughter, and the whole situation relaxed into a slightly hysterical *bonhomie* and over-emphasized relaxation from tension.

Jo plunged her arms into a sink full of bubbles. She had tipped far too much detergent in, partly because Gran said it was too expensive to waste money on, so washing up at home remained a greasy, unpleasant chore. 'Plenty of hot water and a good scourer is all you need. Never had all this fancy washing up stuff in the war so don't need to start now.' Jo allowed herself to enjoy the feel of bubbles up to her elbows. Bridget's children had come down to the kitchen to help: two rather ugly boys of nine and eleven called Mike and Jamie, who were flicking each others' legs with tea towels. Jo felt an inexplicable antipathy towards them. At sixteen, she realized that she was unquestionably their superior, being adult, and yet she had the feeling that they did not recognize this fact. In their eyes she was not only inferior, she was just not there.

'Come on, skivvy,' Mike said. 'Let's have the dishes then.'

Jo was enraged. 'Don't dare speak to me like that or I'll fetch you a fourpenny one.' She swung the dishcloth out of the suds and hit both boys round the head.

Mrs Webb, at that moment, came down the stairs into the kitchen with final clearings from the table. 'That's quite enough of that, I'll have no horseplay in my kitchen if you please. And we don't need nobody else to get in the way. Out, you two boys, before any more damage is done.'

She surveyed the floor with its spattering of suds,

and the sink where the bubbles rose high above it and were beginning to overflow down the side and to spread over the draining board. 'And you're more trouble than you're worth,' she said to Jo, her face becoming redder every moment. 'What possessed Miss Cynthia to think you had the sense you were born with I don't know I'm sure. Clear up that mess before you make it worse and bring the silver for me when you've washed it all so that I can polish it before you put it away.'

Jo became suddenly bored and cross. How could she have imagined this would be amusing? Much more interesting to be out feeding the pigs or the hens, or milking the cows. Grampa was perfectly right: she missed the warm comfortable smells of farmyard, and the wind in her hair or the mist on her face. The romance and excitement in which she had clothed the Petherick family had shrivelled irrevocably and could never be recalled. Their reality was somehow worse than boring – it was vulgar and frumpish and as such had cheated Jo out of part of her everyday, fundamental diversions of the mind. She felt resentful and angry, and could only blame herself for being stupid in the first place. The Prince and the beggar maid indeed – more likely the beautiful and wise princess in disguise to test out her stupid suitors – or at least her one paltry, pitiable admirer, if he could be considered such.

19

'My family are vulgar and frumpish,' Peter told Jo some weeks later. 'I apologize for their bad behaviour. You can see, now, why I want to get out from the whole set-up. I don't belong there. You can see I don't belong there, can't you?'

'Don't really know what it means – to belong,' Jo said, watching the wind blow the sea pinks and smelling the thyme along the top of the cliffs. Funny he should use just the same words as she did to describe his family. It was the first time they had spoken together since the party. She had spent the money she earned there on two cotton dresses and a sweater and copies of Black Beauty and Grimm's Fairy Tales, all of which she had found at the Church jumble sale in St Ives.

Gran was appalled. 'Wicked, wicked waste I call it when you could put it by or put it into War Savings.'

'But the war's over Gran.'

'Don't matter it's over. Don't mean to say there's any more money around; less in fact. There's us scrimping and saving and you goes out and throws it all away like that. Wicked it is.'

Jo, on the cliff that morning, let her mind wander over the arguments with Gran about the dress she was now wearing among the pinks and the thyme. It was pink like the pinks and it was pretty, and Gran and the farm and the pigs were a million miles away.

'I don't belong to Gran and Grampa any more'n you belong up there in the big house. Don't see that it matters all that much.'

Was that true? she thought. Didn't I envy Peter and his family not all that long ago? Why don't I think that way now? All those years thinking abo t those grand people in my mind like that; didn't I know it wasn't real? Course I knew.

This Peter, for instance: this stranger, Peter, who had to be rethought and reassessed: not a king, not a knight who rescued maidens in distress, just another ordinary, weak young man, moaning away about his family and his life. Jo felt irritated and put out, and had a great desire to run away, there and then, from the idea of where she might, or might not, belong. Was it possible that Belonging did matter after all? Could have discussed all this with Charlie a few months ago, but now that alternative seemed to have vanished into thin air along with Charlie himself.

Since that day on the cliff when he had dared her to jump, she hadn't even heard his voice the way she used to. Made her uncomfortable when she thought about the way he'd shouted at her then. And the sort of things he'd said, too; gave her the creeps. But was it *really* his voice? And if not, then whose was it? Had she imagined it all? Not possible: she'd heard it all right. If only he would come back properly, she could ask him. Why would he have wanted her to kill herself? She thought about the cave incident: could've been killed that time too. Whole thing was a bit weird.

Just now, she'd thought Peter was Charlie when she first saw him approaching along the cliff path, and a glow of pleasure had swept through her until she realized that it wasn't Charlie at all, but only Peter, and he was all part of the let down now, when she thought back.

'Thought you was my friend Charlie when I first saw you this morning.'

'Who's Charlie?'

'He's someone I've known all my life. He's my friend.'

An unexplained mind flash, gone as soon as it came: *this has all happened before.*

'Charlie who?'

'Oh I don't know his other name. He probably doesn't know mine.'

But he did, of course he did. He knew everything about her; about who her parents were and everything about everything, Charlie did. She felt a sudden rush of panic, realizing she didn't know Charlie's other name.

'Where does he live? Is he local? What family does he belong to?'

But I've told him this before.

'Belong – belong – all this belonging. People are people on their own.'

'Well I don't know of any Charlie living round here.'

156

'You don't know everything.'

'No, I don't suppose I do.'

He scowled, furious with himself for sounding so superior and condescending. Of course she would know far more about the surroundings and the people than he did because she was part of it all, part of the whole community, while he was only on the outside, looking in. An alien in a hostile environment, in fact. She belonged all right, even if she didn't know it.

There was a very long silence while clouds scudded, turning brilliance into shadow and changing whole areas of sea and cliff top as the shades rushed over them. Sea birds were swept and buffeted; none of the motionless hanging in the sky of the airless days of summer. Jo remembered the stifling, heavy day when Peter had stopped her from sailing out over the cliff, when soaring like the suspended buzzards had seemed a peaceful alternative to living.

'Don't you ever want to get out?' he asked, finally, looking at her properly for the first time. What a remarkable looking girl she was; reminded him of some Nordic warrior princess, with her white-blonde hair blowing over her face. Only the ridiculous pink dress spoilt the picture; she should have been draped in a billowing blue cloak and holding a spear and singing like the Brünhilde he visualized when he played the old Eva Turner records in his room.

Jo turned to meet his gaze and had a slight shock. He did look exactly like Charlie, now she came to think of it; in fact she could not really remember quite what Charlie looked like while she was looking at Peter. Funny, that. That rather longish fair hair, was that how Charlie's hair looked? She couldn't remember, and a further small wave of anxiety slipped through her, leaving a tingling sensation behind.

It was then that she heard the voice again: definitely Charlie's voice it was, not shouting this time, but sounding nasty: 'What you listening to him for? He's no friend of yours; wants to get rid of you, he does –

157

don't make no mistake. Wants to do you in. You watch out what I say! That po-faced Petherick wants to wipe you out.'

Joanne looked all round her; if only she could see where he was she'd throw a rock at him. Who did he think he was? Making all these accusations. She looked back at Peter, who was waiting for her answer about something or other, but she couldn't remember the question. Was it possible that he was some deranged lunatic, just waiting to plunge a knife into her back?

She felt her mind reeling and made a superhuman effort to control the panic: the question, what was the question? 'Er – what? Oh – get out? How do you mean? Get out where?'

'Just away from all this smallness.'

She stared out over the sea, her heart and her thoughts still racing, and wondered what on earth he could mean. 'You mean our own smallness in all this bigness?' She spread her arms out to encompass the surrounding panorama, and felt as though she might be brushing Charlie and his voice right away. It made her feel better.

'I don't like feeling inconsequential,' he said, and wondered if she would understand.

She didn't. Could he be a murderer?

'I was actually thinking,' he went on, 'of the smallness of some people's minds, and the smallness of a small community that makes it its business to know what everyone else's business is,' he said.

Jo managed a smile, and hung on to the feeling that she had swept Charlie and the Voice out of earshot for the moment.

'You do talk different,' she said. 'It sounds comic sometimes. At least to me it do. But it do have a good ring to it.' She found her own talk slipped firmly into the Cornish way to keep the balance.

'Not nearly such a nice ring as yours does,' he said.

'Mine?' She put her hand over her mouth to control

158

the laugh. Charlie was nowhere; it hadn't really happened. 'There's nothing special 'bout my talk. Just common talk, that's all.'

'There is so much to think about,' said Peter, 'and no time to do it. I think I'm going to go into retreat in a monastery sometime soon to think things out, if I can bring myself to face the family displeasure.'

What a strange boy he was. Hardly the murdering type. Retreat? That meant running away didn't it? What did he want to run away for?

'Don't know about that,' she said. 'I suppose it wouldn't be that bad to have the time to just sit back and think a bit, but it would be much better to sit and talk about it. Never done much sitting and thinking myself, wouldn't know if I was thinking right, less I talked about it with someone.'

Unless of course the old Charlie came back; she could always discuss things with Charlie; he always used to give exactly the sort of answer she wanted to any of her questions – or at least explain to her why her own answers might not be correct. Stupid boy, why did he have to disappear like this just when it seemed that answers were going to be needed?

'I don't want to spend the rest of my life mouldering away down here,' she said. 'But then I don't know what else I'd want to do. Don't fancy sitting in a monastery and thinking, though, don't fancy that at all.' They both started to laugh at the very thought of it.

'Just to sort out my thoughts,' Peter said. 'That's all I meant. And after that I want to go to India and Burma and Ceylon and Bali and all the different parts of Africa. Just to find out – there must be the perfect place to live, somewhere in the world.'

'Reckon there must be,' Jo said. 'Though no place is any good if the people in it aren't up to the mark.'

'If the place is perfect, then the population are much more likely to be preferable – not spoilt by things round them.'

159

'That don't follow. They could be lazy, spoilt and self-centred just because they have things easy.'

'When I get there, I'll send you a post card and let you know.'

'Better if I come with you,' Jo said, 'else I might not believe what you say.'

'All right,' Peter was laughing as he said it, 'I'll make all the arrangements and we'll go and see for ourselves. Agreed?'

Jo's whole being blazed with the excitement of the new, imaginative extravaganza that was taking her mind over. 'Oh yes,' she said in a whisper, 'I do go along with that, absolutely and completely.'

You brought it on yourself, Charlie, you only have yourself to blame if you've lost me.

20

In the old house, Cynthia sat at her desk, struggling with the household accounts. She did this once a month, but it somehow never got any easier. She felt her patience leaving her, and a tense, exasperated irritation taking over. It always looked perfectly simple when she started; every month it looked perfectly simple – just one or two bills to pay and bank statements to be checked. No difficulty at all; and yet, invariably, the whole operation seized up into a convoluted, constipated, bloody mess, which her mind refused to deal with. It shut down obstinately after a certain period of time, and would not allow her to sort the whole thing out.

She wanted to scream with frustration; she always wanted to. The fact that the whole business coincided with her period obviously didn't help, but it was just that the stress that always bothered her the week before the period was the thing that reminded her it was time to do the accounts again; always managed to forget them otherwise. And it was far better to have them ready before Bea asked to see them, rather than having to rush them through at the last minute. It was her job, after all; she had been pleased when Bea suggested she should do the house accounts; never felt much use in the family except as a nurse-cum-elder sister to the young ones. And they never liked her for that; resented her really and called her bossy, they all knew that Bridget was the bossy one. But Cyn knew perfectly well that her own bossiness was merely a weak carbon copy of Bridget's. She never did understand why they respected Bridget's strident domination and yet resented her mild attempts to organize things.

And now, after the brief relief of war work, where she was admired for what she did in the community, and where the adulation made every situation a welcome challenge and simple to cope with, she had allowed herself to be drafted back into the consuming family circle as the obvious choice to stay at home and look after Bea. No man in her life, so the obvious choice.

She stubbed her pencil furiously on the paper – where the total figure for the weekly bills appeared as three different amounts, even after four attempts – and scarred a thick black line across the page, before the point broke, and the wood splintered into a splayed and mangled stump.

'Finished?' said Bea, striding into the room in a dripping mac and stockinged feet, with three steaming, soaking dogs at her heels. She wrenched off a knitted woollen hat with a bobble on top and shook the rain out of it across the room. The wet splattered across Cynthia's calculations and incensed her.

'God, what a day,' Bea said, with joy in her voice. Why did she so enjoy getting drenched? Cynthia asked herself venomously; she was somehow so fanatically perverse.

The dogs shook themselves with the same sort of jovial relish that Bea was showing, and started to rub themselves dry on the rugs and furniture.

'Rory! Bounder! Stop that this instant!' Cynthia aimed a kick at the nearest sodden mass, which sent it yelping under the table. 'And in answer to your question, no, I haven't.'

'All right, old girl. No need to snap my head off, is there? What's the problem then?' Bea cast an amused eye over the pile of papers, the open account book and the stubbed pencil. 'Can't see why you make such a song and dance over it.' She laughed genially. 'You never were very good at maths, were you? That's why I thought this would be the ideal job for you. Give you a chance to brush up. But if it's too much for you, I can easily take over. It's not really such a chore you know, at least it shouldn't be.'

'Don't be *silly*, Mother. I do the accounts in this house and that's that. Though it would be easier if you remembered what you paid out when, and wrote it all down as I've asked you to do so often.'

Bea laughed again. 'All so totally unnecessary darling. I mean we don't have to be *that* accurate. I'd never have got you to do it if I thought you were going to be so pedantic. Take my boots into the kitchen and get them dried out, there's a lamb; I left them by the front door. I'll have to get these dogs towelled off a bit or they'll catch their death. Come on then my cubbies, fetch towellies then.' And she made her leisurely way out of the room, with the dogs skittering on the polished floor and sending the Persian rugs into huddles of piled-up folds.

Cynthia seethed, and pulled her heather-coloured cardigan together over her chest; it was a gesture that gave her something to do with her hands, to stop them flinging a cushion at those bloody dogs, if not at bloody Bea herself. What right – what *right* had she to order everyone around like this? She expected everyone to pander to her slightest wish, and then criticized them for not doing it right. And now everyone else had left home, Cynthia was the only one left to pander.

Her thoughts homed in, as they often did in moments of stress, to the tall, billowing figure of the Reverend Cyril Pendennis: until recently, the neighbouring vicar. Cynthia had been pleased at his promotion, but missed the gratitude her work for his church had brought her. All those kneelers she had embroidered, it irked her that they were probably now scarcely appreciated by the elderly, nearing-retirement cleric who had taken Cyril's place. Cyril's wife might be an excellent Vicar's wife, but she wouldn't be able to fulfil all those little extras that made church life that little bit easier. Cynthia sometimes seriously thought of moving over to St Issy; she would at least be appreciated in that parish; instead of being the dogsbody that she was here. No gratitude, no consideration, taken completely for granted. And the new man was much too high church; even wore a cassock when riding his bicycle which was positively dangerous.

She shook out the rugs forcefully before laying them out in their correct positions, and made her way into the hall to fetch Bea's boots.

'I thought it was time to talk to you all,' Bea said, 'now that Peter is approaching his twenty-first.'

'What sort of a party will it be?' Dorothy asked. 'Public, I suppose, with all the tenants and employees?'

'Let's have a dance as well – just for us I mean.' Bridget resented being summoned to a family meeting in the middle of the afternoon, preferring to make a lunch do of it. To come over for tea seemed a waste of a day. In any case, family meetings were her responsibility; she knew of no good reason why this one should be necessary. The last one was only a few weeks ago. 'Local jollity is all very well and can be quite fun, but it's a bit restrictive.'

'I surely don't *have* to celebrate it if I don't want to,'

Peter said. 'And I certainly don't want to, as you well know.' Bea had insisted on his attending this meeting since it concerned him. Usually, he was able to talk himself out of these family get-togethers, but this time, Bea had put on the pressure: 'I must insist, dear boy, because it really does mean a great deal to me. I would be shattered, quite shattered if you didn't come.' It was beyond her histrionic powers to muster tears, but her chin had gone up in the brave attitude of one who suffers. Real emotional blackmail, he thought, viciously; he was pretty sure she didn't really care one way or another. Gave the impression these days that she'd given him up as a bad job.

Jean flung up her hands, angrily: 'Oh you – you'd rather go and sit on a rock by yourself, and not let anyone have any fun,' she said. 'We really can't take into account what you want because you only think of yourself. Never consider anyone else, do you?'

Peter put his elbows on the table and locked his hands over his head. 'That's about it,' he said. 'And when I – Come of Age – as everyone so wittily puts it, perhaps I shall be allowed to do just what I like without being castigated all the time.'

'Makes no difference what age you are,' Jean said. 'Once a freak, always a freak. Don't see why we should all stop telling you how nasty you are just because you're twenty-one.'

'Stop it!' Bea smacked her hand down on the table. 'Will you all stop the argey bargey and bickering. I have a little ceremony to perform before you start deciding how you're to celebrate. I'm doing it before the actual birthday, because it might make a difference to how Peter might view the festivities.'

There was an instant silence. What the hell was she going to jump on them this time? She looked round at her family, ranged about her in recognizably typical attitudes, and savoured the moment of complete control. 'Your father,' she said, very slowly, in order to prolong the moment, 'was very obsessed with cere-mony and tradition.'

'As if we didn't know,' Jean said. 'But why bring that up now?'

'Because,' Bea said, 'he told me he wanted to give Peter a special present on his twenty-first which was to be kept a secret until that time.' She beamed at Peter, as one would at a five-year-old when holding a birthday parcel behind one's back. 'He didn't even tell me exactly what it was, so it will be a surprise for all of us.'

She had no doubt that it was a nice, fat cheque, and a statement of the actual terms of the inheritance he came into on his coming of age. She hoped that Humphrey had reckoned with inflation and had not made the cheque too small. It would be good for Peter to have some money of his own to spend; might give him a better sense of responsibility.

The silence in the room deepened and became manifestly ominous.

'He wrote a letter to Peter at that time,' Bea went on, opening up the blotter on her desk and taking out an envelope. 'Here it is, darling boy. You'd better read it straight away and tell everyone what it says. He wanted it that way, such a romantic he was, silly old fool.'

Peter slit open the envelope slowly, not so much for the effect it would have on the others, but because he wanted to postpone the act for as long as possible. He was quite petrified with fear as to what he was about to discover, thinking, from the look of devilish glee on Bea's face, that it was bound to be shattering. Where was the cave, the burrow, the bottom of the bed, the safety of the secret hide-out where he could uncover his reactions to no-one but himself? Here, in the stifling bosom of his family, he would be forced to react or not react in full view of all.

The letters on the page, as it was unfolded, blurred and wavered as though seen through tropical heat: Dear Peter dear Peter dear Peter . . . *Get on with it for*

Heaven's sake. Just in case I do not live to see you grow up, I still want to tell you myself of the decisions I have made concerning you, your sisters and the family inheritance . . .

'Well? Go on – read it out – what does he say?' Daphne was undaunted by Hans' restraining hand on her arm. 'Don't keep us all in suspense.'

'That's exactly what he'll enjoy doing.'

'For God's sake, give him a chance, he's only just opened it.'

'It is written to him after all. Leave him alone.'

'What a bloody fuss.'

Peter got up abruptly. 'You can go on arranging my birthday celebrations,' he said. 'When I've read my letter, I'll tell you what it says – if I think it concerns you.'

Bea frowned. 'That's really not necessary, Peter. Why not just read it out to us? As far as I know, it's only about what you inherit when you're twenty-one, but it does concern everybody else because . . .'

'Mother, please be quiet,' Peter said as he walked towards the door. 'Father wrote to *me*, and nobody else. I will decide what to do about it after I have read it.'

Good heavens! he thought, I've actually defied her, and the wrath of God hasn't hit me. And he walked from the room, climbed, briskly, upstairs, and shut himself in the tomb-like cupboard under the eaves in his bedroom. Crouched under the cobwebbed light of the glass pane let into the roof, he read his father's letter, without having to worry about how his reactions would look to anyone.

Dear Peter, Just in case I do not live to see you grow up, I still want to tell you myself of the decisions I have made concerning you, your sisters and the family inheritance. You know all about the old family traditions and the ancient curse that was supposed to take effect if ever the inheritance was allowed to pass on to anyone who was not a male Petherick of direct descent from Tristram of Petherick. I told you all about that when you were very small, and I am sure you have remembered.

You must have realized how delighted I was to welcome another man to the family when you were born! Not only, of course, because of the old traditions, though I have to admit, I was sufficiently superstitious to have been a little anxious about the ancient curse, surrounded as I was by such a bevy of female dominance!

So, Peter, I decided that I would arrange my will in such a way that your mother and the girls would share the inheritance between them, in trust for such time as you became old enough to decide for yourself. My solicitor knows all about it; your mother thinks you are about to come into your share, no more than that; but in truth, I am bequeathing the whole of my fortune, the farms, and all the income therefrom to you, solely and une-quivocally, for you, from this day forward, to do with it as you think fit.

Thus, I am fulfilling the old tradition of the Petherick family, that the inheritance shall pass to the direct male descendant of Tristram Petherick, and the Polwagle curse can therefore not be effec-tive.

We men must stand together and not allow ourselves to be dominated by the female element – however much we may love them! This is our great responsibility.

Look after your mother and sisters, and *carry on the great tradition*, for the sake of your proud and loving father, Humphrey Godolphin Petherick.

Peter put his head on his knees and shut his eyes to blot out even the small amount of light that came through the skylight.

'You devil,' he whispered through clenched teeth;

then putting his head back, he shouted it out at the top of his voice, 'YOU DEVIL INCARNATE!'

Giving him the very thing that he had been demanding all through his life – the possibility to do exactly what he wanted without being told, advised or instructed. Free to do what he wanted – just so long as he took the entire responsibility for his actions – what sort of freedom was that?

21

'I don't believe in psychiatrists,' Bridget told Bea, 'but Harold thinks you ought to get Pigs to see one.'

The sisters had assembled together several times during the three weeks that had followed the drama of Humphrey's letter. Peter had refused to speak to them at all, and had spent most of his time closeted in his own room when he was not striding along the cliffs or sitting on rocks dangerously close to the sea's edge. The twenty-first birthday had come and gone, with no celebrations and no clarification of the situation. The solicitor had been contacted, which was the way the rest of them had learned of the letter's actual instructions. The confusion and upset that ensued created a sense of desperation.

'Psychiatrist? Rubbish,' Bea said sharply. 'They're all charlatans and it's not as though he's mad, after all.'

There was a suppressed groan, and Jean gripped the arms of her chair. 'Mother, he *is* mad. Totally and completely loopy. And the sooner you recognize that, the better. It can't be legal to allow a lunatic to run the business and deprive us all of our livelihood.'

'He does seem to be mentally disturbed at the moment . . .' Daphne suggested.

'Mentally deranged, more likely . . .'

168

'Get the doctor to commit him . . .'

'They'll need a strait jacket to get him out of the house . . .'

'Tell the solicitor to make a power of attorney, or make him a ward of court or whatever they do in these sort of circumstances . . .'

Bea started to cry. 'How could Humphrey have been such a fool? He knew Peter was the last person to be able to cope with this sort of thing.'

Peter, meanwhile, slipped out of the house and made his way to Tremayne's farm. Jo was mucking out in the cow shed and was pleased to see him.

'Hullo, stranger. Thought you'd gone off to your desert island or run away to your monks' place. Haven't seen you for something like an age.'

'I have to talk to somebody.'

'And come to me for that? You got plenty of people round you to talk to, surely? But p'raps it's that you don't want answers back; is that it?'

'Not exactly, but at least I know that you aren't against me, that you aren't biased, and that you don't know any better than me.'

'A great deal worse I would guess.'

'Certainly not worse.'

'All right then, I've got my off time now, for a short while. Charlie and me, we used to talk in the hayloft. You want to share my tea and sandwiches?'

They walked towards the barn. It was like a great rush of air, this time, blowing against her, so that she could hardly move forwards, and then that ruddy voice again: 'Don't you go with him, you baggage. You do go and see what you get – I warned you didn't I? He'll do for you.'

Jo pushed against the force. 'Get lost, Charlie,' she said under her breath. 'Leave me be.' And the blast of air subsided, and the movement returned to her legs.

'What?' said Peter, close behind her.

'Nothing, nothing – I'm for ever talking to myself.'

They climbed the ladder and settled themselves into the nest of hay that Jo had tunnelled out for her quiet times, when the weather was not good enough for roosts outside among gorse and heather or on cliff edge. Solitary habitats they had been lately, because Charlie did not come any more.

'What a great place this is,' Peter settled back into the secluded refuge, and wondered if she remembered the last time they'd been there, when he was trying to avoid going back to school. But she was busy unpacking the sandwiches, giving no sign of remembering anything. No sense in reminding her. 'Does anyone else come up here?' he said.

'Not now they don't,' Jo said, pouring tea, already mixed with milk and sugar into the top of the thermos. So he didn't remember, then. Odd how memory worked; she could recall every detail: the fearful dread of getting caught; the thrill of adventure and of ganging up against the grown-ups. 'Grampa can't get up the ladder these days, and Gran don't ever do the cows. It's my job to send down the hay for them. Course Charlie used to come all the time, but he doesn't do that any more. He's long gone; don't know where, he never said.' She halved a thick pilchard sandwich and gave Peter the bigger half. 'What do you want to talk about then?'

He told her the story of the grim afternoon, three weeks ago, and relived the harrowing moments under the eaves when he had first read the letter, only gradually allowing himself to understand the full implications of the contents, because it was too shocking to take in all at once. He found tears forming in his eyes as he spoke, and turned away so that she should not see them. The relief of the telling was surprising; clouds seemed to be lifting off him. Jo and he took it in turns to sip at the sweet, hot tea – a drink Peter thought he abominated. When the tale finally came to an end, he turned his head towards her, and returned, with a sense of shock, to the here and now, and the cosiness of the soft smells of hay and farmyard, hot tea and pilchard sandwiches.

'What shall I do?' he said.

While he had been talking, Jo had travelled with him through his ordeal, only she had somehow visualized the whole thing as a black and white film, acted out with all the exaggerated gestures and wild gesticulations of the twenties film that had once been shown in the village hall. She saw Bea clutching her bosom and tearing her hair, and Bridget looking scornful with hand on hip and eyes outlined in black. Daphne was the silly, weeping, heroine-type, forever at the mercy of the harsh, black-browed father who had spent all their money in drunken, gambling orgies. Just off-screen were the dashing young couple, Peter and his fearless, flaxen-haired companion, rushing bravely to the rescue.

'What shall I do?' said Peter, and the screen and the character melted abruptly.

Jo wiped her mouth with the back of her hand, and brushed the crumbs off her dungarees. 'Well . . .' she said, screwing the top back on the thermos, 'I reckon you should go and have a long talk with the law man who did the will, and arrange with him just how things have got to be organized for your mother and sisters, and then I reckon you should take a great chunk of all that money and really go to that place you told me about before.'

The words came out of her mouth so confidently, gave her quite a turn. She realized that no-one had ever asked her advice before, and was pleased that answers to questions like this were so simple and obvious to her way of thinking.

Peter stared at her without seeing her, because the euphoria that had accompanied the unburdening of the anxiety nightmare did not survive the telling. It shrivelled like a spent balloon, so that he retreated, immediately, back into the very depths of the darkness inside himself. That same darkness into which he had

171

withdrawn when he had taken in the contents of his father's letter: when he realized that he held in his hand a mandate that condemned him for ever to the stark obligation of managing and being responsible for the lives and well being of his six female relatives. Something he felt he was totally unable to take on. A charge he could never fulfil. He was no Hercules; never had been, never would be. He could only eke out existence as a common drone – an unwilling one at that – the only safety was darkness and solitude.

He became conscious that Jo was sitting beside him, her mouth full of sandwich and her expression quite unconcerned at the appalling tragedy in which he was involved. He pulled himself up, painfully, from the depths and looked at her with astonishment. Of course she couldn't be expected to understand. She was a simple, uncomplicated person who had probably had no such horrors to contend with. Brought up by uncomplicated grandparents to cope with the surface essentials of life, what would she know of the torments he was going through? Why should she be expected to understand?

'I'm sorry,' he said. 'I should never have bothered you with my troubles. I have to work through this problem myself. No-one can get me out of my disaster except myself.'

'Disaster? Trouble?' she laughed. 'You got all this good fortune spilled in your lap and you go calling it a disaster? You soft in the head or something? All you got to do is talk to that law man who knows all about everything, and then go off somewhere. Can't call that a disaster.' The picture in her mind changed from black and white melodrama into glorious technicolour beaches and sunshine.

'I gather you think I'm stupid?' he said rather testily, trying to think where the catch was and why things that had seemed unsolvable to him, were, to her, perfectly straightforward and manageable.

'Not stupid exactly,' she said, 'a bit silly like. But

172

then they say I'm a bit silly. I suppose we all are, come to that. P'raps it's just that I don't dwell on things if they're going to cause me upset. 'Tisn't worth it, is it? You got to think of something good to blot out the bad, and then, often as not, the bad'll go away.'

'But that's running away from the problem.'

'Maybe it is; same way as you run away from people when you ought rightly to be facing up to them. Like George and the Dragon,' she added, suddenly inspired by the beloved knight and all that beautiful silvery, flashing armour. She could hear the clash of steel and see the dragon's fiery breath shooting out of its flared nostrils. 'But I'd best be getting back,' she said. 'Grampa'll need some help with the pigs.'

They stood up in the mass of hay which clung to their clothes and their hair. The sun shone in straight shafts through the small roof lights; light shafts which were alive with brilliant specks of hay dust, floating aimlessly with the flies. She stood directly in the shaft of sun, looking positively angel-like, and he suddenly became irrationally convinced that she was the one good thing in his life, and that whatever else happened, there might be a possibility of his escaping from the darkness with her help.

'You're just wonderful,' he said on the spur of that momentary conviction, and he pulled her towards him, locking his arms round her waist. 'You're so *real* and down to earth and sensible, and you make me feel like someone that matters.'

'Don't need me to make you into someone that matters,' she said, embarrassed at the unexpected closeness, but not wanting to push him away in case it made him feel unwanted. Fancy him flattering her like that, just as if she'd said something clever. A small shock wave of excitement burned through her at being so close to him. She was reminded of the turbulent moment on the cliff, and before she knew it, there they were, bonded together in a breathtaking, intoxicating, impassioned kiss, the like of which her imagination had never touched on. His tongue met hers, and the explosion that overtook her was like a fountain of tiny stars shooting straight up her body and out through the top of her head.

'We belong, you and I,' he said. 'Do you remember holding my hand here, that day you helped me to run away?'

Jo made a great effort to bring herself back to the barn and the pigs waiting to be fed. So he *did* remember! But she had to get herself back to what was here and now, because in some strange way, her mind and her body were uncomfortably mixed up, and that was a new feeling. They'd always been separate before – what she thought and what she did – two different things, satisfactorily and separately packaged, so that they didn't intermingle. So what was this chaos going on inside her now? No matter if he felt unwanted, she had to get out of the situation before it took her over completely.

'Course I remember,' she said, and then gave him a sudden push backwards. 'Aw my life,' she said with a little burst of laughter. 'What're you doing to me? Don't know if I'm coming or going.'

As he released her and she felt herself gaining control of the uncontrollable, she started to laugh with the delight of the whole incident. 'Lord sakes!' she said, standing back and smiling at him, 'All this talk about belonging again. Can't you never get it into your head that I am me and you are you?' She started down the ladder. 'But that's not to say we couldn't be quite close together because of us thinking the same sort of things. There's no saying we couldn't be quite close I reckon.'

She vaulted right over the gate that afternoon, after running across the yard; she'd never been able to do that before, however much she'd tried.

22

Mr Tibbs, of Archibald Tibbs and Son, Solicitor and Commissioner for Oaths, of Penzance, had dealt with Petherick affairs for all his adult life, taking over from his father before him and his grandfather before that. It was one of their more important accounts, and in spite of the difficulties that accompanied dealings with large, moneyed families such as they were, the account was closely and jealously guarded and maintained.

'They may not be the easiest people to deal with,' Tibbs Senior told his son, when he first came into the family business, 'but they are none the less gentry, and should be treated as such. Few enough of them around these days,' he added. 'You expect them to be a bit eccentric.'

The younger Tibbs had been brought up to treat everyone with respect, and though the smallest glimmer of dissent had begun to creep into his thinking, it had not yet burgeoned into any sort of rebellion. In any case, he would not have enjoyed entering into any disagreement with Beatrice Petherick or her formidable daughters. He enjoyed working things out on paper with the help of legal books, but arguing cases in court or privately with clients, was not his strong point. However, being the senior partner in the firm now that his father was getting on, the Petherick dilemma was planted fairly and squarely in his lap, and he had no option.

'Of course I shall expect you to get us out of this ridiculous situation,' Bea said, having summoned him to Petherick Hall so that he could tell them of the true contents of Humphrey's letter. 'I had no idea what he had actually written in the letter; he just said he

175

wanted to tell Peter himself exactly what he was inheriting. Naturally I presumed he was telling him that the whole estate was in my hands, in trust for all six children on my death. I never dreamed he was putting him in control of the whole cahoot – I mean, what utter madness! He knew the boy was incapable of any sort of farm business dealings. I can only hope he'll come to you for advice, Mr Tubbs, and you'll tell him straight away that the whole thing is illegal. He's just not capable, you see, and anyway, he's not at all himself at the moment.'

'Absolutely himself, as it happens,' Bridget joined in. 'Which means he's not the sort of person who should be allowed near a fortune as large as this one.'

'He's mad,' Jean said. 'Bonkers, looney, of unsound mind, backward, disturbed . . .'

'Jean, *really* . . .' Daphne looked anxiously at Mr Tibbs. There was no need to explain unnecessary family details.

'I shall expect you to stop it.' Bea carried on as though no-one else had spoken. 'The family enterprise is running perfectly well, as it always has done, under my management. Just as it always did when Humphrey was alive. He didn't have a clue about business matters either.'

'We manage everything together,' Bridget explained, 'and it runs extremely well. I presume you'll be able to find some legal snag that will prevent things from becoming a shambles?'

Alec Tibbs had opened his mouth several times during the various conversations, but had not been quick enough to start his prepared speech.

'I'm afraid . . .' he said, overloudly, at last, 'that Mr Petherick did consult us when we drew up this document, and he was very insistent that it should be made absolutely legal, and able to stand up in a court of law, and this instruction we followed implicitly.' In spite of the satisfaction he felt at being able to report an assignment commendably executed, his voice faded as

176

the statement ended, and finished on a note of apologetic anxiety in the stunned silence that followed. 'We are subject to our client's wishes,' he added, with an unconvincing smile.

'And what about *us*?' Bea thundered. 'Are we not your clients also? Such insidious infamy! Why was I not told of this when it was first mooted? Did you have no duty to me, as your client? Why was I not told? I shall sue – have no doubt about that, Mr Topps; I shall sue the company.'

'We did attempt to advise Mr Petherick,' Alec Tibbs felt himself shrinking in the face of such rage. 'But he was adamant that no mention of the matter should be made until Mr Peter came of age. Quite adamant, he was.'

'Infamy!' Bea repeated, striding majestically out of the room.

'My mother is perfectly right,' Bridget said as Bea left, 'but I suppose we shall get no satisfaction from you or any other firm. You stick together like clams, you law people. Disgraceful, I call it.'

'Father could never fight free of tradition, could he?' said Daphne. 'Totally bound up in it, poor old dear; had to do what his forefathers told him. What a mess, but I'm sure Hans will be able to think of a way round it.'

'Can't think why he should,' said Bridget. 'German law is probably totally different.'

'Really, Bridgie,' Daphne rounded on her. 'Can't you ever get it into your head that Hans is now a British subject?'

'That doesn't make him an expert in British law.'

Alec Tibbs coughed, delicately, and started to collect his papers together prior to putting them away in his brief case. This was really embarrassing.

The women all turned their heads towards him and stared with surprise, as though they had forgotten he was there.

'Hope you realize what a mess you've made of our family,' Bridget said. 'Go away and think about it, and

177

don't forget to tell your father what a swine we think he is.'

What impossible people these Pethericks were. He certainly would tell his father no such thing; *he* still believed that the gentry had good manners and a sense of justice. And probably there were still some that had. They were supposed to be very good to their servants; but then there weren't many servants around these days for them to be good to. Alec Tibbs pondered on this idea for most of the way back to Penzance in the firm's Ford Prefect.

It was probably jealousy that made them so unpleasant and rude to people like him; jealousy and fear. Because after all, the lower middle classes were on the way up now, after the war. The upper classes wouldn't have it their own way for much longer. Bea's attitude had fanned the small, smouldering spark of rebelliousness into a feeble little flame inside him. Next time he dealt with them, he would meet rudeness with dignified scorn; if he couldn't persuade his father to take him off the case, that is.

'What a perfectly horrid little man,' Dorothy said just before the sitting-room door closed behind him.

'Odious,' Bridget agreed, 'but probably legally accurate. Little worms like that invariably are.'

'That's a bit unkind,' Daphne said. 'He was only doing his job.'

'Perhaps we could find a really corrupt one to fight the case,' Jean suggested. 'Families do fight wills and win.'

Cynthia spiked the ball of wool on to the needles and put her knitting back in the flowered cretonne bag she had made at the beginning of the war. 'That sort of talk is unworthy of any of us,' she said. 'Of course we can't fight the will. Just imagine the publicity we'd get. All our dirty laundry washed in public – it's unthinkable. We shall just have to try to influence Piggy, that's all. He must be made to see the sense of us running everything rather than him – solicitors or no solicitors.

I'm pretty sure he would be only too glad to come to some sort of arrangement with all of us. He's a sweet, gentle boy, after all.'

Jean laughed. 'How do you know?' she said. 'He hasn't spoken to us for years. We can't even find him since he had the letter. How do you expect to influence a demented, absent misanthrope?'

'In any case, Cyn, you'll be far too busy trying to keep Mother from murdering someone and having a stroke in the process.'

'We shall have to get another solicitor, whether we fight the will or not, that's the first objective. We shan't get anywhere with Tibbles and son; I'll talk to Harold about it.'

'I'm sure Hans will think of a way round it all.'

Nobody bothered to answer her; Daphne's ideas never got anywhere.

Peter took his father's old Humber from the garage, where it had been kept since Humphrey's death, and drove it into Penzance. The car had been lovingly tended and kept in perfect working order by Sam Snagle, who had joined the family as a stable boy in 1910, when he was fourteen. When the carriage had finally given way to the first Daimler, Sam learned to drive and became the chauffeur, as well as being in charge of the stables, with a new stable boy to look after the girls' ponies. The Humber was acquired in the thirties so that the girls might learn to drive and then use the car for their own outings. At the beginning of the war, the Daimler was sold, but Humphrey was allowed a special petrol ration in order to fulfil farm duties in the Humber.

'Farm duties my foot,' Bea said at the time. 'I need it for shopping in St Ives and fetching food from Penzance. I shall get exemption for Snagle, and he can drive me round. He can be considered a perfectly bona fide farm worker, and he's just about over age anyway, and quite unfit after being gassed in the last war. Can't

179

see why I should learn to drive, I have absolutely no desire to, and I refuse to be driven by Cynthia and put in peril of my life.'

So the Humber and Sam Snagle were both kept on, and used a great deal during the war years. Afterwards, the girls all had their own cars except for Cynthia who preferred to do shopping for herself and Bea in the village where possible. Sam had taken on the gardening, and Bea resented taking him off the garden to drive anyone anywhere. She also expected her family to come visit her rather than that she should visit them, so the car sat in the garage for most of the time.

It was years since Peter had driven it. They had all insisted that he should learn, but he had never been keen; he was frightened at being in charge of such a lethal weapon as a car, always had been. It took him a long time to get the hang of it, though Sam was a patient, understanding teacher. Sam was someone Peter liked to be with; about the only person he actually liked to be with; didn't have to talk or be afraid that Sam would talk to him. They had quiet, satisfactory sessions together.

It was the same when Sam had taught him to ride, another skill Peter had found difficult and not at all enjoyable. It seemed that he could always see the pitfalls and the possibilities of disaster ahead. But Sam was a stabilizing presence, whatever they did together; Peter had learned most of the good things he knew about from Sam. He was only sorry that he could never shine at the sort of things Sam was constrained to teach him, like riding and driving and fishing – though fishing was better, because there were those long, long intervals between catches, which could be silent, or interspersed with Sam's utterances: quiet, often monosyllabic and always to the point. The only bad thing about fishing was actually catching the fish: killing the poor, beautiful thing and dragging that dreadful hook out of its throat – callous and cruel.

Peter put his foot down harder on the accelerator with disgust at himself for not being bold enough to become vegetarian. He had tried once or twice to suggest it, but the whole family had laughed noisily, and ridiculed the idea.

'Oh Pigs, don't be such a wet.'

'For God's sake grow up, darling.'

'It's a rule of nature: big fish eats little fish who eats littler fish. You can't go against nature.'

And Bea putting the final kibosh on the whole idea. 'I'm not having Mrs Webb bothered by having to make up special menus for you, my boy. You'll eat the same as everyone else and like it.' He had found it impossible to stand up against that. His foot went down a little further: what a miserable drip he was.

The fox ran straight out of the hedge in front of him, and the brakes only slammed on after he had run right over it; he felt two distinct bumps – and did he hear a scream above the screech of the brakes? He thought so. He ran back in horror, and wished he hadn't. Fur and blood and entrails were smeared over the road and there was nothing he could do about it. If it had died off the road, buzzards, crows, and maggots would have cleaned up the remains; here other cars would finish the job quite tidily – backwards and forwards, like rolling pins, until the fox became an almost unnoticeable extra layer of the tarmac. Dust to dust.

But the irony of the death being caused by his own fury that he hadn't the guts even to become vegetarian, stayed with him as he drove on to Penzance. It was just the sort of situation he was forever finding himself in, whatever he did or thought, which was why it was so much easier to sit back and do nothing; let things happen around you.

So why not turn round now and go back home? To set out by himself, in the car he had only before driven when requested by one of the family, in order to go and discuss with the solicitor how best he could run his family and his life. The whole thing was ludicrous;

just doing what he was told again – only this time he had been told by Jo rather than by the family. Stupid, wasn't it?

He started to look for a gap in the hedge where he could turn round. Let them decide. They would, if he refused to; they always had done before. As he drove on, at a snail's pace, looking for a gate into a field that he could turn into, the thought kept nagging at him that Jo's suggestion had seemed very sensible at the time; just that he was sure it wouldn't work out because things never did for him, something always went wrong – like running over that wretched fox for instance.

And anyway, what did he think he was going to say to the solicitor? He had heard the family talking about this same solicitor the other day, and saying how dreadful he was, how unsympathetic and useless, and Bea saying he was deceitful and underhand and wily. There was no way he was going to be able to deal with an underhand, wily solicitor.

But there were still no gaps in which he could turn the car. This winding lane went on for miles, and the further he went the more he began to think that he had nothing to lose anyway, and Jo had seemed to think that it would be a perfectly easy, straightforward thing to do. And it *would* be very uplifting to have a large sum of money in his hand to do exactly what he liked with, and no-one to ask him where it had all gone afterwards, because they needn't even know how much he had taken out in the first place.

By the time he got to Penzance, he almost felt that Jo was sitting next to him, egging him on and suggesting just what they could both buy with the money afterwards. It was really quite exhilarating, and made him forget about the fox that must, by then, have become an almost invisible part of the tar macadam of the road between Zennor and Penzance.

Alec Tibbs had never met Peter before, and so was full of foreboding when the secretary announced over the phone that Mr Peter Petherick was downstairs.

182

Could he be madder than the feminine side of the family? They all seemed to think so. Probably resentful too, having heard of the meeting at Trewethy Farm in which he was not included. Might even have brought a gun. You never knew with these people. They always had plenty of guns around for shooting game.

Tibbs sat down at his father's heavy mahogany desk. The old boy never came in on Mondays or Tuesdays, unless there was something special to attend to. Just like him not to be here when he was wanted – he checked himself quickly – thank God he's not here, he told himself firmly; much better that only one of them would be shot. He rearranged the big, Victorian ink stand on the desk exactly opposite where he sat, and placed his attache case also on the desk, upright, facing the chair in which clients sat. Now, anyone would have to stand up in order to aim and shoot off a shot gun, that would allow a few seconds to dodge.

'Ask him to come up Miss Moyle.'

Peter walked up the stairs of the rather grand old house, that had recently been turned into offices, with a sense of doom. He knew exactly what this wily, unsympathetic solicitor would be like: tall, smooth, sardonic and supremely confident of his own ability. How does one deal with types like that?

The main shock was that he was so small. Not being particularly tall himself, Peter had to stretch up to see him sitting behind all the paraphernalia that was crowded on to the desk. He felt a terrible desire to laugh, but controlled it because of the difficulty of explaining why he was doing so. Was this little creature, in round, owlish-looking horn-rimmed specs, who looked lost on the vast chair he was sitting on, was this really the assailant he had dreaded meeting? Peter imagined telling Jo the joke when he got home. It was hilarious.

Alec Tibbs peered out from behind the desk lamp and the flowers Miss Moyle arranged in a vase each day, and saw that there was no gun. He saw a fair, fragile-looking man, looking as though he was just about to laugh, standing hesitantly in the doorway. Could this possibly be Peter Petherick?

He got up from the chair and came round the desk to meet him. 'Good afternoon Mr Petherick, I'm so very glad to meet you. There are lots of little things we ought to discuss.'

They got on like a house on fire.

23

'It was so *funny*,' Peter told Jo afterwards. 'There was I, expecting some dragon of a man who would frighten me to death, and he was so small, I couldn't even see him behind that great enormous desk which was covered with everything under the sun. I was left with nothing to fight, I had the feeling he was more frightened of me than I was of him.'

'Thought you were going to be like the rest of your family no doubt. And you got it all arranged did you? Did he tell you how it could be done?'

'It's all so simple, just like you said.'

'There! Didn't I just tell you?'

'I always get so afraid because of what *might* happen. You're lucky not to have that fear all the time. I just get paralysed by it into doing nothing, because I know I couldn't cope with the sort of things I imagine might happen.'

'Daft I call that. You got to think of all those good things that's going to come your way, and that makes you want to get on with it and get started. You don't want to think on miseries. If you got miseries, then the first thing you got to do is push 'em out and get your mind back on the good things.'

Peter smiled to himself at the childishness of the

idea. 'What about the disappointment when things don't live up to the expectation?' She really hadn't grown up yet, he felt satisfactorily superior and warm towards her.

Jo remembered the let-downs, but quickly swept them out of her thinking. No good letting them spoil what could be exciting news that Peter was about to tell her. 'Well?' she said. 'Go on then, tell us what happened. You got your money, did you? You got all them women fixed up did you? Have you thought where to go? You going to all them eastern places like you said?'

The fear returned abruptly. 'Yes, I got all them women fixed up. That was the easiest of the lot; just had to, sort of 'employ' them to do the jobs they're all doing already. And then I pay them a kind of salary, which is the same amount they have been getting out of the estate anyhow. They were pretty good at keeping accounts, so we were able to work out just how much they all ought to get. Don't know how they'll take it of course.'

Jo rocked with laughter. 'You paying them *wages*?' she giggled. 'Aw that's rich, I must say. You going to put it in packets with their names on? I'd like to see that I would.'

'Well, not packets exactly, just a nice big cheque into their bank accounts each month, plus allowances for themselves.'

'Which you'll stop if they don't behave theirselves,' Jo hugged him with delight. It was right that they should have had the tables turned on them; they had made him very unhappy, even if they hadn't meant to be unkind to him. 'And you?' she said, letting go of him in order to hear the next step. It was just like a fairy tale: the poor woodcutter's youngest child getting the best of the bargain in the end. The beginning of the happy ending. 'What you going to do then?'

Peter blushed; now came the difficult bit; the bit he couldn't decide. At least he didn't feel he had the guts

185

to bring about his decision, so therefore couldn't really make the decision. It was all far too impossible and unlikely. Quite impossible, and silly into the bargain. He slouched back into the dried up cow parsley and meadowsweet that grew beside the stone wall where they were sitting, picked off a head of clover and started to suck at the base of the flower to taste the honey.

'Go *on*,' she said, 'tell us what you're going to do with all that money you got?'

'I don't have to do anything special straight away,' he said.

'What d'you mean – you don't have to? You were telling me off for not wanting to get out and see things, and now you've got the chance to do that, you say you don't have to.'

Peter looked at her miserably. 'Well, I did get to the solicitor's on my own, and that was difficult enough . . .'

'You just said it was easy . . .'

'Only easy when I got there – it was very difficult to go. Frightening I mean; I was rigid with fear all the way. And I ran over a fox, so I nearly turned back. I would have done if there had been a place to turn round; only there wasn't. I kept thinking, if only I hadn't done anything at all, if I hadn't tried to do what you told me to, then I would never have killed that fox and it would still be living and enjoying life today. Because of something I did it's dead. I kept thinking of that when I was trying to turn round and go back. I thought if only I had gone on living quietly without getting in anyone's way, then the fox would still be alive.'

'And you'd be dead, or as good as, any road – aw my life, what a frightened jellyfish you are.'

He turned to look at her again, and was sorry that he had irritated her.

'I'm not nearly so pretty as a jellyfish.'

The tension eased at once, and she laughed again. 'That surely you're not, and you don't sting neither.'

'I do realize I'm impossible, you know.'

'You're not impossible my dear; it's just that you've not been treated right, and now you don't know how to fight back. You haven't got the habit yet, but it'll come, given time.'

Jo took his hand in hers and saw him as a helpless baby, probably left out in the woods to die by an uncaring family – she restrained her thoughts a little – well, not actually left out in the woods like in the stories, but left out, in more ways than one, by that self-satisfied, stuck up family of his. No wonder he'd growed up timid and fearful. But she'd look after him; she'd help him along; she wouldn't leave him out in the cold no more.

'I'll look after you' she said out loud without meaning to. She remembered saying that to Charlie Doll often. She used to wrap him in Blanket – the old scarf that Mumma left behind which had been the necessary accompaniment at the time for a thumb sucking session. Bit silly to say something like that to Peter, but it was out and she couldn't take it back now, so she put her arm round his neck and pulled him towards her. 'Don't you worry none,' she said, and put her thumb in her mouth as she rocked him backwards and forwards in the long grass.

He told her the second part of his plan quite a long time later; and in the meantime he ran away, because he was afraid of what he had done, and because he was afraid of the ensuing, frightening turmoil he had created at Petherick Hall. Ran away from the wrath and unhappiness of his family; ran away because he suddenly became mortally afraid of Joanne herself. He had always been so certain that the only safety and satisfaction in his life was his separateness from the rest of the world. His belief that only by avoiding contact with others – more particularly women – could he avoid fear and disillusion. If he relied on nobody, then nobody could cheat him or frighten him. And yet here he was, allowing a dangerous relationship to develop. Why should Jo be any different from the rest of them? Bound to be devious or dominating, or just plain dependent in the long run. And he would be left with no place to run to; he would be trapped before he knew it, and before he could get away to find his own particular Shangri-La.

He crept quietly away to the monastery he had read about, and asked to be allowed to retreat into the impersonal safety of its silence. Keep safe and in hiding for a little time longer before taking the next step.

By the new arrangement, drawn up by Peter and Mr Tibbs, Bea was dubbed Bailiff-in-Chief, and considered to be in charge of all operations. 'Damn cheek!' she stormed on receiving the letter of designation. 'The little fiend's actually *paying* me a *salary*, can you believe it? And calling me *bailiff*. God, what impertinence. Just wait till I get my hands on him.'

'You probably never will if he knows what's good for him.' Cynthia said sadly. 'As soon as he gets some money he just slopes off somewhere without telling us where. It's extremely hurtful after all we've done for him. Does he dislike us all so much? Shockingly ungrateful. I just can't somehow imagine that this is my little baby brother behaving like this.'

'Stop being so ridiculously sentimental,' Bridget looked up from reading the screed from the solicitor. 'What I can't get over is that two such inept creatures as our dear brother and that revolting little Tibbs man, have managed to draw up such a Machiavellian-type document as this one.'

'It was probably Tibbs senior who drew it up.'

'Rubbish, Tibbs senior is practically senile. And anyway he's always appeared to be terrified of us.'

'Small wonder, when he knew what a disgraceful secret he was hiding from us for all these years.'

'So I suppose,' said Bea, 'I shall now have to go, hat

in hand, to Harold every time I want to employ a gardener, or raise someone's wages, or buy Websie a little present. It's positively humiliating.'

Bridgie smiled. 'Mother darling, when have you ever given Websie a present, large or small?'

'And you *are* a bit careless with money, Mother dear,' Cynthia reminded her. 'You so seldom remember where it's gone.'

'I see you're all against me, but what right has Harold to tell me what I can spend I'd like to know? Careless indeed! You just forget to write it down when I tell you what I've spent.'

Cynthia bridled. 'I *never* forget to write anything down when people tell me. It's just that nobody ever remembers to tell me.' She was still smarting under the title of Assistant Accountant (household), under the shadow of Bridget's husband as Chief Accountant. Bad enough to be accountable to Bea and have her carping and breathing down her neck all the time, but to be at the mercy of Harold and Bridget – well, that was too much. Also unforgivable that Harold would be paid three times as much as her for the work. Albeit his ability was certainly of more professional status, but it still looked demeaning on paper like that. Naturally, her personal allowance made up her share to a great deal more than his, but all the same, written down like that, in a bald statement, it was extremely degrading. And as for Bridget herself, as Management Overseer in Charge, one could immediately see the subtle change in her already overbearing character that the title had effected.

'I'm sure Harold will manage everything very efficiently from now on,' Bridget said, somewhat smugly. She began to have the slightest suspicion that the whole document was, in some strange way, a dubious send-up of the family. But of course it couldn't be; not really; because neither Tibbs nor Peter had the remotest hint of a sense of humour between them. Apart from which, they wouldn't dare; didn't have the intelligence either. Of course not. But it was quite amusing that Hans should be termed Interpretative Controller of Foreign Contracts and Assignments Overseas! Really quite amusing that. Daphne would be delighted, without having an idea what it actually meant.

Life was never the same for Jo after the afternoon in the barn with Peter. Whether it was the result of that particular meeting and the rather strange turmoil that made itself felt in her mind at the time, or whether the upheaval to her thinking had begun before, she was not absolutely sure. But something surely happened then. And it was because of this happening that she felt that the bottom had dropped out of her world when he disappeared without a word.

Every day after their last meeting, she had waited for him to turn up at the farm. Certain, she had been, that he would be wanting to spend time with her whenever possible, because he had suddenly started to occupy all her thoughts, and she had imagined that it would be the same with him. Day followed day, and he didn't come. Whenever there was a footstep, or any slight sound behind her, she would turn with the belief that he would be standing there. The despair she began to feel was like a black chasm surrounding her.

And all the time, Charlie's voice nagged at her: 'Didn't I just tell you? Only got yourself to blame for not taking no notice of what I said. He don't want you, never did. Just wants to do you in, that's all. He's crazy, that one. If ever he comes back, you want to watch out he don't get you.'

So it was true: no-one wanted her; no-one would ever want her. It must be something about her that caused everyone to run away from her. What had she done to frighten Peter away? For the life of her she couldn't imagine. Suppose he was crazy like Charlie said? Perhaps he'd actually tried to push her over the cliff that day, not pull her back. Just when she had thought that her life was taking off in some new and exciting direction, she found herself back to that realization that she was once more alone and abandoned: first Mumma, then Charlie, then Peter.

Viciously, she raked up the straw and the muck, and tears came into her eyes. Well, if he had up and left her, it wasn't the end of the world was it? There was lots of other things in life she could do. Just needed thinking about, that was all. She'd think of something tomorrow.

24

The tomorrows seemed unending to Jo. Winter came early and wet, and day followed day in a slough of mud, wet hair clinging to her neck with rivulets of rain dribbling down her back and the mouldy smell of sodden clothes, drying off in the kitchen. Nothing ever dried properly, and the whole cottage oozed damp.

Gran's temper worsened with the weather, and Jo found the silence into which Grampa and she retreated had, of late, become ominous and dangerous, rather than being the welcoming refuge it used to be. She could no longer conjure up the adventures and the brave deeds, or even the blatantly magical havens of delight; it was only despair that waited for her: the empty dejection of finding herself abandoned and alone. There had been a short time like that, just before she re-met Peter. That time when floating with the birds had seemed to be the only possible pleasure left for her. This time it was worse: now there was the added humiliation that, quite apart from Mumma, the two people round whom her life had previously revolved, had deserted her without explanation.

Charlie had not only disappeared, but kept on yelling and shouting at her at irregular intervals: 'Told you he'd do for you. But you wouldn't listen, would you?'

All the time, whenever she was at her lowest ebb, the voice came at her, loud and clear. There were times when she was driven to shout back, shaking her head, hands over her ears: 'Leave me alone can't you!'

With the desertions and the melting away of the helpful fantasies, the hopes and convictions shrivelled too, and all the buried anger surged to the surface. Things would never have been like this if she had had a mother and father like anyone else. And who was this mother who could have abandoned her in this way? What had made her such a monster? Why was she never talked about?

Must've been Gran that drove her away. It was Gran's fault, not Mumma's. And as soon as the thought entered her head, back came Charlie's voice: 'It was the old bitch what drove her away with her spiteful tongue; made life impossible. Went on and on at her and made her feel no good and not good enough to be a proper mother even. Made her think she couldn't look after a baby proper, else she never would have gone off like that. You ought to pay her out for that; ought to put her away for good for that; shouldn't be allowed to get away with it. Why don't you pay her out? Go on – why don't you?'

Jo's hatred boiled and seethed inside her, all the more venomous for having been confined for so long. But behind all the anger was still the dispiriting thought that perhaps it wasn't just Gran's fault. It could be that, somewhere along the line, she had somehow brought it on herself. Perhaps she had cried all the time until Mumma could take no more. Perhaps she had been just the sort of child that nobody could possibly like; perhaps she was still that unacceptable sort of person. What was wrong with her? Did she smell or something? The kids at school had always said so.

'Why don't anybody like me Grampa?' she asked, when they were alone.

They sat together in the barn, with their sandwiches and their thermos of tea, as they had so often done before. As she had done with Peter all that time ago. Couldn't expect a hot meal in the middle of the day, Grace told them, specially when the days were so short. They could have their hot dinner at five o'clock, when it got dark, and they were lucky to get that; there were women she knew that wouldn't do as much as she did for their men; it wasn't as though she was getting any younger, and if Will insisted on keeping Jo out in the fields with him and not letting her help in the house, then there was no knowing how long a hot dinner every day would continue, because she would likely drop dead from the strain before too long.

'Nobody *like* you?' Will stared at Jo in astonishment. 'But *I* like you don't I?'

It was crazy to ask, of course. Poor ol' Gramp, didn't know any different, did he? If he put up with it, there was no reason why she shouldn't. He wouldn't have no idea what she was talking about. But in spite of the commonsense that told her this, the whole dilemma was suddenly too much, and Jo put her head down on his sodden knee and bawled like a baby.

Will had shed a good many tears himself over the years, but he put it down to the wind or the sun or a danged old cold in the head and hadn't taken that much mind. But the sight and sound of his grand-daughter sobbing away on his knee loosened something inside of him, and this time the tears weren't caused by the weather, nor by some danged rheumy-eyed cold in the head.

He gathered her up and held her close, and the two of them sat clamped together, rocking backwards and forwards while the wetness dripped off them and the steam from their body heat hung round them like a sea mist.

'Mumma never came, Grampa, she never came and fetched me so she couldn't have liked me could she? And Gran doesn't want me here, and my friend Charlie

193

has just gone off and doesn't come and see me no more, and . . .' But she couldn't tell him about Peter because that had been a secret; couldn't tell nobody at the time – and certainly not now. Couldn't let on how silly she'd been.

'Aw my dear life, don't fret so,' said Will kissing the top of her wet head. ''Tisn' true that we don't love you, it's just we don't do much showing off of it, that's all. And your Mum, well I reckon she couldn't fetch you my dear love, else she'd be sure to have come; no way she wouldn't have come. And as for your Gran, well, she's just made that way i'nt she? It's just her way, that's all. More's the pity.'

Jo choked over an explosive giggle that interrupted the sobs, and felt better. She sat up and tried to wipe her face with the end of her shirt. Grampa had survived through endless years of this; he must often have felt bad, but he'd survived, and he loved her; she wasn't entirely alone.

Will rubbed at his stubble chin and decided to take a plunge: ''Tis strange,' he said. ''Tis very strange that we didn't hear nothing from her, I'll grant you that.' He put his hand over hers. 'We did hear at first. Always asking after you she was, and she sent that old doll along to keep you company, so it wasn't that she didn't love you my old love, wasn't that at all.'

'She *wrote*? She wrote and you didn't tell me? Why Grampa? Why didn't you tell me? Why didn't you let me write to her? Why didn't you tell me?' The tears welled up again, accompanied this time by a fury at the injustice of it.

'Your Gran thought it best, thought you'd settle best if you didn't keep expecting her to turn up like. Wasn't sure that she was right, mind, but then I didn't know much about little kids at all, so didn't like to interfere.'

'You *should* have done, Grampa, you've always known better than her; you should have told me. It's all Gran's fault, everything is Gran's fault. She stopped my Mumma coming to fetch me. I could have written if

I'd known, I could have written and asked her to come if I'd known.'

'But we didn't have no address for her, 'tisn't all your Gran's fault, Joanie; you mustn't be hard on her, she was for ever telling me to find out where your Mum was, only I never could get round to it somehow. Didn't really know how.'

Jo sat up straight, excited anticipation sweeping away the great cloud of grief and fury. 'But I can; I can find out, can't I? That's what I'll do, Grampa. I'll go up to Exeter or London even, and I'll find out where she is. You'll help me Grampa? Lend me a bit of money to go there will you?'

Will hugged her. 'Course I will, old love, course I will if that's what you want. Got a little nest egg hid away from prying eyes for rainy days. But you be a bit cautious and don't you expect too much. There's no knowing what's happened to her after all these years. Be a bit cautious and ready for shocks.'

'Shocks? What shocks? I bet she's just too scared of Gran to come down, and I expect she thinks I might not remember her after all this time, and she doesn't want to upset me. That's why she didn't get in touch. She's just thinking what would be best for me, that's all.'

'Maybe, maybe; but just you be cautious all the same.' A wave of anxiety caught up with him, but he pushed it down. Much better that she be given the chance to find out for herself, else she'd never be satisfied. And what a treat it would be to see them together again. Best all round for everyone.

'Reckon you and I'll go down to the pub before we do anything else,' he said suddenly. 'It's time you knew what a half pint tasted like, and what if you are a mite too young, old George, 'e won't say nothing if I say we're celebrating.'

'Oh yes!' Jo felt the laughter gurgling up, 'let's celebrate, I feel so like celebrating just now.'

They set off, down the road, for the pub, hand in

hand, Will whistling between his teeth. He felt a whole load lighter, like a great weight lifted clean off him. Been preying on him all these years; wasn't sure they done right in keeping any news of her mother away from her. Good that she wanted to do something about something; somehow shifted the responsibility a bit.

Jo's mood had swung in a complete arc from the depths to the heights. Of *course* that was what she had to do; why ever hadn't she thought of it before? Whatever she might find, and she wasn't really able to imagine that the finding could be anything but good, but whatever happened, when a mother met a daughter and a daughter met a mother after long, long years of absence, then there was bound to be fireworks, you couldn't escape it, and fireworks was exciting. Some danger, some shocks, but above all exciting, and excitement, she felt sure, was just what the doctor ordered at this moment.

25

If retreat was supposedly synonymous with escape, Peter did not find it so, though at first, the peace and the isolation he sank into, transported him immediately to the land of Erehwemos. This is it, he thought to begin with, this is what I always wanted: peace, quiet, space to move about and complete anonymity. At last I can be master of my own identity without worrying about who is going to invade my territory. A splendid, triumphant situation; but it palled all too quickly, and guilt came rushing back in.

Thus, in spite of the sympathetic surroundings, he seemed to persist in condemning himself for something or other. In spite of his own denials, he didn't seem able to convince himself. The unnecessary pain he had caused everyone, his mother, his sisters, Jo – just walked out on all of them; left them to stew, not even thinking of the unhappiness they might feel. To take off like that: despicable; forever running away to Erehwon, not to Erehwemos. Why could he not climb out of childhood?

He attended services at the monastery, not because he believed or wanted to believe, but because he hoped the chanting and the ritual might assuage. It didn't. He even confessed his sins to the Abbot in charge and asked for forgiveness, only to find he did not want God's forgiveness, he would have preferred to know that Jo understood the reason for his going, but he realized that she wouldn't. He disciplined his life: eating little, rising early, meditating, reading, keeping silence, exercising, trying to keep his mind on what he was doing. He couldn't. He took part, to excess, in the tasks that were asked of those in retreat, hoping to exhaust himself into dreamless sleep every night. But sleep was fitful and crowded with nightmares. He grew thin and felt ill most of the time, but could see no way out of the situation. If this was not the answer, it would seem obvious that there was no answer anywhere.

And all the time, at the back of his mind there was this insistent unease, because he wanted to go back, and sit with Jo on the cliff-top at Zennor. Wouldn't be much good sitting and thinking, she had said, much better to talk about things. Was that true? Couldn't imagine it working for him. The problems were his, nobody else's. She was really just a child, without education and without experience. What could she possibly know about his problems? What right had he even to think that she might listen to his talk? She wouldn't be able to do anything for him, so why was he even considering the idea of making a companion of her? Of making a companion of anyone in fact? His problems could only be sorted out by himself.

He was digging over a patch of earth in the vegetable

garden, along with another – guest was he? Surely not a brother, he wasn't wearing the habit, his head wasn't shaved. Much too scruffy looking, with beard and long hair hiding much of his face. But he had this air of quietude that most of the brothers had too. Set them aside from others, and this man too, he was somehow set aside as well.

Peter slid a surreptitious glance at him, feeling that he wanted to study him further, but his glance was caught and held. 'You got trouble?' said the man, straightening his back.

Peter was taken unawares and felt rather indignant and defensive, as though he had been spying on the man. 'No more than anyone else I suppose.'

The man continued to look at him. Trying to read him? It was uncomfortable, being considered such an open book. He went on digging, very conscious of being watched.

'You a visitor?' Peter said, after a few minutes, in an attempt to shift the discomfort, 'or do you belong?' And immediately he thought of Jo saying, 'Belong? Belong? What d'you mean, belong?' And what exactly did he mean? Why did belonging matter to him? He was trying to get away from belonging, wasn't he?

'Bit of a permanent visitor. Don't rightly belong, but they let me hang about on the edges, doing this and that. I get on with the animals.'

'You work on the farm?'

'Not really; not officially. Fact is, I'm not really here at all according to the records, but the Brothers like the way I know what's wrong with the livestock, so they let me hang around.'

'Sort of faith healer for the stock? Is that what they call you?'

The man smiled. 'They call me Francis, Francisco, Cisco. It's not my real name, but it's good enough to be going on with for now.'

Odd, how enforced silence made conversation much more agreeable than usual. The desire to talk took

Peter over quite forcibly; words, words – they came jumbling into his mind with the demand to be spilled out all over the place. And here he was, bound into a convention of silence; not a hard and fast rule, but you felt constrained, on account of the gentleness and kindness of those who surrounded you. Nothing to rebel against, so comply, mildly and willingly.

'I would suggest a pint in the pub in about an hour,' said Saint Francisco, hoeing away, quite gently, at the weeds in the red, overturned earth, 'if that's all right with you. Feel in need of a good chat.'

Peter wondered who he was. A tramp? A drop-out from society? An alcoholic? A mental case? A bit frightening to take up with someone you knew nothing about; perhaps he just wanted to get him on his own in order to rob him. Well, he'd be disappointed if that was what he was after; wouldn't get anything of value if that was his game.

Rather silly to consider socializing with someone like this in a pub! Run away from it all and then drift back at the first opportunity. He began to wonder if he had any backbone at all. Glumly, he came to the obvious conclusion: no, he hadn't.

The pub was small, crowded and relaxed. It was several months since Peter had been in one, and the first time he had not just been in tow, trailing behind one of the family. Bea always stopped off at the pub on her way back from anywhere, and if she had been able to drag Peter along to carry shopping or help her with some other chore, then he had accompanied her to the pub as well, sullenly, silently and disapprovingly. He remembered those times now, and to his surprise, found the memory of them amusing. They had seemed horrific at the time; he could still feel the cold distaste that he had felt then; the terrible fear of all those noisy, red-faced monsters, pouring gallons of beer down their throats. So threatening they had seemed.

This lot appeared to be mildly good-humoured and not at all frightening. He drank cider, and felt his defences crumbling. The words came tumbling out: hundreds of them, sometimes a little confused in their rush. The story of his life, or very nearly, because some of it was not quite sorted out, and some he forgot. Some incidents he remembered as he started the telling – almost as though he was making it all up, and yet he knew he wasn't; it was all absolutely true and important.

'Why on earth am I boring you with all this?' he said suddenly, filled with embarrassment at such a lapse.

The saint-who-understood-animals smiled over the table at him. 'Not boring,' he said. 'Not boring at all. You could be talking about me; circumstances were different of course, but reactions just the same. This getting away from it all, being alone, not talking, not trusting people, I felt exactly the same.'

Peter was surprised, one could almost say a little disappointed to find that his problem was obviously not exclusive to himself. 'But you coped with it, didn't you? You didn't run away from it all; at least you carried on living.'

'Did I? Do you call what I do living?'

There was quite a long silence as Peter considered the question. 'Well, I suppose I wouldn't particularly want to live your sort of life, but that doesn't mean anything. You chose that life and you are living in the way you have chosen, no matter what anyone else thinks.'

'So are you.'

'No I'm not. I'm not living at all at the moment. I'm just hiding.'

Francis sprawled across the table, his head resting on his hand, and stared long and hard at Peter without saying a word. And the longer he stared, the more Peter heard his own mind ticking over in his head, arguing the case against himself: You are doing exactly what he is doing; you chose to live your life in hiding and in silence, and up till now, that is precisely what you have done. 'I do quite enjoy hiding,' he said. 'It's especially satisfying when you get a hiding place that is so good that nobody at all can find you. Gives you a great sense of achievement. I've always been pretty good at finding unfindable hiding places.'

He felt aggressively pleased with himself.

'And once you've found it, what do you do?'

'I – er – I sit. I sit and think.'

'Does that give you pleasure?'

'Well, yes, of course it does. I mean you've fooled everyone, haven't you? They can't find you, so they can't pester you. I don't let anybody into my hiding places.' He looked at Francis rather aggressively; did this man think he was going to barge in?

'But when you've stopped being pleased with yourself, it's all a bit boring, isn't it? That's what I find, because you can't sit there for ever, so you have to crawl out again to go to the bog, or get something to eat. To carry on living – or existing, perhaps you would prefer to call it. I find I feel a bit stupid then.'

Peter shot another glance at him; he certainly knew it all. Coming out of hiding was a big anti-climax and tended to make him much angrier and more disgruntled than when he had first run away. A vicious circle that could be considered rather pointless.

'Are you feeling like that now?' he asked.

'I'm not hiding any more,' said Cisco. 'I'm out of that phase; into the one of trying not to be so completely self-absorbed. It's much more interesting.'

Peter was riled by the criticism, but kept quiet, realizing that it would be useless to argue against it. Most people were more or less self-centred; it wasn't such a sin.

It was inescapable that Peter should gravitate towards Cisco. To find an image of himself in the middle of the uncommunicating and detached assembly was like finding a desert island after spending a lifetime floating in a still and silent sea. Francis, he decided, was not trying to winkle him out of anything; he was

201

just a handy refuge, so he clung, because otherwise he would drown.

But he decided to leave the retreat, which he was beginning to find suffocating, and to move into a rented cottage in the district. 'I shall grow vegetables and keep hens,' he said, and in his mind he saw himself living there with Cisco, who would know what to do about cooking and poultry feed and how to deal with vegetables. He telephoned instructions to Alec Tibbs.

'You needn't tell anyone that you heard from me,' he said. 'Just put the money into the Post Office, so that I can draw out what I want.'

'But don't you want to let your family know that you are safe and well?'

'No I don't. They wouldn't care a fig if I was unsafe and ill. No need to tell them anything. Much better for them if I'm both out of sight and out of mind, otherwise they might get into their usual state of fury and frustration about me.'

He had not bargained for Cisco's reaction to the idea; there was a marked hostility in his manner.

'You shouldn't tie yourself down with property,' he said. 'No-one is free when they have goods and chattels.'

Could his sisters be considered chattels? A stab of amusement caught Peter in his midriff, and he laughed. 'I'm already tied down,' he said.

Cisco did not smile. 'Then break free; you know what Jesus said about the camel and the eye of the needle.'

Peter wanted to say that he had no desire to enter the kingdom of Heaven, but thought it might offend. A ripple of laughter was still milling about inside him as he thought how Jo would have laughed if he'd told her: I'm thinking of driving my chattels through the eye of a needle to enter the kingdom of heaven. What was the matter with him? What was there to laugh at? He'd told Alec Tibbs that it was better for him to be out of sight and out of mind. There was nothing whatever to laugh at.

And Jo? Was it better for her that he should be out of mind? Of course it was; she would scarcely remember him after all this time. One kiss and a few conversations – why should he ever imagine that she would recall such trivialities? He was right to stop it there and then, before either of them became involved.

'I was involved with a girl,' he told Cisco, 'but I found I wasn't ready for a relationship. I didn't want her in my life, she could never have put up with my moods and my odd ideas. Stopped it before it started.'

He was disappointed when Cisco did not respond for some considerable time, just continued to sit in silence in the kitchen of the cottage, steeped in disapproval. Peter stirred some vegetable concoction that was on the stove. He had managed to find things out for himself, without Cisco's help, but he still demanded approval and guidance; only felt capable of dealing with the basic necessities of life.

The silence became irritating to Peter; he found he was always wanting responses these days; conversation somehow reminded him of Jo, and of the sea and of sitting on the cliffs. When he thought about these things, a pain clutched at the middle of his body. The sentimental would call it heartache, he thought; the idea made him smile with its absurdity.

'What d'you feel about girls then?' Cisco said finally.

'Girls? Well, I don't seem to have needed them. I mean – not as *girls*. Er . . .' He wound down, embarrassed.

'Still a virgin then.'

Peter studied Cisco's expression. Mocking? Pitying? Denigrating? He couldn't be sure.

'Well – yes.'

'Do you prefer boys?'

'NO!' The violence of his reply shocked him, but he hadn't expected the question and so was unprepared for the deluge of shocking memories that flooded out the sentimental nostalgia. Pain, humiliation, disgust, fear, it all came back. Certainly not boys. He shook his head from side to side. That all had to be blotted out and forgotten. 'Had enough of that at school.'

And Dimple? What about dear, gentle old Dimple? But you don't talk about having a relationship with an old man: it would be misunderstood; you would be considered perverted.

'Bad experiences can't be allowed to mess up good ones; they bear no relation to each other.'

'Of course they don't.' The brief sexual arousal he had felt with Jo was one of the good experiences, but it might have turned sour. He hadn't wanted to risk that. Hadn't wanted to risk any sort of disillusion. Hadn't wanted to risk anything at all. Much safer to back off.

'Some risks are worth taking,' Cisco said, taking the bowl of soup Peter handed him.

'Like trying some of my inedible soup.'

'Exactly, and think how silly it would be to refuse it in case I burned my tongue.'

What was he getting at? 'All right, you've made your point. With a bit more encouragement, I expect you can induce me to climb out of my bolthole.'

'You haven't made such bad progress already,' Cisco said. There was silence as both concentrated on the meal.

When Cisco came to visit, he always stayed for something to eat, which Peter considered a compliment: meant he had to make an effort; might not have done if he'd been alone. The idea that Cisco might teach him how to cope was misguided. There was no help, only company and conversation, much of it fairly heated because of Cisco's criticism. The small garden was cleared and planted by Peter, while Cisco sat and watched. It might have been annoying if Peter hadn't decided that Cisco's plan was to make him find out things for himself. He bought two hens and a goat, and books to find out how to deal with them.

The whole set-up was idyllic, Peter told himself;

couldn't be better. But at the back of his mind there was the conventional 'and yet – and yet . . .' drumming away incessantly. The annoying cliché insisted on hanging about. He leaned back in his chair and looked long and hard at Cisco. A perfectly satisfactory companion he was: warm, understanding, practical, sensible; all the things Peter, himself, wished that he was. All the things he felt that he was not. And as if that weren't enough, Cisco was one of the most beautiful looking men he had seen. How could he ever have looked on him as an unsightly tramp? Possibly because of all that hair; the only thing you could really see were the eyes, clear blue, positively glinting out from under the long fringe that kept catching in his eyelashes. It almost looked like he was doing a bit of hiding as well.

The warmth, the affection, the intimacy was all very conducive to the next obvious step. Was that what he meant when he talked about taking risks? Sitting by the fire after supper, one evening, Peter drank his can of beer, and worked himself up into a fever of anxiety. How did he really look on Cisco? Just as a pleasant companion? Wasn't he something more than that? Wasn't there the danger of another relationship forming? Had it not already formed in fact? What were Cisco's real feelings towards him? Were they in danger of becoming just another couple, living together?

No way would he make the first move; wasn't up to him, but how would he react if Cisco made any sort of advance? He felt an urgent desire to make for the door on the pretext of feeding the hens or collecting the eggs, or untethering the goat – anything at all to get him out of having to cope with a possible situation. His mouth was quite dry, and there was no more beer left.

Cisco suddenly laughed, and made him jump. 'Relax, you idiot, I'm not about to rape you, though I'd quite like to. But don't you think we should, by now, be able to say to each other Brother, I love you, without feeling frightened to death of getting – involved – as you put it? We are already involved, have been since we first met, and will probably be for the rest of our lives.'

Peter panicked immediately: involved *for the rest of his life!* Was that what he wanted? He sat rooted to his chair, but in his head he was already at the end of a mile long rabbit warren, folded up small with his knees up to his chin and his head tucked down, in the classic foetal position, eyes closed, arms enclosing head: deaf, blind, unbreathing – but safe.

Cisco came over, knelt on the floor in front of him, and put his arms round him. 'Don't be so afraid of life,' he said. 'I'm not going to take you over, any more than you're going to take me over. We can both do exactly what we like with our lives, but whatever either of us do, it's bound to affect the other, isn't it?'

He hugged Peter to him, and they kissed. Perfectly natural thing to do, Peter thought, to someone you loved and who loved you. He was astonished to find the rush of passionate excitement he felt was really exactly the same he had experienced with Jo, only this time he didn't feel at all like running away. Cisco was part of his present life, and Jo was part of his past. She didn't love him the way Cisco loved him. Absurd of him to think of their relationship as a love relationship; they had been little more than children: not at all grown up in fact. Where was the problem? He came out of the rabbit hole and found nobody was chasing him.

26.

With the confidence of Grampa's nest egg behind her, Jo made the announcement to Gran that she wanted to take some time off.

Grace's heart flickered with the shock of encountering

something she knew had been concealing itself round the corner for years. This child was her mother's daughter all right; it had to happen, she was going just the same way. Grace had allowed herself to hope that perhaps this one could have been influenced along the right lines; but she knew all along that there was really no hope. When the worst actually came about, it was all the more painful because of the dread that had preceded it.

'Time off?' she shouted. 'And when have I ever had time off? Tell me that. Never would have dreamed of it; didn't have no holidays in my day, no money for that sort of thing. School holidays just meant a bit more work on the farm, that's all. And I didn't have the sort of schooling you did either – for all the good it did you. So I didn't get no chance of idling away my time with books all day long, did I? Took on your grandfather when I was no more than a girl and promised to stand by him no matter what. And that's what I done, and that didn't include no time off, not on a farm it didn't.'

Grace's small, miserable world shrivelled about her, and she felt herself moulder within it. Life was unfair; God was unfair; she did not deserve this sort of punishment when she could not even work out the sin for which she was being punished. What was the point of it all? But despair must not be admitted, less still shown to others; weakness in a state of emergency was despicable and not to be countenanced.

'I'm sorry, Gran, really I am, but I'm not the same as you and times is different. Grampa says he'll get old Isaac down the road to lend a hand, and I shouldn't be that long.' *Not that long?* It could be for ever; she could be moving into a new life. Her mother might need looking after. She saw a small, brave, careworn figure bravely fighting to keep the wolf from the door. There was so much she might be able to do to help.

'Just have to have a break.' She wanted to tell her why, it was only fair, and she might be pleased if what Grampa said was true. He said that she was always on

207

to him to find out what had happened to Mumma, but he didn't want to be the one to tell her.

'I'm going to find Mumma,' she said, and there was a long drawn out silence as the information hovered round the room.

Grace was caught mid-track with the surprise of it. Had to collect her thoughts together for a minute or two. She felt uncontrollable rage building up inside her. Something to do with Jo doing something she had not been able to tackle herself; she felt she was somehow being blamed. What cheek!

'We're not good enough for you? Is that it? Find your mother indeed! And a lot of good that's going to do you, just supposing you ever do find her.' Supposing she did. Supposing she did. But she never would, that was certain. No sense worrying over that; that one wouldn't come back unless there was something worth coming back for. And she wouldn't want no grown child cramping her style, sure as eggs is eggs, she wouldn't want that.

'It isn't because you're not good enough – what a silly thing to say. I just want to find her, that's all. I want to see for myself. You never told me nothing but bad about her. I just want to find out, that's all.' She wished she hadn't told her; and how to explain about the money? Grampa's life would be made more of a misery than it already was if she knew about that.

'Needn't think we're going to pay you pocket money if you're not going to be here,' Grace said. She wouldn't get far, that was certain.

'I saved some,' Jo said, her heart pounding with the anxiety of it. 'And I've been doin' a bit of gardening for Mrs Barnes on Sundays.'

'You been spreadin' it around that we keep you short? There's gratitude for you I must say.'

Jo clenched her teeth. Keep quiet, for goodness sake keep quiet. Don't say nothing at all. Don't make it worse than it is. Nothing must get in the way of this turning point. She was darned if she was going to feel

guilty about it. Finding Mumma was the most important thing in the world. That knowledge made her feel
very much stronger. After she'd found Mumma, then
she could sit back and take stock and work out what to
do next. So got to succeed; no two ways about it; there
must be a way to find things out, and if there was a
way, then she would discover it. Quite a blessing she
was all on her own with no-one to turn to, because it
meant she'd have only herself to rely on; much better
not having to rely on other people. She felt sure God or
somebody would help her out if she really got herself
into a scrape. She suddenly had a moment of almost
tearful regret that Charlie wasn't there. The wretched
runaway deserter. Well, she'd jolly well show she
didn't need him – or anybody else for that matter. Even
if she didn't have the know-how at the moment, then
she would no doubt pick up skills on the way.

She felt quite drunk with the intensity of it all, and
set off on the bus to Penzance the following day, in her
best dress and shoes, with Grampa's nest egg, her
belongings rattling about in Grampa's old carpet bag,
and her heart and her head jammed full of expectation.

She found that she was perfectly right about having
the stamina and the ability to pick up skills along the
way. It was really not at all difficult if you were
determined. Officials were sometimes frightening and
often rather rude, but if you were persistent, and gave
back as good as you got, then you were able to find out
pretty well all you wanted to on the whole.

So many people to ask, from the first, disinterested
clerk in the library, on to the Town Hall in Penzance;
kind people, bored people, bossy people, interested,
helpful people. And then all these little bits of information heard, some useless, some leading her on to
other possible leads, sorted and written down pain-
stakingly in a notebook. The more she enquired, the
more she began to enjoy.

As she proceeded on her extraordinary journey,
many of the pictures she had held in her head for so

long were shattered, one by one. There were a few disappointments, and sometimes a great deal of astonishment that her imagination could be so much at fault. She had never, for instance, conjured up sounds to go with the vision: thoughts of train journeys had merely been accompanied by the choo choo of childhood, so that the biddlydum biddlydum, with a biddly-da-da-da over points and the terrifying explosive force of two express trains passing each other were a revelation. She marvelled at the discovery that telegraph wires seen from a moving train seemed alive as they flew up and down in graceful curves outside the window. The sad suburbs of South London that went on for ever, made her feel like crying with the sameness of the view of roofs, chimneys and smoke, but the echoing clatter of Paddington Station excited her. She was finally able to see the specks of dust, described by her teacher all those years ago, clear in the sun shining through the glass roof, and she gasped with astonishment to think that the world, floating in space, was no bigger than one of them. Where was the need for imaginary worlds when the real one was beyond belief?

The quest for Mumma was like a frantic treasure hunt, with a priceless treasure that it was imperative to discover; life depended on it. It was a malevolent game, with death at the end if you failed to find the treasure. A game you could never give up; it had to be played out.

Jo sat, finally, in her YWCA hostel room, with very little money left. In her hand was a small piece of paper, torn from the notebook that she had bought in Penzance at the start of the great treasure hunt. On it, there was a name and an address: Mrs Jennifer Bowen, who lived in Woking, Surrey.

The treasure hunt clues, as she had come across them, had been difficult to decipher, because they had been impossible to believe. First the vague knowledge, from something – overheard perhaps? Mumma's a soldier — was this true? Women soldiers were called ATS in the war, now they were called WRACS: this from books in the library about the war. Then finally, many questions, interviews and enquiries later, the name on a list: Private ATS 372413 TREMAYNE Jennifer. There, on paper, was a perfectly unidentifiable Mumma, who had to be conjured up in the mind as a strange figure in a khaki uniform, standing strictly to attention. Jo could see the figure, but couldn't really identify it as Mumma. It was all too unlikely.

Then the journey to London, to find more clues: great buildings, endless traffic, thronging people, red buses, tube trains, moving staircases and a strange, hostel bed in the YWCA. Jo found the adventure beginning to pall, because she could not believe in this little khaki cut-out figure, standing to attention: it seemed to bear no relation to the treasure at the end of the search. Must be that she would soon uncover some new fact that would make it all real again. Must be that.

What she did find out next didn't really do anything at all to turn unreality into reality:

'Private ATS 372413 TREMAYNE Jennifer,' she read. 'September 1944: Married BOWEN Martin S. Captain, Parachute Regiment. November 1944. Released from duty because of pregnancy.'

The world took an extra turn at that moment, and Jo swirled with it, returning to earth dizzy and sick.

Mrs Martin S. Bowen, with a husband and child *her Mumma*? Not possible; obviously a mistake. This was another Jennifer Tremayne; could easily be; not such an uncommon name.

This peeling off of layer after layer of certainty and misconception was also a stripping of part of her own childhood. With every new discovery, Mumma had become less and less like herself, until there she stood, stripped of all her finery, changed from that soft, gentle-smelling dream of comfort and security, first into a rigid, khaki-clad soldier and now into something known to the world as Mrs Jennifer Bowen who was

211

pregnant. What, at the beginning of the search, had been buried treasure, had become a name and address on a piece of paper. Could Mrs Jennifer Bowen, living in Woking, really be Mumma? It was quite beyond belief, but the clues had led up to this, so it had to be checked out. Possibly a further clue would be waiting for her there, and that would lead her to the real treasure.

It meant another train journey. She had just enough to get her there; a one-way ticket. Must be meant, thought Jo, it's an omen, means I'm going to stay there, means she won't be able to let me go. She supposed she should write or telephone first, but there wasn't time to write, the money would run out, and the idea of claiming the treasure by telephone was an impossibility. Tring Tring. Then, 'Hullo Mumma, this is your daughter, Joanne.' It was unthinkable. All this confused thinking, it was driving her mad. Was Mrs Jennifer Bowen really Mumma or wasn't she? She'd just have to go and see; much better that way. Mother meeting daughter must be a wonderful moment and would have to be acted out for real, otherwise it would be a let down and an embarrassment. There'd be no embarrassment between a mother and her long-lost daughter when they were actually facing each other; couldn't possibly be.

The whole adventure then turned into some vague sort of dream. The search had been real and exciting, and had carried her forward in a great surge of ebullience and ferment, but now it was different, because the search was done, the striving had ceased, and all that was left was the uncovering of the treasure that was beginning not to sound like a treasure at all. She ate half a sandwich that she had bought yesterday and set out.

The journey was not at all real, but this time, the unreality was like a vacuum, because it was not filled with comforting fantasies of dancing telegraph wires or magic noises off; it had no sparkling vision of a warm, loving fairy-tale mother waiting expectantly at the other end. Jo felt herself suspended, as though she was floating under water and waiting to die. There was no sound, and movement was involuntary and restricted because of being in this buoyant sea full of emptiness.

The walk from the station was a long one. She had looked up the route on a map before she started out, and knew exactly which turnings to take. The only difference being that she found it impossible to match the uncluttered lines on the map with the houses and trees along the way. The lines on the map had not prepared her for the extraordinarily unfamiliar look that the whole district had. She had never seen houses like this before, they seemed far too clean and well kept, and had unnaturally tidy gardens all round them. They all had garages with very clean cars standing in front of them. She saw the windows, veiled discreetly with net, looking out at her with closed disapproval. What was a country farm girl doing here, in all this respectability? Her best dress and coat were quite out of place, and all the well-mannered, newly-painted doors were firmly, though quite politely shut against her.

She looked at the map again; bound to feel out of place in new surroundings; nothing she could do about it, so get on with the business in hand. But a tremor of anxiety shot through her; she felt like an alien and had the sudden dread that the people behind all those closed doors would speak in some outlandish language that she wouldn't be able to understand. Silly idea, she'd grown out of all these stupid imaginings long ago.

Second right and then straight on till you get to a church. Shouldn't be all that difficult to find. More posh, detached houses, red brick or painted white, with their gardens full of dahlias and marigolds and well-controlled shrubs. Number thirty-seven it said on the paper, and here was a three and a seven in brass stuck on a gate post, so she walked up the path and rang the bell. Ding-dong. Ding-dong. She'd heard one of those sort of doorbells before, but only once. There was a scuffle and a thump, and the door was opened by a girl of about ten, with a younger boy peering round her shoulder: no thoughts, just two strange children.

'Is Mrs Jennifer Bowen at home?'

The children chased each other back through the hall and out into the garden beyond without answering.

'Mum! It's a lady for you.' A *lady*! What a funny idea. And she was left on the doorstep with a long, empty hall stretching away in front of her. Thick, patterned carpet on the floor, walls, cream paint, and a hatstand with children's coats and a man's hat and two umbrellas.

Was there a small 'Tchk' of irritation before the quick footsteps started down the stairs? Jo wasn't sure, but she felt very strongly that she was being an intolerable nuisance, and her mind filled up with apologetic opening gambits.

A neat, smart figure appeared at the end of the hall, silhouetted against the light of the open door into the garden: obviously Mrs Jennifer Bowen.

'Yes?'

Jo kept her eyes fixed on Jennifer Bowen's shoes: black patent leather court, with rather high heels.

'I'm Joanne,' she said in a voice that croaked. 'Hallo Mumma,' and she looked up but felt quite unable to move.

There was total silence between them, which was disturbed only by sounds of the children shouting in the garden, a dog barking and a blackbird singing in a lilac tree by the front gate.

'Jo-Anne?' Jenny said it very slowly, and clung on to the door to stop things reeling about her. *'Jo-Anne?'*

No kisses, no hugs, no glad cries of delight, no explosion of sentiment. Jo waited, transfixed, on the doorstep, because this wasn't Mumma. This was a lady

214

in a tight black skirt and a white frilly blouse, clinging to a door in a state of shock. Nothing at all like the real Mumma: the face was wrong, the expression was wrong, even the smell was wrong. Better start apologizing.

'I'm sorry I didn't warn you I was coming but . . .' Couldn't say she hadn't enough money; she might think she was begging, 'I only just found out and I thought it would be difficult to explain on the telephone.'

Jenny felt the foundations of her life rocking about her. Because this had become her life now; she had finally settled into accepting it and believing in it – enjoying it even. It had seemed safe for quite a few years now.

'I can't believe it, I just can't believe it.' She covered her mouth with her hands, and tears welled up into her eyes. 'Can't be, can't be. Not little Jojo.'

They still stood on the doorstep, a long, cold distance apart. Jo didn't feel like crying; she didn't feel anything at all, except sadness 'that she had caused her mother distress. As she continued to stand there, the realization that the two children were her brother and sister made her jerk upright in surprise; how extraordinary.

Jenny came suddenly down to earth. 'You'd better come in,' she said, opening a door out of the hall. 'Come in here and let me look at you. How on earth – why didn't you let me know? It's such a shock – I can't take it in at all – you're so *big*. I can't believe it's happening. Why did you – I mean what made you – why didn't you write first? You never wrote to me and I thought – I thought . . .'

The room was full of white hard light and white soft furniture with cushions and late roses and more dahlias in vases, and a piano and a cabinet full of china ornaments. Nothing like it was at home, where everything was dark and restful and unfrightening.

'They never gave me your letters, they never told me

where you were. They didn't know where you were, so I thought I'd come and find you.'

Still no kisses, no hugs, no delight. Just nothing at all, except that she felt a bit sick. All this whiteness made her feel sick.

Jenny also felt sick, and panic attacked her suddenly without warning, making her catch her breath. Martin would be coming home soon; what a hideous situation.

They still stood, several miles apart, until Jenny indicated one of the soft, white chairs, 'Sit down, sit down for a minute – where are you staying?'

'I'm not, I came down from London.' With no money to get back, but that couldn't be mentioned. No kisses, no hugs, no love, no Mumma.

'You living in London then? What are you doing? Aren't you with Mum and Dad any more? I thought you'd be so happy down there on the farm with them. What happened? Did you misbehave or something? Didn't get yourself in trouble or anything, did you?'

'No, I just came up to look for you.' Wanted to know what sort of a mother it was who could abandon her own baby. Resentment flared very suddenly, and with it something like black hatred for this unknown stranger living in Woking with a husband and two children. 'Sorry if I've made things awkward.' Keep control, keep control, don't let things upset you. Made a big mistake it seems.

Jenny suddenly wanted to cry but fought it back; no good to give way, something had to be worked out to make this whole ghastly situation surmountable. 'Oh Jojo, you don't know what I've been through. I thought you were happy and contented with Dad and Mum, I didn't want to bring you back into all the difficulties I've had to go through. You just don't know what it was like. Losing Steve first of all – you didn't know I lost Steve I suppose. He was killed early on, and then I went through hell, being ill and depressed and nearly out of my mind, and it's only lately that I've felt that life was worth living. Only recently that I've been strong enough to cope. I got married to Martin who's just wonderful to me, just wonderful.' She paused for a moment. 'He doesn't know about you.'

The two children burst into the room, 'Mum, is it lunch time? We're hungry. Can we have some biscuits?'

Jenny composed her face into a tight smile. 'No – at least, I haven't had time to do the lunch yet, you'll have to wait. I suppose you may have a biscuit. Just one each, that's all.' She caught the boy by the arm as he turned to go. 'Jeremy and Lucy, this is a long-lost cousin of yours; come and say how d'you do.'

They stopped, sulkily, in their tracks and stared at Jo aggressively, 'How d'you do,' they said, without enthusiasm, and Jo disliked them immediately. Spoilt little brats. 'Hallo,' she said, in an equally hostile tone, without smiling. They looked a little shocked and flung themselves out of the room to find the biscuits.

Jenny turned back to Jo, apology in her expression. 'Can't break it to them so suddenly, I'll have to do it gradually. It would be much too much of a shock to come straight out with it.'

Of course it would; almost as great a shock as discovering that this strange woman was your mother.

'Would you like some lunch?' Jenny said, remembering Martin never came back to lunch on Wednesdays. 'I expect you're hungry. Are you going straight back home or are you staying in London for a bit?'

Straight back home! That was rich, that was; home was where your mother was, wasn't it? All Jo knew was that she wanted to get out of this strange place that wasn't her home and away from this strange woman who wasn't her mother.

'Once I've had a bit of time to pull myself together,' Jenny said, 'perhaps you could up and stay with us for a few days; so that we can get to know each other properly.' Her laugh had a very false sound, Jo thought. 'Hope you won't mind being a long-lost cousin for a bit, just until I think the children are old enough to understand the situation.'

Mind? Of course she'd mind. She, Joanne Tremayne, was Mumma's real daughter, wasn't she? Not that stuck up, bad-mannered Lucy type. Furious tears stuck in her throat but were not permitted to appear.

'If you could give me a sandwich and a cup of tea and some money for my fare to London, I should be much obliged, because I shall be getting back to Penzance on the night train. I have my return ticket. I will send back the money as soon as I get *home*.'

Jenny heard the anger, and found herself responding with some irritation. Jo was surely old enough to realize the situation she had put them all in? What a thing to do, drop a bombshell like this. Then immediately came the rush of guilt again, causing her whole body to shake in a kind of rigor. This was her little Jojo, her own baby; how was it possible for her to view her with such disaffection? What a trauma she had been plunged into. Just not possible to sort it out in a few stressful moments.

'You have to give me a bit of time to sort myself out. You've given me such a terrible shock, turning up like this without writing or anything. Of course I'll give you some money, look, here's five pounds to be going on with; perhaps I could arrange to send you something regularly if you'd like that.'

Jo didn't bother to answer that bit. 'Thank you,' she said, stuffing the note in her pocket. 'I'd best be going now.' She couldn't wait to get out. It suddenly became difficult to hold back the great storm of distress that was building up inside her; building up, building up all the time, but it had to be controlled until she got out.

'No, no, you can't go so soon. Stay and have lunch, and then I'll drive you to the station.' The least she could do, and all quite safe. Joanne was the grand-daughter of one of Will's brothers, just turned up out of the blue. Could be quite easily explained, even to Martin, because the children would be sure to talk. Jenny's composure began to return; that's what she

218

must do. Couldn't send her packing like that; never forgive herself. 'Wait there a minute and I'll make some coffee and biscuits, and then you can go out and make friends with the children while I get the lunch.' She was smiling now, because she saw a happy way out. 'You just make yourself comfortable, dear, I'll be back in a minute with some coffee.'

She left the room and Jo heard her walking down the hallway. She waited a moment or two, listening to the kettle being filled and cups clinking on a tray, and then she crept out of the room, out of the door, down the path, and away down the street as fast as she could run.

Her mouth was open with the exertion and with the horror, and tears streamed down her cheeks to be swept away by the force of the wind in her face. She needed to get away from all this pretence. There was nothing real here – must get back to reality. Had to go home. It was difficult to draw breath fast enough, and each gasp made her throat raw, it was like running in a nightmare when your legs won't move properly. Everything hurt, particularly both her feet, which were painfully in contact with the unrelenting ground beneath them.

27

Nothing, then, to do, except run back home with the help of Mumma's five pound note. Buy a present for Gran and Grampa in Penzance, and then home on the bus. And that was it. Very peculiar, how *ordinary* she felt; just as though nothing much had happened, other than her having a few days off from the everyday work on the farm. First time she'd ever done that, so altogether a new experience. She slept a little on the milk train back to Penzance, but saw, through the train windows, the dawn come up slowly, with pink clouds in an azure sky. Red sky in the morning, shepherd's warning – so it would probably rain later.

As the train steamed into Penzance station, Jo was surprised to feel a glow of pleasure at recognizing familiar landmarks. They were like old friends, welcoming her back. She was no alien here. Had she really only been away a few days? Seemed like a lifetime. For a second, there shot through her mind a shattering flashback of a distant horror, but it was gone almost as soon as it had surfaced, and she emerged from the station, bought a brass toasting fork with a Cornish piskie on the handle for Gran and Grampa, before catching the bus to Zennor.

They were both sitting in the kitchen when she opened the door, drinking tea in total silence. The relief she felt at seeing them there, in the small dark kitchen, with the fire, burning slowly away in the range and Grampa's long pants hung up, along with a shirt and some socks on the airer strung up to the ceiling, was overwhelming. She ran in and hugged them both, which left them startled and uncomprehending.

'I've got you a present,' Jo said, putting the wrapped toasting fork on the table. 'Go on, undo it and see,' and she watched as Gran fumbled with the paper. 'We wanted a new one, didn't we? Because doing it on an ordinary fork always burns your hands, doesn't it? Do you like it Gran? I thought you'd like the piskie, and you've got other brass things, haven't you? Do you like it?'

Grace managed a smile, which went along with a small flush of pleasure that caused her quite a bit of surprise. 'Very nice,' she said, 'very nice indeed. We'll hang it by the fireside.' And they both looked at Jo, full of questions kept under control.

She sat down opposite them and poured herself a cup of tea. 'I found her,' she said. 'She's quite all right;

married to someone called Mr Bowen and they have two children called Lucy and Jeremy.' She glanced at both of them anxiously. 'Two more grandchildren for you,' but their expressions didn't change, so she went on. 'I think they're quite rich; they have a smart house, quite big, with a garden. I didn't like the children much, but then I didn't get much time to talk to them, I wasn't there long. She asked about you, wanted to know all about you.' Might as well pretend a bit, because there didn't seem much else to tell them.

They both continued to look at her, silently, waiting for more, but what more was there? 'I could never fit in with that sort of life,' she told them. 'Not our style at all. All cold and clean and smart. She asked me to stay with them, but I didn't fancy it at all. Wouldn't feel at home there, so I made a suggestion . . .' The idea came to her as she related it; such a very good idea it was. 'She wanted to do something for me, so I said well I think you ought to do something for Gran and Grampa because of what they done for me and because you do owe them something for my keep all those years.'

Grace opened her mouth to say something, but thought better of it and remained silent, and Jo continued describing the idea that was busy forming itself in her head as she spoke. 'I told her that the farm could do with a bit of a boost, and what with you two getting on a bit, it needs money to bring it up to date with some machinery, perhaps, to make things easier for all of us. So she's going to send us some, regular like, so that we can buy new things and get a bit of help. Not charity, mind, but just some of what she owes you for all you've spent on me. Said she wanted to do that, was very pleased with the idea she could do something in return.'

What a wonderful idea! And Jenny would make no fuss about it, she was positive certain of that, because she wouldn't want the new family to know anything about it. Her old man would just think he was helping

221

out some of Jenny's poor relations. Jenny would see to it that he wouldn't mind doing that.

It was a tremendous relief to be back home with no thought of what could be waiting outside for you, but only the knowledge that you had a task to complete, here and now, and in the midst of things warm and familiar. She wrote off to Jenny that night and proposed her plan, promising to send, later, an itemized list of things they might need to make the farm into a more profitable affair – or should she, she asked, write to Mr Bowen to explain the idea?

Quite soon after Jo had thought of her splendid idea, Peter discovered that his own life was devoid of any sort of ideas at all. With the problems gone, nothing appeared to have moved in to take their place. Life was soft, gentle and extremely boring. He should, he thought, be relishing the deep satisfaction of living the sort of life he had always longed for. So why this empty sensation of existing in a void?

Cisco seemed to be a perfect companion, even to the extent of somehow sensing Peter's irritation and depression on occasions, and taking himself off for a few days until the air had cleared. Peter was unsure whether he appreciated or resented this, but was always so pleased to see him when he came back that explanations never seemed necessary. But where did he go?

'Just dropped in on some friends of mine.' So then there was the jealousy. He shouldn't have friends Peter didn't know about. But at the same time, his occasional absences did clear the air. Peter sometimes looked on them as sharp slaps that brought him, Peter, to his senses.

'You're a bit of a disciplinarian,' he once said. 'You don't let me sulk.' He paused to think how best to put the next thought: 'Do you think the time has come for us to move on?'

'Trying to tell me you're tired of me?'

'No, of course I'm not.'

'So you want to split up and it's kinder to make me the one that wants to do it.'

'I didn't say I wanted to split.'

'But you're realizing you want more out of life than a cottage, two goats and me.'

'You forgot the hens.'

But it wasn't a funny enough remark to laugh at, and Peter didn't pursue it. It was several minutes later that he started up the conversation again.

'Of course you're right,' he said. 'I'm getting restless. Being here on our own doesn't seem to be the answer for me. I feel I'm living in a void.'

'Which you are.'

'You feel it too?'

'I don't *feel* it, because I am perfectly content to live in a void with you. Doesn't worry me at all. But then I would be perfectly content to live in a maelstrom if you were there too.'

'Meaning your love is stronger than mine?'

'Meaning nothing of the sort. I just like being with you.'

'And all these friends you go and see, you like living with them too?'

'I would if they felt the same, but they don't. They wouldn't want me to live with them.'

'But I'm too weak to stand on my own feet, is that it?'

'You're being tiresomely obtuse.'

It was a short time after this conversation that a telegram arrived from Alec Tibb's office. *Your mother seriously ill suggest you return* it read.

'I shall have to go,' Peter grasped the opportunity with guilty satisfaction.

'Why will you have to go? You walked out on your family because they were unsatisfactory and because they were ruining your life. Why do you have to return because one member of them is dying?'

'It's my mother.'

Cisco picked up a large earthenware bowl full of potatoes and flung it on the ground, smashing it to pieces. 'And who is your mother? By your own description, she is an insensitive, selfish tyrant, so why should you go running back to her? If you do, they will only trap you again, and you will be lost.'

Peter felt his hackles rising. 'You're being ridiculous.' He started to pick up the potatoes and the broken pieces of pottery, shaken by Cisco's reaction and the fact that he had destroyed a bowl both of them had chosen together and treasured.

'If you go,' Cisco shouted, 'I shall follow you. You belong here and to me – not to that material sort of life that you rejected. I shall follow you wherever you go.'

'Well, if you do, you could have one of the cottages on the estate, you'd be very welcome.'

'I don't need your bloody charity. I have friends in the district – known the place since I was a boy.'

'Really?' Peter was startled: he'd never mentioned that before. But Cisco didn't wait for an answer, he stormed out of the house, pushing past with such force that Peter fell on the floor and was left, shaking and distraught, in a kind of whirlwind of emotional horror.

He drove back to Zennor that night.

There was a brisk atmosphere of organization and efficient management at Petherick Hall when he arrived early the next morning. All the sisters were in the dining room, having breakfast.

Bridget put down her cup with a clatter. 'My God! Look who's here. We thought you must be dead. What on earth are you doing here? Come to make sure we're doing our jobs properly? Did you know Mother is dying?'

Cynthia and Daphne both showed distress. 'Bridgie, really . . .'

'I was told.'

'Told? Who told you?' Bridget glanced round the table. 'D'you mean to say one of us—?'

224

'I was in touch with Tibbs.'

'The little rat, so he knew where you were all the time. I thought he did, but he's so ultra devious.'

'Come and sit down, Piggy.' Daphne pulled a chair out for him. 'You'd like some coffee I'm sure. Cyn, pour him some coffee.'

Piggy! He'd forgotten all about that, and as he looked round these sisters of his, he felt a tremendous desire to laugh. How ridiculous they all were! Just like a troupe of circus clowns. He felt a great affection for the whole group.

'How's Mother?' he said. 'What's wrong with her?'

'A stroke. She's pretty bad, can't talk. Doctor says another one could finish her. One almost hopes . . .'

Cynthia set the coffee in front of him. 'Bridgie, *really.*'

'Well, I don't relish the idea of Mother paralysed and speechless for years to come; don't know about you lot.'

Peter picked up his coffee. 'I'll go and see her,' he said. 'No,' as Daphne and Dorothy got up to accompany him, 'I'll go on my own.'

'You sure?' Daphne asked. 'You're not used to things like this, Piggy. She's not the same as when you last saw her.'

He left the room without answering and walked up the wide staircase. Scarcely could remember when he walked up this staircase last: always seemed to be running up it before – escaping from something or other. He rested his hand on the oak banister and enjoyed the smoothness.

Bea was propped on pillows, and a nurse hovered. 'I'm Peter Petherick,' he said, putting down the cup and extending his hand. 'I'd like to spend a little time with my mother.'

The way the nurse shook his hand with what appeared to be respect, surprised him greatly. 'Oh yes, of course, Mr Petherick. So glad you could get here, I'm sure your sisters will be much relieved that you have come to take charge of things.' She left the room silently, humbly almost, he thought. How extraordinary.

Bea looked ghastly: a pallid white, with her face dragged hideously down to one side. He felt a wave of pity and love sweep through him, leaving him with his eyes full of tears and his throat restricted. What a great indignity for such a fine old war horse. He squeezed her hand and found himself agreeing with Bridget.

'Hullo Mother,' he said, and her eyes swung round towards him. Was it fury? Was it desolation? He preferred fury. 'You don't have to worry,' he said. 'I've grown up a lot since I've been away. Not frightened of you any more, nor of any of that lot downstairs.' You could imagine that the eyes had a twinkle; it was comfortable to imagine that. 'I feel absolutely capable of dealing with them, and I promise you I'll see that the farm is properly and profitably run. Sorry I've been such a pain.'

There was no mistaking the firm squeeze of his hand in hers. She had fully understood and fully approved. Impossible to know whether or not she was surprised at the metamorphosis of her disappointing son, but he had the feeling that she wasn't, so he gave her a big wink and a kiss and went downstairs to take up the reins of government.

28

Bea took no time at all to die. It was the night after Peter's arrival that she had a further stroke from which she never recovered consciousness.

'Well, you got your wish, Bridgie,' Cynthia said, tearfully, as the family gathered the next morning. 'Scarcely time to say goodbye.'

'And isn't that just how she'd have wanted it? No

fuss, no histrionics, and we'll arrange the funeral just the same way; nice quiet cremation and a notice in the *Times* too late for people to attend.'

Peter, who had been the only one with Bea when she died, finished his mouthful of toast and marmalade. There had been a time, hadn't there, aeons ago, when he had spat out an overchewed mouthful, to Bea's intense fury? He remembered vaguely and smiled at the memory. 'Bea would not have liked that,' he said, wondering at himself for using her name in that way, and being aware of the shocked silence his remark brought about.

'What?' Bridget's exclamation was less of a question than a shout of amazement.

'Bea would hate to be shovelled away into the fire without so much as a cheer,' he said, smiling round at his astonished sisters. 'She would prefer a slap-up do, like Pa had. I suggest we order the champagne and make arrangements with the vicar for the family grave to be prepared. We'll have a great party, to make up for the one I didn't have when I was twenty-one.'

And that's how it was. Peter found himself enjoying the preparations for his mother's final, outrageous gesture, set to shock the neighbours. A celebration, he told himself, of death and resurrection; but the resurrection was his own.

Down at Tremayne's Farm over the past few months, Jo had been caught up in the new and exciting occupation of taking over and reorganizing her grandparents' lives. Grace found that her sound and fury seemed to have little effect any more. It was an extraordinary turnabout, and one she could not rightly fathom. 'The cheek of the girl,' she said to Will. But the venom was no longer obvious in the way she said it. 'Thinking she can lord it over us. Don't know what got into her when she was up in London. Coming back here thinking she can turn our lives upsidedown when

227

we was perfectly content and comfortable with the life we had. Cheek, I call it.'

Will was tickled to death with the change in his granddaughter. 'You're a bloody little marvel,' he told her. 'Getting money out of that Jenny like that. Don't know how you done it.'

'It's called blackmail,' Jo said, laughing with him, 'or waking up out of a dream, or getting down to brass tacks. I grew up, that's all. Not sure if that's altogether a good thing, but I think it might make life a little easier.'

She hired a farm hand and made enquiries and a down payment on a milking machine, bought more cows, renovated the pigsties, and kept detailed accounts. She increased butter production and started to advertise in Penzance papers. The farm began to take off, and even Grace found life easier and complained far less. Couldn't quite let go, mind, but Joanne had certainly perked up a bit and become quite useful. Things was definitely easier.

The news of Bea's death reached Jo, through village talk, a few hours after it had occurred, and back came the memories, the depression, the painful hurt of having been rejected and Charlie's venomous voice once again. She swore at herself silently. What an idiot: thought she was over it; been far too busy to mind all that, but now it swept back with a rush, because Peter would be here again; sure to come back, and there was all that unfinished business to deal with. Why was it more difficult to cope with that, than it was to recover from the Mumma shock? Just because it was unfinished, she supposed; like a sore that wouldn't heal. No proper conclusion. And Charlie's voice keeping on about him being a madman.

She heard there was to be a big party for everyone, villagers included, and was faintly shocked. What did those old women think they were up to? *Celebrating* their mother's death? But she had to smile in spite of herself; just what the old girl would have liked – to be celebrated; but the Petherick women would never have

228

thought of it like that. So why—? Sounded much more like an idea Peter might have had, but he'd never be strong enough to carry it out with that lot on his back. Anyway, she certainly wasn't going; much too much to do. And she wasn't going to go on up there as one of the crowd. Not likely.

Winter set in with a vengeance that same week, with freezing gales and heavy snowfalls. Jo felt her spirits decline with the weather. Why didn't he come and see her? Had he noticed that she hadn't been at the funeral party? Had he so completely wiped her out of his mind? Or had the whole thing been an illusion? One of her old mind pictures perhaps. Had anything really happened between them? Had it just been a great big pretend, like all those other pretends?

'Don't say I didn't warn you.' Charlie droned into her ear every night. 'He'll do you in, just see if he don't.'

It was about ten days later, after a heavy snowfall, and when she was helping to shovel the snow from the doors of the more helpless old in the village, that Jo looked up from her efforts, and saw Peter approaching down the road.

After the first seizure of mind-blowing shock that raced through her, she retreated into a frozen numbness, while her heartbeat took hold of itself again.

'Get him before he gets you,' said Charlie.

In the blank space where thoughts had evaporated, she remembered a time, not all that long ago, when she had mistaken Peter for Charlie. Today though, there was no mistaking him: it was not Charlie, but Peter, dressed in heavy snow boots, bulky anorak and scarf, and looking nothing like the Peter she had last seen – was it only six months ago? It seemed like a lifetime. He was recognizable, but strangely different. She could have sworn he had grown taller, and had his hair ever been as long as that? It was over his collar, and his cheeks were positively glowing red – they had never, ever done that before; he had been pale as a ghost, with his fair, curly hair cropped short. This was no dangerous maniac approaching: it was the person she loved.

She stopped her shovelling, panting with the effort she had been making, and with the shovel grasped in both her hands. The painful churning of her stomach made her clutch at it through her coat.

She could find nothing at all to say, as this familiar stranger came towards her. Why had she never thought of him as a man before? Boy, yes, but never a *man*.

He came bounding up to her, slithering on the icy path, flung his arms round her, shovel and all, and hugged her. 'I've longed for this moment for six months,' he said. 'Thought about it at odd hours of every day, wondered just what it would be like – whether it would ever take place at all. Whether you'd remember me, whether you'd ever want to see me again. Can I help you sweep?'

She handed him the shovel silently, and took up a broom. It was all rather embarrassing; a great many people must have seen the hug. The secret, if it could be called a secret at this late date, was certainly out now; the whole village would hear of that greeting before the day was out. Did it matter any more? He obviously didn't mean nothing by it, after all. Hugs was probably the way his sort greeted everybody. Didn't mean nothing at all. 'You dig it out to the gate,' she said, 'and I'll sweep up after you. Don't want poor old Mrs Barnes here to slip up when she sets out.'

'Absolutely not,' Peter said, flinging a heaped shovelful of snow on to the mound beside the swept path. 'Can't have Mrs Barnes slipping up. You look wonderful, Jo. Different and yet the same. I have so much to tell you.'

This was madness; did he think he could just waltz back into her life as though nothing had happened? But then *had* anything happened? Was it all in her imagination?

'How could you have gone off like that without saying nothing?' She swept furiously behind his shovelling.

'But I didn't think, I mean I didn't know – I mean – I never dreamed you would be interested in what I did.'

So why had she expected him to tell her? There had been nothing between them except a few conversations and one solitary kiss. How could she possibly expect him to inform her about his movements?

Peter stopped shovelling: 'I thought it would be cheek to tell you I was going away for a bit. I didn't think I had the right to imagine you would be interested.'

And of course, she didn't have the right to be interested. She looked at him, confused. 'I missed you.'

'Did you? Did you really? Oh Jo, I'm so glad you did. You always seemed so confident and so secure, I didn't believe you'd give me a thought.'

'You're loopy, you are. I've been so lonely since you been gone, I nearly died of it.'

Peter leaned on the shovel, and stared at her, but she kept sweeping to hide her confusion.

'I've got so much to tell you,' he said. 'So much has happened. And I would just love to kiss you again. Do you remember that kiss in the barn? Do you think I could kiss you now? I have a tremendous urge.'

'Indeed you cannot,' she looked round anxiously and saw the Vicar pass the gate. 'Good morning, Vicar; big storm last night, weren't it?'

'It certainly was, Miss Tremayne. How good of you to come out and give a hand. And you too, Mr Petherick. Haven't seen you around for a very long time. Did I hear you had been visiting – now where was it? Some Franciscan brotherhood – Cerne Abbas was it? Most interesting to hear of such leanings, I had not realized . . .' There had been so much idle talk and gossip about the boy during his absence; good that he was back. Only hoped he hadn't been up to some mischief and bad ways. Such a strange, surly lad he had always seemed; so secretive. And now the extraordinary party he had arranged round his mother's funeral; quite shocking. But someone had reported seeing him at the Franciscan community at Cerne Abbas. Sounded most unlikely.

How on earth had that got out? Peter wondered. He didn't think anyone knew. 'Yes ... er ... yes, I did spend some time as a visitor.' Did Jo know? If not, he would have to explain – sort of apologize – rather than tell it as an adventure.

The Vicar raised his hat and passed on his way, leaving a hint of anxiety between the two of them at the need for explanation. Peter stopped shovelling, and his arms hung limply by his side; confidence gone.

Jo continued to sweep briskly. 'What's this Brotherhood then? And how did Vicar know you was there? Did you tell him?'

'No I didn't tell him. I didn't tell anyone. Haven't an idea how he knew. It's a monastery – like I told you, you remember?'

She remembered all right, but he didn't say he was definitely going; he never told her that. He could have said; could easily have said.

'A lot happened there,' he went on. 'Such a tremendous lot. I want to talk to you about it. Can we go somewhere?'

Jo stopped sweeping, unconvinced. He could have told her before; probably just wanted to make excuses and she wasn't interested in excuses. He shouldn't never have put her through such an agonizing time.

'Like where?' she said. 'Gran would have a fit if I took you home, and your sisters would do likewise if you took me. I don't fancy sitting out in all this snow either.'

'We could go into St Ives. There are plenty of cafés and tea shops where we could sit.'

They were both silent, thinking of the embarrassment of sitting in an empty café, with their conversation echoing round the void, and the humour struck them both at the same time.

'We could as well take a megaphone and broadcast our conversation from the church steeple,' Jo said, beginning to laugh. 'Truth is, there's no place round here that you and I can go to in winter where we'd not be noticed.'

He was laughing too. 'Let's go to Penzance. That's big enough to lose ourselves in.'

'Penzance? That'd take the morning. How d'you think I'm going to take the morning off and not be noticed? And how do we get to Penzance anyways? Don't expect buses will be running in this weather.'

'I've got a new car. I bought one with some of my money. And perhaps your grandfather would let you off if you asked him nicely.'

Jo smiled; funny, he was thinking things were just as they were when he left, having to ask Grampa's permission and that. He didn't know anything about anything. 'I've got quite a bit to tell you and all,' she said.

To go to Penzance with Peter in his new car seemed an excellent idea. All the gloom, all the annoyance, all the resentment melted into the air at the thought; she could recall none of it. The sun had just come out and life was about to shoot off again into one of its more brilliant phases. How was it possible for feelings to turn turtle like this? For life to stand on its head?

'You stay here and finish off the path,' she said. 'And then you knock on the door and tell old Mrs Barnes that it's all nice and safe for her now; and I'll go and tell Grampa where I'm going.'

She ran off, sliding and slithering on the ice, crunching on the snow, her cheeks scarlet with the exertion and excitement of it all. How could she have dreamed he would desert her? And sucks to Charlie, with all his silly scaremongering.

He watched her go with a great glow of love and delight; and only a short time ago, he had been closeted in his bedroom, afraid to approach her in case she had forgotten him. In case she showed no interest. In case she said no.

*

But they never got to Penzance that day; a blizzard closed in around them before the car reached the main road, and in the blindness of the storm, Peter ran it into a snowdrift. The car burrowed quite deeply, and the overhang collapsed on top of them so that they were almost completely enveloped. The silence that ensued was total.

Finally, Jo let out the breath she was holding, into a long drawn-out 'Aa-a-a-aah,' and Peter relaxed his foot off the brake. 'Hell's bells,' he said. 'Now I've done it.' He felt a sense of urgent horror on the one hand, and of deep, satisfied peace on the other.

'Are you frightened?' he asked, after a moment or two.

She thought for several seconds before she answered, because she realized that she should be frightened, yet for some strange reason she was not. 'I know it's daft,' she said, 'but somehow I'm not. Are you?'

'When I think about it, yes, but I seem to have the certain belief that we are quite safe here.'

'What do you think we ought to do? Don't people die when they get shut in cars like this? Because of using up all the air?'

The simple answer to that was, 'Yes, people do,' but there didn't seem much point in saying that. 'We're not going to die,' he said. 'We've only just started living.'

'Sheep that are buried sometimes live for days and days.'

'Air pockets,' said Peter, and they both felt something like laughter welling up inside them at the idea of being like a sheep in an air pocket, but both quelled the feeling, for fear it should turn into crying. This calm was only a hair's breadth away from panic.

'The snow shouldn't be too deep above us on the road side,' Peter said, 'so if we wind down the back window a bit, then perhaps we could push the broom handle through the snow so that someone might see it.'

'Didn't you give the broom back to Mrs Barnes then?'

'No, I forgot.'

'She'll likely be upset; she told me it was her special broom and I'd got to be careful with it. And anyway, who's likely to see a broom handle?' Jo said, allowing a tiny burst of the laughter to escape.

Peter's restraint slipped a bit further, and he let fly an explosive spasm that was impossible to check, and in a second, they were both convulsed and helpless with hysterical laughter.

'It's really nothin' to laugh at,' Jo gasped, wiping her eyes.

'But it's so much better than crying,' said Peter, and they collapsed into laughter again.

As control gradually began to creep back, Peter said, 'We're quite near to the main road to Penzance I think, and there should be snowploughs in action. If we tie my scarf to the broom handle and push it up through the snow out of the back window, there's quite a chance of its being seen once the blizzard dies down a bit.'

'Funny not knowing whether or not it's still on. We seem shielded somehow against all that storming going on all round us.'

Peter's scarf was red. 'What luck I wore this one today and not that brown one I usually wear,' he said, tying it in a knot round the end of the broom handle. 'Now if we open the back window just a little, so that too much snow doesn't get inside, I'm sure the top of the handle will poke out of the snow and wave about a bit.'

After being busy and occupied making all possible arrangements for their rescue, a period of empty anxiety returned, and they climbed on to the back seat and, because they were numb with cold, crawled into the sleeping bag Peter kept in the car for emergencies.

'It's quite cosy,' Jo said. 'Bit of a tight fit, though.'

'Better than a tea shop, and much more private.'

'So now you're going to tell me all about why you took off like that.'

'You'll probably be bored.'

'So then I'll go to sleep and it'll help to pass the time.' His arm tightened round her, the desire to kiss built up in both of them.

She lay on her back, staring up at the roof, because if she faced him, their noses, and possibly their mouths would probably touch unless they held themselves apart. Her heart was bounding, and she was breathing much faster than usual. She wondered if they were going to die and then be found in each others' arms. People would think they were lovers. How difficult, because they weren't, and everyone would get the wrong impression and they would be dead, so they couldn't put it right. Gran would be terribly shocked; probably have a heart attack, and die as well, so that would be two of them gone. Poor old Grampa, it would be very upsetting for him.

What an unbelievable, make-believe situation this was. Was it really happening? Or was it just another of those mind stories she had lived with for so long? Could she actually be clamped together with Peter Petherick of Petherick Hall in a small sleeping bag, buried in a make-believe snowdrift, awaiting death? If this was reality, then it was more far-fetched than any unreality she had conjured up previously.

Peter's voice came as quite a shock when he started speaking again.

'How old are you, Jo?'

What a funny question. 'Turned seventeen these two months. What you want to know for?'

'Just a crazy idea I had. Didn't know you were as young as that.'

This couldn't really be happening, he decided, it was all madness; part of the fantasy in which he had spent so much of his life. He hadn't pulled out of it after all. And Cisco? That inspiring period he had spent with Cisco, struggling out of the mind's burrow? Was that part of the fantasy? Surely not. This snow womb was real all right; and this gorgeously warm girl creature he held in his arms at the moment, she was real too: living, breathing and loving, all in one. The other part of his life: the part Cisco wanted him to abandon.

He could hear Cisco's voice in his mind even now: 'She's no good to you, that one. Get rid of her; push her out – now. She'd freeze quick enough, and no-one would know. She'll be the death of you if you let her. Go on – push her out.'

'I met this extraordinary chap,' he said. 'He just about changed my whole life. That's what's been happening to me since I've been away. Made sense of most things; made me see things differently. I'm a different person now, to what I was.'

Jo tensed, and felt herself draw away from him, in spite of the physical closeness. Two people wrapped in a cocoon, how could one draw back in such a situation? If she'd been able to move her arms, she felt she might have pushed him in the chest and escaped there and then. So it was all an illusion. He wasn't thinking of her at all; never had been; of course he hadn't.

'So am I changed,' she said. He needn't think he was the only one that changed. He didn't mean any more to her than she did to him. They'd both grown up, that was all. 'I went and found my mother who'd abandoned me when I was little.'

There was a silence as Peter cast about in his mind for an adequate response. How to answer that sort of remark? 'Oh did you', or 'Good for you', didn't seem at all expedient, but Jo went on:

'It was awful. She wasn't anything like I'd imagined. But it made me realize that I had to rely on myself and not think I had anyone to fall back on.' He needn't think she was helpless or needed support; didn't have any reason to think that. He was at liberty to go off with this precious friend of his if he wanted to. Nothing to stop him; nothing at all.

'It may sound crazy to you,' he said, 'but I realized when I was away from you how much you and I seem to belong together. I know you're very young, and it isn't fair to ask you to consider anything before you've had time to find out about life and people, but – well – well, it would be wonderful if – if you could, perhaps start considering.'

Jo was thunderstruck. 'Me?' she almost shouted. 'Me, consider? I've done nothing else this last twelve-month. But what about this friend of yours? The one what changed your life?'

'Cisco? But he was the one that made me realize you were a part of my life.' By his condemnation, he'd made him realize. How contrary. 'Once he's met you, he'll see at once how right it is for us to be together, and then he would be a pretty useful person to have around, because he's older and much wiser than me. Be a great back-up if we needed it; because people probably aren't going to take us all that seriously. Can't imagine anyone will approve of you and me setting up house in Petherick Hall, can you?'

Gales of laughter overtook them again, and relief and delight were all mixed up in the laughter this time.

It was easy to kiss, because they were so close. Scarcely needed to move at all. It was a long, fierce, and very passionate kiss, causing both of them to flare into an erotic frenzy – but in their confined state, there was very little they could do about it. Peter considered struggling out of the sleeping bag, but it would be far too much effort, and that would destroy the spontaneity and the magic. On no account could he spoil the magic.

'I love you very much, you know,' he said. 'That was one of the reasons I had to go away. I couldn't stay on here and see you every day and yet not be with you, so I had to go away.'

'I thought of you all the time. I nearly died of lone-liness and fear that you weren't never coming back.'

There was never such happiness; no-one else could ever have felt such happiness as this.

'If we are going to die,' she said, 'it'd be quite good to

do it feeling like we do, wouldn't it? I couldn't feel better'n I do now.'

'Don't think I could either; but it would be a pity if we didn't survive, because being together with you and loving you for ever must be better than only having an hour or two in a cramped sleeping bag in a snowdrift, don't you think?'

'I'm not so sure it would be,' Jo said, struggling and squirming to get her arm round his neck and failing. 'Oh blow,' she panted, 'perhaps you're right.'

'What do you think of the idea then, if we ever get out of this?'

'I think it's a smashing idea.'

The kiss was gentle this time, each clutching on to control.

'There won't half be a shindy,' Jo added a moment later. 'Oh lordy, are we going to be able to face up to that?'

'I've thought about it continuously all through the last few weeks. We can't tell them, because they'd stop it. They could, you see, because of you being under age. We'd just have to get on and do it.'

'What d'you mean "do it"?'

'Er – I think we'll have to get married, because otherwise there'd be so much fuss about our living at the big house. It would sort of make it legal. Would you mind?'

Jo laid her cheek against his: 'Funny sort of proposal that, but I certainly don't mind at all.' She drew her head back. 'But I might not suit; I don't know nothing about sex, you know, except what I seen in the farmyard, and I don't reckon that's much to go by.'

'I don't know much myself,' he said. 'But I don't think it would take us that long to learn. I'm almost sure you'll suit extremely well; only hope I shall.'

They stopped talking then, and just looked at each other, each trying to drink in every detail of the face opposite, it was an altogether enthralling experience.

'Love is just as wonderful as everybody says . . .' Jo

said after a bit and, whether it was the exhaustion of the trauma they were both experiencing, or whether it was the lack of oxygen beginning to have an effect, suddenly, and quite without warning, she fell fast asleep.

There was no dramatic rescue. Will took it for granted that she had been caught by the storm in Penzance and had stayed with someone or other. The telephone lines were all down anyway and no-one could get messages through. The thaw set in almost as quickly as the blizzard had taken them over, and when Peter and Jo stirred in their sleeping bag in the early morning, steady, driving rain had washed away the enveloping snow, and they looked out of streaming car windows at grey, disintegrating shapes of slush, pitted with the bullet holes of the rain.

It was an unromantic predicament, made no better by the struggle that ensued when they tried to get out of the sleeping bag.

'I have to pee,' Peter said, finally extricating himself and forcing the door against the remnants of the snow. But no way did Jo have the time to allow herself the indignity of squatting down in the frozen, drenching surroundings. She wet her knickers in an agony of embarrassment.

29

'It's all so completely unreal,' Cynthia spoke tearfully, and with a waver in her voice. She realized that she was still suffering from the shock of Bea's death, but felt that there was quite a bit more at the back of her acute anxiety of the moment.

'You don't look well, Cyn.' Daphne was full of

irritating concern. 'You must take a long holiday somewhere; Mediterranean cruise perhaps. Once you've got over the shock, you'll enjoy the freedom, my dear. After all, you've been dreadfully tied, having to cope with Mother.'

Bridget frowned. Cyn had been about as much use as a honey bee in a block of flats. 'Cruise or no cruise, I can't imagine you'll want to go on living here on your own. Much more sensible for you to take over one of the estate cottages, don't you think? Might be an idea if Harold and I moved in here, I thought. Can't sell the place of course, only wish we could.'

'Of course you can't sell it,' Dorothy said, 'but I don't see why you should take it over, Bridgie. What about the rest of us?'

'Don't panic, girl; we'd come to some financial arrangement, naturally, but it would be good to have a business base for the firm. We could turn the ground floor into offices.'

'That would be awful,' Daphne became emotional at once. 'Petherick Hall is a *home*, not an impersonal, inhuman office block.'

Jean lit a cigarette. 'So let's all move in together and be a jolly happy family – Bridgie, Harold and the little darlings, Cynthia and the cats, Daphne and Hans, Dorothy and John, and me and several of my friends – what a good idea'!

No-one even smiled; it was too dreadful a solution even to joke about.

'And what about Piggy?' Daphne said.

'Piggy?' Jean laughed this time. 'Oh he can live in the air raid shelter at the bottom of the garden.'

'You happy with the way things is going?' Jo asked her grandparents. 'Farm's doing well, you know. We've made enough to hire another hand to help in the dairy.'

'I don't need no-one to tell me how to run my dairy,' Grace started, but Will cut in: 'Don't be so daft woman,

241

you'd be telling him, not the other way round. And you'd like that, you know you would.'

'Maybe I would and maybe I wouldn't. Can't see how it's come about that spending out all this money means we got more to spend. Can't see that at all. You mark my words, it'll all end in tears before long.'

'It won't, Gran, I promise it won't. For one thing, I want you two to be able to sit back and do a bit of retiring when you find the work gets too much.'

'Retire? Sit and moulder? That's not for me,' Will said.

'But it would be good to have no worries about things,' Jo persisted. 'If our farm was a part of the big Petherick estate it would mean no worries at all.'

Will wheezed out a cackle of laughter. 'That'd be a fine thing,' he said. 'Them women buy up a little bit farm like ours? They wouldn't give that their blessing, now would they? Chance'd be a fine thing!'

'They might,' Jo said. 'You never know.'

Emerging from the snowdrift experience had been a sobering return to reality for Jo and Peter. The soul-stirring event that had up-ended both their lives shrivelled into an unnoticed, unreported accident where Jo wet her knickers and Peter couldn't get the car to start.

They had walked together, through freezing sleet and slush, to the main Penzance road, where a lorry finally picked them up and took them to a garage. The whole escape back into real life had taken several hours, by which time they were drenched with icy spray from passing cars, and frozen practically solid. The recovery from the experience took a good deal longer.

It was even difficult to bring the subject up again, once they sank back into their everyday lives; time was taken up in immediate, everyday things. The notion of arranging times for both of them to meet together became a highly-charged, formidable operation. The

Tremayne cottage had no telephone, and there still lay the awkwardness of secrecy around them.

Jo received a letter by post and Will brought it to her. 'Bob gave me this down the lane,' he said with a bit of a laugh. 'And who's writing a letter to you then, postmarked local?'

The blush rushed up her neck and face, and she put the letter in her pocket before carrying on with mixing the cattle feed. There was no way she could answer, so she smiled and said, 'Must be my sweetheart.' A blessing Gran wasn't around, or she'd never have heard the end of it. Will just enjoyed the joke without probing further, and she restrained the overpowering desire to turn tail, dash away and search for a private corner where she could read it immediately. Carry on as normal; pretend it wasn't the most important communication in the world – but what was in it? Did it say that he still loved her? Or was it a note to say that he'd made a big mistake – things were far too difficult to be considered possible? Because of course they were, when you looked at them in the light of day. It was just a mad fantasy induced by the extraordinary circumstances they had found themselves in. After all, they might have died in that snow igloo; you say lots of things when you think you might be going to die.

She controlled herself for all of ten minutes, and then slipped, secretly, into the house. Gran was in the kitchen. 'Whatever are you doing in the house at this time of day?' Every movement checked; secrets were not possible.

'My nose keeps running, got to have a good blow. Fetching a handkerchief.'

'Well take your boots off then; can't traipse across my clean floor with all that mud.'

Jo took off her boots and walked slowly up the stairs; no undue haste, or it would be noticed. Was she seconds off a catastrophe? Was life going to collapse yet again? Perhaps it wasn't from him at all; she'd never seen his writing.

Dear darling Joanne, This is really too awful, being apart like this, quite ridiculous, we just have to have some arrangement to be able to see each other. We have to talk and be together without the whole world knowing, but how? What about the old gun emplacement on the cliff? Could you get there at lunch time? I'll be there tomorrow, Wednesday, at twelve. I love you, always and for ever. Peter. PS Isn't this absurd? Just like a cheap thriller. I love you.

She bounded down the stairs, two at a time, with an impulse to burst into song. Boots on, head up and out into the open where one could leap and dance and sing with only the pigs and cows and hens to see.

'Got your handkerchief then?'

Momentary panic: she'd forgotten it. 'Yes, it's in my pocket, and I've had a real good blow. See you later alligator.'

Saucy minx; but you couldn't help laughing. Grace sat down and had a cup of tea. Nice to put her feet up for a bit.

Inside, the concrete look-out smelled terrible, so they leaned on the outside wall, the wind tearing at their hair and the waves smashing on the rocks below. He undid his jacket and wrapped her into the front of it, so that it felt a bit like being back together in the sleeping bag. Clouds streamed and birds were flung about over their heads. Blown spray glistened on their eyelashes and in their hair, but they felt nothing at all except the heat of their love for each other.

'What are we going to do, Petey?'

'First of all, I'm going to introduce you to the house. You have to get to love it like I do. Cynthia's gone away, and Mrs Webb only comes in the morning. Will you come tomorrow evening after work? Then we can talk and decide.'

'But all them women?'

'They're not there. They've all got their own places now, except Cynthia, and she's away on a cruise at the moment.'

Jo could only imagine Petherick Hall as being the big, bustling family house, crammed full of women. She could not, even now, connect it with Peter.

'You mean it's empty?' What an extraordinary thought.

'Well, not exactly; I'm there. Cynthia's moving out into a cottage when she gets back.'

Jo looked at him, laughing, trying to see him on his own in that great castle of a place. 'Bet you don't half rattle about,' she said, 'you and all the ghosts.'

'They're nice, friendly ghosts. It's quite extraordinary how differently I feel about that place, now that I have it to myself. When I was young, I was for ever trying to find places to hide in, now the whole house seems like a refuge in itself. I'm sure you'll see what I mean, once you get to know it.'

It was impossible to imagine such a thing. Petherick Hall was not a *real* place: it was that great house on the hill where all those women lived. However they lived – in medieval splendour or boring, frumpish everydayness – they were an unreal, illusory lot. Was the house not just a castle in the air as well?

'You really going to live there, all on your own?'

'*We* are going to live there.'

She put her arms right round him and hugged him to her, 'Oh Petey, Petey, isn't it all just a great fairy tale that will never come true, however much we try? This great enormous step we want to take makes me frightened. It all seems so unreal and hopeless, and really quite silly. Can't see that anybody could think their way round it.' But Peter put his hand up her shirt and found her breast so that she almost fainted with pleasure and forgot everything else until it was time to get back.

'Tomorrow evening then, come to the house.'

'Shall I come in by the kitchen like I did before?'

'No, silly, come to the front door and ring the bell. There'll be nobody there but me. The lady of the house uses the front door, she doesn't slink in the back way.'

It was all too ridiculous.

Petherick Hall stood, gaunt and forbidding against the dusk sky; shrubs and bushes, and a few trees clustered round it protectively in its isolated position, set among its acres of sparsely hedged and slate-walled fields. There was not a soul about, and Jo shrank to the size of the smallest field mouse in the vicinity. Talk about a speck of dust in Paddington Station, this must surely be one step further down the line of disparities. But as she started up the never-ending drive to the house, a light went on in one of the upstairs rooms, and the whole scene changed. One small square of orange light, and the house became a welcoming haven of refuge out of a wicked world of darkness. One just had to burst into song with relief: 'Star of wonder, star of light, star with royal beauty bright,' sang Jo, trying out the carol they had been rehearsing in the church for the Christmas concert.

As she approached, she discovered that all the lights were on on the ground floor which had been hidden by the bushes, and the house became a palace flooded with magic light from a thousand chandeliers. 'Stop it,' she told herself out loud. 'This is for real, so don't you forget it,' and she heard the bell pealing away behind the closed front door – not just a silly ding-dong, a real *peal*.

He was there in a second – must have been waiting in the hall – and at once they were locked together, like one person in a cocoon of affection, love and mutual protectiveness.

'Welcome home, Joanne Tremayne-Petherick of Petherick Hall in the county of Cornwall,' he said. 'I've prepared a sumptuous feast of bacon and baked beans, but we can pretend it's roast swan and venison and larks' tongues.'

'We can pretend no such thing, you wicked, meat-eating piggy; beans are much more humane.'

'If I didn't love you so much,' Peter said, 'I should probably have killed you by now for calling me Piggy. All Piggies are, from this moment henceforth, banished from the House of Petherick.'

'All right,' said Jo, without worrying what he meant. 'No piggies. I'll leave them at Tremayne's.' Shame really, she'd always loved the pigs.

They feasted, sitting at the big dining-room table, and he took her on a tour of the house, from bottom to top.

'You like it? You like it?' he kept asking at various stages of the tour.

'I love it,' Jo said.

'You like it? It's yours.' He waltzed her round the library, his father's library, he told her, which had been shut up ever since Humphrey had died. Too much to dust, Cynthia had said. 'But I found out where she kept the key, so I used to creep in and lock myself inside for hours. It was one of my best hiding places.'

'But you don't need those hiding places any more, do you?'

'Haven't done so far; of course there's no knowing what you're going to drive me to in my old age.'

'Can we really deal with it all, Petey?' The rosy picture of King and the Beggarmaid wasn't really true at all. Was being practical and down to earth enough to deal with such high romance? 'We're so alone – sort of us against the world. Can't think we'll ever be able to win through.'

Peter felt a tense waver of doubt catch at his heartbeat, making it surge unpleasantly. When he had thought up the whole idea, down at Cerne Abbas with Cisco, everything had seemed positively plain sailing. He had been certain, finally, of what he wanted to do. Bea's illness and Cisco's violent reaction to his return-ing just made his conviction stronger. But now, when it was actually taking place, could he be so sure of success?

'Of course we'll win through. We have at least three friends on our side: Alec Tibbs for one . . .' and they both collapsed into laughter. 'No, I mean it; he may be little and insignificant, but he represents "The Law", in inverted commas, and he's on our side, so that's one friend. Then there's MONEY, in capital letters, which is an even better friend, and lastly there's Cisco; he will be the best friend of all, you'll realize that as soon as you meet him.' Once Cisco had met Jo, he was bound to realize his mistake.

Jo tensed up a little. 'This Cisco – is he going to live with us?' Who was this best friend she'd never even met? Might hate the sight of him for all Pete knew; sounded much too good to be true. 'Don't know if I'll take to him.'

'Of course he won't live with us – he'll just be there when we want him, as a sort of friend and advisor. I wanted to rent one of the cottages on the estate to him, but he wouldn't have that, said he knew the district; used to live here when he was a little boy and knew somewhere he could stay. He just wants to be a kind of farmhand, dogsbody sort of thing, and you *will* take to him, I promise you.'

A sense of pique invaded Jo's thinking. Peter couldn't possibly know who she would take to. 'How d'you know I will? And he probably won't like me either, be jealous or something. He might spoil everything.' Friend or foe? She wasn't certain, but she recognized jealousy in her own mind, and was afraid of it. 'Where did he live? I didn't know anyone round here called Cisco . . .'

'It's really Francis – I just call him Cisco . . .'

'Well Francis then. There weren't no boys called Francis round here. I would have known.' Didn't trust this Cisco bloke somehow; probably just a scrounger playing on Pete's good nature. 'I had a friend too, when I was little,' she wished to goodness that Charlie was still around; so much better if she had a special friend to back her up as well. 'But he ran out on me.' She gave a small laugh. 'He didn't turn out a bit like I imagined him.' Warn him that friends weren't always as good as they seem. 'His name was Charlie.'

Peter held out his hand to her, and they twined their fingers together for reassurance. But Jo felt suddenly cold and alone and sadly insecure. Peter might be all right with his Mr Tibbs and his money and his Cisco, but what sort of back up had she got to help her face such a situation? A few years ago, she thought ruefully, I could have thought up all sorts of happy endings and been confident that things would magically work themselves out, but now, all the magic's gone: Charlie's gone and Mumma's gone. Nothing left, nothing at all but clear, chilly reality. She wanted to cry, but couldn't even do that. It would be silly to cry because of wishing you were still young enough to believe in magic; and that was really all it was.

'I'd best go home,' she said, with certainty in her mind that should she step out of this present world of fantasy, she would never, ever be able to step back in again.

'This is your home, Jo. Please don't leave it. Please stay with me.'

It would be the height of brazenness, now, she thought, to let him know that she had already told Will and Grace that she was staying the night in Penzance; told them she wanted to consult an accountant and arrange for a bank loan: told them she wanted to check on some farm machinery while she was there. Must have been out of her mind. Much better to get out now, while the going was good. It wasn't going to work out, was it? It was all a silly dream: all make believe. Go now – run – scoot – skedaddle – turn tail – and immediately she had the vision of thousands of little rabbits skedaddling all over the place, white tails bobbing, fleeing to the safety of their warm, dark burrows.

She wrapped her arms round Peter, and laid her face against his. 'I'm not going to do no running away,' she said. 'Not now, not ever.'

The log fire Peter had built up in the huge fire-place in the sitting room, the oversized, over soft sofa and end-less cushions were conducive to luxurious sensualism and abandon; almost too conducive. Peter felt the pressure of something being expected of him, and was frozen, suddenly, into the old obstinacy of non-response.

Jo's brave statement of no retreat collapsed back into panic, and she withdrew, rather primly, from the sensed detachment, to stand near the fire, warming her hands and feeling that she had been shamefully immoral to have considered making arrangements to stay the night. Whatever had possessed her to imagine he had meant her to *stay the night*, and all that that entailed? What a horrible mistake. She was painfully embarrassed in case he should ask whether her grandparents would be expecting her back. Impossible to explain that they weren't, because that would mean admitting that she had made all these arrangements in anticipation. She kept her back turned to him in an agony of sheepish confusion. How stupid she was.

Rooted in childhood obsessions, Peter stood a few feet away, staring at her, seeing an isolated, dejected backview, silhouetted drably against the irrepressible geniality of the firelight. Couldn't bring himself to do more than just stand and look, with his mind and feelings locked away in a dungeon-like recollection of things past. It wasn't until Jo turned from the fire, filled with the certainty that however cowardly fleeing rabbits might appear, flight was really the only possible action to take, only then did real life hurtle painfully back into Peter's suspended animation.

'It's no good,' he said, advancing towards her with his arms outstretched.

'Better face up to it,' she said, without looking at him.

'Absolutely essential that we do.' His arms locked round her.

Back to reality: down to earth. She looked up at him then, and started to smile.

He was smiling too. 'We're just going to have to grow up.'

'You mean we've got to recognize the whole thing is an impossible dream?'

'Yes, as long as we carry on dreaming it.'

'For real.'

'For real.'

They could scarcely kiss for laughing, but the urgency of their need for each other very soon overwhelmed any thought – real or unreal. And so their love-making, this time, was an erotic consummation of fact and fantasy. It surpassed all expectation.

30

It goes without saying that the next day dawned bright and clear. Frost had turned grass, bushes and trees to glistening white, and in the depths of the morning silence only the small snap of contracting iced twigs could be heard.

'Magic,' Jo whispered, her breath condensing into mist on the window. 'We must get out into it before it vanishes.'

'Tour of the estate? Or a bit of it anyway.'

They wrapped themselves in coats, boots, gloves and scarves which were hanging in what Peter told her had been known as the gun room when his father was alive. The guns still stood in a glass-fronted case on the wall and mackintoshes, scarves and dog leads hung from hooks in dusty neglect. Another world, Jo thought as she tried on a tartan-lined burberry.

The freezing air was as exhilarating as the beauty of the frost world all round them, and stimulated them into wild chases, leaving pristine white fields bes- mattered with crazy tracks. When their breath finally gave out in gales of laughter, it hung round them in an enveloping mist as they made their way, a single entity, arms entwined, towards the cliffs and the sea.

But something nagged away at her; had to keep picking.

'That Cisco, I don't believe he's really the friend you imagine he is.'

'What d'you mean? You haven't even met him. Are you jealous of him or something?'

'No, of course not. Well, yes, I suppose I am a bit. But he sounds somehow quite unreal; he sounds like I thought Charlie was: a sort of perfect person; too good to be true.'

They stopped walking and looked at each other.

'So did you – do you – think Charlie wasn't – isn't real?'

'Of course he's real; a real friend to me he is, always was.'

'The way Cisco is for me. Couldn't have survived without him.'

'Nor me without Charlie.'

So what was she niggling about? She slid her arm round his waist, and they strolled on, full of euphoric content and certainty.

The figure appeared way in the distance, on top of the high cliff that they were approaching.

'Who on earth's that?' Peter said, shading his eyes against the sun, and feeling an extraordinary seizure of anxiety grab at his guts.

Jo screwed up her eyes, but could only make out an unrecognizable male figure. You didn't often come across strangers in winter on this part of the cliff. They made their way towards the approaching figure in silence, both straining their eyes to see. This is where I saw Charlie for the very last time, Jo thought suddenly, and she felt immediately panic-stricken for no good reason that she could think of.

'You know, I do believe it's Cisco,' Peter said. 'He

said he'd follow me down here. But he looks so different; no beard and his hair's cut short. I can scarcely recognize him.' A deep fear crept up his spine, making his blood seem to congeal.

The figure disappeared again behind a mound.

Jo approached slowly, also full of strange foreboding. There flashed through her mind the moment that she had re-met Peter, that day when Charlie had urged her to jump; at this very spot where she was walking now. It was here that she and Peter had had that momentous encounter. What if he had let her take off as she had intended? She'd never have known what love was all about. He had rescued the damsel in distress, so perhaps he actually was the fairy prince or the knight in shining armour after all. 'My hero!' she thought, with a giggle. A confused jumble of fantasy thoughts seethed in her mind now, as she walked, a little behind Peter, with slow, deliberate steps towards the obscure stranger.

'What's Cisco's other name?' she asked, racked through with suspicion. Lived round here as a boy? What nonsense, she would have known him. She remembered telling Charlotte that Charlie lived in a tree. But this odd unknown being in the distance, where had he lived? How could he have been one of the village boys? Her suspicion was coupled with a fearful anticipation, as she saw him come into view again over the brow of the hill: something about the springy walk – as though he was bouncing along; almost as if his feet weren't really on the ground. 'I'd be sure to know his name if he lived round here as a boy.'

Peter stopped walking, and seemed confused. 'Er – well, I know this sounds silly, but, well, d'you know I don't *know* his other name. It never sort of cropped up.'

They looked at each other with the memory sharp in both their minds.

'I didn't know Charlie's other name,' Jo said, with

253

the beginning of an explosive giggle. 'Don't think I'd even recognize him now that we're both grown up.'

She strained her eyes to see better who this person might be, and was suddenly sure: it was Charlie, wasn't it? Know his walk anywhere.

'That's not Cisco,' she said. 'That's Charlie! I remember the way he walked.'

Peter laughed out loud. 'So let's go and see who's right,' he said, catching hold of her hand. 'Find out who this mysterious person really is. He doesn't seem to have seen us; look, he's making off towards the sea.' He started to run, pulling her along with him. 'Come on! Quick! We don't want to lose him.' And, breathless with the cold and the laughter, they ran together, hand in hand, towards the cliff to search him out.

But when they got there, there was no-one on the cliff; no-one on the beach. Just the floating sea birds, and the sea, swirling and splashing against black rocks.

'Zennor mermaid must have got him,' Peter said. 'We'll come back tomorrow and see if she's let him go.'

THE END

Sins of the Mothers
by Patricia Angadi

'PATRICIA ANGADI ATTACKS HER STORY IN THE
HIGHEST OF SPIRITS'
Penelope Fitzgerald, *The Standard*

Iphigenia – Iffy – stands over six foot tall, weighs
seventeen stone, has a wonderful operatic voice, and is the
daughter of a black prostitute and an English Duke. And
Iffy's personality is as magnificent as her appearance.

Iffy has many wonderful and flamboyant friends in her
life, but her oldest and most faithful is pink and white
Rosemary, nicely respectable, nicely middle-class, who
spends her life doing everything right, unlike Iffy who
does everything wrong. In Rosemary's life is one man: in
Iffy's many (including Rosemary's). Rosemary's child is
beautifully groomed into discontented adolescence: Iffy's
bastard son is outrageously reared to an unconventional
but outstanding success. And yet the friendship prevails,
naughtily, wittily, and lovingly.

'ROSEMARY'S NAIVETY OVER HER FRIEND'S
LIFESTYLES ADDS A DELIGHTFUL HUMOUR TO THIS
FRESH AND ORIGINAL BLACK COMEDY'
East Anglian Daily Times

'ANGADI USES HER SOPHISTICATED WIT IN
ENTERTAINING FASHION'
Publishers Weekly

0 552 99385 9

BLACK SWAN

A SELECTED LIST OF FINE TITLES
AVAILABLE FROM BLACK SWAN

THE PRICES SHOWN BELOW WERE CORRECT AT THE TIME OF GOING TO PRESS. HOWEVER TRANSWORLD PUBLISHERS RESERVE THE RIGHT TO SHOW NEW RETAIL PRICES ON COVERS WHICH MAY DIFFER FROM THOSE PREVIOUSLY ADVERTISED IN THE TEXT OR ELSEWHERE.

☐	99248 8	THE DONE THING	*Patricia Angadi*	£4.99
☐	99201 1	THE GOVERNESS	*Patricia Angadi*	£3.99
☐	99385 9	SINS OF THE MOTHERS	*Patricia Angadi*	£3.99
☐	99322 0	THE HIGHLY FAVOURED LADIES	*Patricia Angadi*	£3.99
☐	99351 4	BLUE HEAVEN	*Joe Keenan*	£4.99
☐	99243 7	CONFESSIONS OF A FAILED SOUTHERN LADY	*Florence King*	£3.99
☐	99376 X	REFLECTIONS IN A JAUNDICED EYE	*Florence King*	£3.99
☐	99377 8	WASP WHERE IS THY STING?	*Florence King*	£4.99
☐	99375 1	WHEN SISTERHOOD WAS IN FLOWER	*Florence King*	£3.99
☐	99337 9	SOUTHERN LADIES AND GENTLEMEN	*Florence King*	£3.99
☐	99239 9	BABYCAKES	*Armistead Maupin*	£4.99
☐	99106 6	FURTHER TALES OF THE CITY	*Armistead Maupin*	£4.99
☐	99383 2	SIGNIFICANT OTHERS	*Armistead Maupin*	£4.99
☐	99373 4	SURE OF YOU	*Armistead Maupin*	£4.99
☐	99384 0	TALES OF THE CITY	*Armistead Maupin*	£4.99
☐	99086 8	MORE TALES OF THE CITY	*Armistead Maupin*	£4.99
☐	99302 6	THE LOVE OF GOOD WOMEN	*Isabel Miller*	£3.95
☐	99126 0	THE CAMOMILE LAWN	*Mary Wesley*	£4.99
☐	99210 0	HARNESSING PEACOCKS	*Mary Wesley*	£4.99
☐	99082 5	JUMPING THE QUEUE	*Mary Wesley*	£4.99
☐	99304 2	NOT THAT SORT OF GIRL	*Mary Wesley*	£4.99
☐	99258 5	THE VACILLATIONS OF POPPY CAREW	*Mary Wesley*	£4.99
☐	99355 7	SECOND FIDDLE	*Mary Wesley*	£4.99
☐	99393 X	A SENSIBLE LIFE	*Mary Wesley*	£4.99

All Corgi/Bantam Books are available at your bookshop or newsagent, or can be ordered from the following address:

Corgi/Bantam Books,
Cash Sales Department
P.O. Box 11, Falmouth, Cornwall TR10 9EN

Please send a cheque or postal order (no currency) and allow 80p for postage and packing for the first book plus 20p for each additional book ordered up to a maximum charge of £2.00 in UK.

B.F.P.O. customers please allow 80p for the first book and 20p for each additional book.

Overseas customers, including Eire, please allow £1.50 for postage and packing for the first book, £1.00 for the second book, and 30p for each subsequent title ordered.

NAME (Block Letters) ....

ADDRESS ....

....